To, Steve

2047

Best Wishes

Enjoy!

2047

A.A. CADDY

Library of Congress Control Number:		2017907679
ISBN:	Hardcover	978-1-5434-8552-3
	Softcover	978-1-5434-8551-6
	eBook	978-1-5434-8550-9

Print information available on the last page.

Rev. date: 06/02/2017

To order additional copies of this book, contact:
Xlibris
800-056-3182
www.Xlibrispublishing.co.uk
Orders@Xlibrispublishing.co.uk
757619

CONTENTS

In memory of my father, Bill

Thank you to my wife, Moira; my daughter, Alexandra; my son, Sam; and dear friend Sharon for your love, encouragement, and support.

CHAPTER ONE

DISCOVERY

She had only been asleep for about two hours when Natasha awakened her. This was earlier than expected. She had worked late into the night, and the shock of being suddenly roused made her feel quite ill.

"Maria, you must come and see this!" screamed Natasha.

"Surely, it's not daylight already," she said.

"No, no. You must come down to the lab. I need you to verify something."

She was still feeling quite nauseous as she climbed out of her sleeping compartment and pulled on the white all-in-one lab suit. She didn't like wearing this garment. It always made her itch all over, and the paper and silicone construction was rough against her bare skin. The silicone in the suit absorbed odours and kept the occupant dry. It never needed changing unless someone damaged it. The only drawback was that it caused slight skin irritations, but it was light and made moving around the space laboratory trouble-free.

She grudgingly followed Natasha.

Natasha Kuzuhara had been Akira Yamoto, whose mother was Japanese. She took her daughter's first name, Natasha, after she died. Natasha was thirty-eight and now single and dedicated to her job. She was a couple of years younger than Maria was and didn't have any dependents. Her husband and daughter had died in a car accident back on Earth, she came from an orphanage so she didn't know her father. Her mother was a scientist but had passed away. Natasha was determined not to find anyone new, as the thought of losing someone again would kill her.

Maria was hoping this excursion to the lab would be brief because all she could think about was getting back to bed so she could dream about her next leave on Earth. Their tour of duty was due to be completed in four days on 30 June 2047, and she would be back on Earth for two weeks. She was looking forward to seeing her two children, Alana and Sean, and her partner, Adam. They lived in an apartment in England, in a town called Millennium. This town was situated on the site of the year 2000 Millennium Dome and was now in the forty-seventh year of its existence.

As towns went, it wasn't that special, except the Millennium Dome concept was kept in the design of this town. There were one thousand homes on the site, all constructed with polymer-based materials, even the windows were made from plastic, all the homes were fitted with the latest high-technology appliances. No fossil fuel vehicles of any description were allowed in the town. Each residence came with its own urban-friendly six-seat vehicle. These vehicles were solar and fuel cell powered. What made them special was the fuel: water or sun! The other feature that made this town unique was the polymer dome that covered the whole town, making the need for weatherproof dwellings unnecessary. All the essential drinking water came from the rainfall collected by the dome and the electrical power from the solar-powered cells all over dome.

Natasha pushed open the door to the lab and rushed in. Without thinking, she let the door swing back. Fortunately, it was only a glancing blow on my forehead, as these doors were titanium alloy for their lower weight properties, but even in the space lab with zero gravity, they can give you a nasty injury. The doors were made to withstand huge pressure surges. If an object penetrated the lab from the outside, like a small meteorite, normal plastic or steel constructions would collapse under the extreme pressure drop.

"Maria, will you stop dawdling and come over and look at this?" Natasha was peering through the on-board space/planetary telescope and waving her arms frantically as if she were being choked.

Maria ventured over cautiously, just in case one of her flailing arms gave her a left hook.

"Look at that and tell me what you see," Natasha said.

She looked through the optical viewer, and what she saw made her angry. "Natasha!" she shouted. "You got me out of bed just to see a hole in the ozone layer, something that we've been aware of for weeks. I could absolutely throttle you!"

"No, no, Maria. Take another look. I have the long-range telescope trained on an area of sea just a few degrees south of the Azores. Can you see it?"

"See what?" she said. "All I can see is water, acres and acres of it." And then suddenly something caught her eye. "What the hell is that?" This telescope had the ability to spot a mushroom from eight hundred miles away and see through the water to the ocean floor. "Natasha, it looks like a building! But under the water."

"Yeah, yeah, that's what I've been trying to tell you. That must be over two miles below the surface of the sea."

"Do you know what that could be?"

Before she could get out the whole sentence, Natasha cried, "Atlantis!"

Back on Earth, Adam was preparing for Maria's return from the space station; the three-month tour of duty was almost over. They normally communicated weekly over the video link, but that wasn't the same as being with each other. They had a trip planned to see Maria's mum in Scotland. She lived in a small town called Carnoustie, in a cottage close to the sea, and you could walk through a gate at the bottom of the garden straight onto the beach. The children were excited about going, as they loved the beach, Granny Mary's cakes and scones, and Granny Mary, of course.

Adam also liked going to see her mum, as he could slink off to the local golf course for a few rounds and drinks with her uncle Tom, her mother's younger brother.

On the way back from Scotland, they were planning to visit Adam's brother, Gerald, who lived in the Lake District. They didn't see Gerald and his family often as they lived in a remote location not far from Lake Windermere. They never really ventured far from Ware Gardens, the name of their small cottage. It used to be called Lake Gate, but they renamed it after the town in Hertfordshire that they'd moved from ten years earlier. Gerald decided to opt out. He sold his small engineering business and bought the land and cottage to go "back to basics," as he called it. They didn't even own a UFV. That made travelling any distance out of the question, as he only had an old BMW.

You had to have a special government permit to drive a fossil fuel vehicle any further than ten miles.

It was always a treat visiting Gerald and his wife, Valerie. They could relax and put their feet up. He always had an open house. The garden was about five acres in size and full of so many "surprise and delight" features. There was a small lake at one end and a fruit orchard. At the opposite end, a large vegetable plot ran between the lake and the orchard, and to the west was a small farmyard. To the east was a grazing pasture. Sean and Alana loved to play in the orchard. They were planning to visit in early July, which meant they could pick all varieties of fruits, from apples to bananas.

The other distractions for the children were their cousins Lauren, Jade, and Jamie. Jade was fourteen years old, and Jamie was twelve, the same ages as Alana and Sean. Lauren was at university studying anthropology.

Back on the space lab, she was still in shock at the discovery of this city under the sea. "Natasha, do you really think this is the lost city of Atlantis?" she enquired. "Or is it maybe an optical illusion?"

"Why do you think that?" Natasha said.

"Well, I'm sure I could see a roadway with white lines down the middle. Correct me if I'm wrong, but the Atlanteans didn't have cars in that time, did they?"

"How can that be?" asked Natasha.

"Let's take another look through the telescope," Maria said.

They moved on down to the lab again and refocused the telescope to the south of the Azores. Maria set the scope to its maximum range with the filters on to eliminate the distortion of the atmosphere and water. This telescope wasn't just for scanning the earth. They also used it for looking into deep space. At the time, they were tracking two huge asteroids heading towards Earth or maybe they would harmlessly pass by. One of the asteroids was discovered in July 2019 by Sir William Caddy; they named that one William 6. The reason it had been defined with a number was because of the size of it: six miles in diameter.

The other one, Mona 3, was discovered in 2020 by celebrated astronomer Monalise Gerrard-Shalford. Mona 3 only came into view after William 6 had obscured it. Mona 3 was about one month behind William 6 from crossing Earth's orbit. William 6 was due to come close or cross Earth's orbit at the end of July 2047, with Mona 3 following one month later.

There seemed to be very little panic back on Earth regarding these life-threatening events. I suppose that stemmed from the other predictions that had been wildly wrong. Two other asteroids were predicted to strike Earth.

Jupiter 4 was supposed to strike in 2016, and Venus 2 was due for 2017, but both missed by thousands of miles. Jupiter 4 was so called due to it passing into Jupiter's orbit, causing a slingshot effect to propel it earthwards. Likewise, Venus 2 would pass into Venus's orbit and do the same.

Maria looked through the scope, and again she could make out a road with white lines on it. "Natasha, look through the scope now that I have it trained on the area we were viewing earlier." Natasha moved over to the scope and peered excitedly down its lens.

"God, Maria, you were right. I can see a road with white lines running down the middle. What does it mean? We should contact the WSOA [World Space & Oceanic Agency] and let them know what we've found. They can send out a survey team to investigate our findings."

"Now can I go back to bed, as I have already wasted two hours of my sleep period?"

"Okay, okay, Maria," Natasha said. "I'll see you in the morning."

She went back to bed and must have fallen into a deep sleep. She awoke still feeling tired. It only felt like a few minutes, but the clock did not lie. It was eight in the morning; she had slept for six hours.

Natasha was on her way back to their sleeping quarters when there was a loud thud and a huge bang. This caused their space laboratory to judder violently. "What the hell was that!" she heard Natasha scream.

For the second time today, she quickly exited her sleeping compartment. The space lab consisted of a sleeping quarters section that could sleep eight astronauts; two labs, one for experiments and one for analysis; and a toilet block, as they called it, with showers and toilet facilities and a living area for relaxing and eating. Attached to the station was the Earth/space telescope. They had a docking area for relief ships and travel to Earth space RTEs (return to earth) pod. The pods could carry supplies and eight astronauts, and they had a short range, only travelling to our space platform. This was attached to an Earthbound tether, which at its base on Earth had a three-kilometre diameter. The tether was anchored in the shallow seas around the Thames estuary over the eastern side of England. This allowed the waters to be used in the cooling of the pod runways. It also projected from the earth sixteen kilometres into space and was adjustable to take up slack or for planetary movements. The pod flew the short distance from the space lab to the platform and then attached itself to the tether. It took about ten hours to reach the base on Earth from start to finish. There were also two escape ships docked on the station should we be unable to use the tether. These can carry eight astronauts each and would have enough fuel on board to manoeuvre and fly to the earth's atmosphere so there was no room for any flight errors. Fortunately, the flight to the earth's atmosphere was computer controlled, but the descent to the earth had to be completed manually and wasn't powered. You would free-fall and then glide back to the home base, which was a runway built on the Maplin sands at the mouth of the River Thames. Strange that the computer could control the flight to the atmosphere but not to Earth. Rumour had it that the WSOA who were based in Houston directed funds elsewhere so no base computer program was developed for return to Earth. Part of the training prior to time on the station was how to fly the escape ships.

Natasha came running into the sleeping compartment shouting, "Maria, Maria, wake up! Did you feel the station judder?"

"Yes," she replied. "Am I ever going to get enough sleep? God, what a racket."

"That's exactly what I was thinking," said Natasha.

"No, I meant you're making so much noise that you would think the station was falling apart."

"Let's get down to main control and see what that was."

They made their way to the main control room, which was part of the analysis lab. "Natasha, you check the outer hull," Maria said. "I'll check for any system failures."

When they arrived at main control, several lights were flashing blue, which meant there were a few problems with some of our systems. "Maria, my God!" Natasha shouted. "We have a hull breach. Look, the outer casing lights are flashing blue!"

"Which part has the breach!" she shouted. It was difficult to hear each other, as the warning lights flashing caused the high-pitched klaxon to sound. This was so we could hear it even if we were at the other end of the station.

Natasha checked the indicator lights, and it seemed as if they had a problem with the experimentation laboratory. Maria checked the external cameras, which were mounted all around the outside of each section of the station to enable them to quickly identify any impact areas should they be struck by space debris or meteorites/dust particles. Yes, even dust particles could cause a breach, even if they were minute metal fragments or rocks, as they travelled at over sixty-five thousand miles per hour.

What they saw on the recordings from the cameras was unbelievable. They had only been hit by a rogue satellite that had been launched back in the 1950s. Fortunately for them, it was just a glancing blow, but it left them with a tear in the outer casing of the experimentation lab. The breach was about two hundred millimetres long, and they were venting oxygen. That would mean they had a breach on the inner hull as well. Natasha would need to do an outside repair; they needed a patch on the tear to seal the leak. The station should automatically seal the experimentation lab from the rest of the other units, checking first to make sure no one was in there.

Natasha suited up with her OLS (outside lab space) suit and went down to the exit hatch with a titanium Kevlar patch. This was made up of three layers, Kevlar sandwiched in between two sheets of titanium. She would need to fix it in place using a special bonding adhesive that did not need air to set. It was set using an ultraviolet torch, and the whole operation would take about two hours. Once the patch was on, the self-repair liquid system would go into operation. It would only work if the outside environment was sealed. Within the three-skin wall of the station, flows a new substance called "timinium repair", a compound of titanium and aluminium in a liquid form. This compound stayed in a liquid state and ran around the secondary wall of the station on all units. If it vented to space, it would stay in a liquid form. If it vented into the station and encountered oxygen, it underwent a chemical change and hardened instantly, forming an airtight seal.

Natasha climbed into the airlock, and the hatch closed automatically behind her. She did not like space walks, as being in the suit made her feel claustrophobic. She was quite agitated, and her breathing became more rapid. Even though she passed this test on the simulator and underwater, this was her first time outside the station. The suit contained monitors for everything from heart rate to body temperature and beyond. It also incorporated high-pressure jets should you become detached from your safety umbilical. With all the safety measures in place, Natasha was still nervous about this walk. What if a piece of debris should hit her? All these thoughts raced through her mind as she was exiting the outside hatch.

Back on Earth, Maria's family were still preparing for her return from the space lab. Adam, her husband, was looking forward to seeing Maria again, as she had been away for almost three months. Adam had been planning something special for Maria's return. He had asked his brother, Gerald, to prepare a party for her, and Adam had invited all her friends from around the country. One of her best friends she went to school with and had known for longer than she had known Adam was Stephanie, who was godmother to both their children. She worked for the local city council in London as the director of education and was looking forward to catching up with Maria when she returned. The party Adam planned was to celebrate Maria's fortieth birthday, which would have happened at the end of March, but she had to go to the space lab at that time.

Natasha was now outside the space lab and working her way towards the experimentation lab section. She had made sure that the safety line was firmly secured to the docking port tether arm, and she had about twenty metres of secure line to work with. The experimentation lab was about thirty-five metres away, which meant she would have to unclip her line and secure another one that was in her chest bag to the next tether arm, which was on the outside of the experimentation lab. She nervously moved towards the next tether point.

Maria could hear her heavy breathing through the two-way communication module. "Natasha," she said, "are you all right?" She did not get an immediate reply, which worried her a little. She spoke again into the com module. "Natasha, can you hear me?"

"Yes, I can hear you, Maria. I can't seem to locate the next tether point."

"It's next to the lab viewing port up to your right, about two metres from you," she replied.

"OK, got it," she said. She moved towards the tether, and as she took the next line out of her chest bag, she could see something in her eyeline that made her freeze. Moving rapidly towards her were a couple of small objects about the size of tennis balls. She had just unhooked her tether when the first object glanced off her helmet. The shock of that impact made her let go of her handhold, and she started to float away from the station. The other object passed harmlessly by. "Maria, Maria!" she screamed in absolute terror. Help me! I didn't manage to clip my line to the tether, and I'm floating away from the station." She was also leaking oxygen. The object had cut a hole in her suit. It was probably only pinprick size, but it was enough to cause a problem.

Back on Earth, the world space centre was frantically trying to contact Maria on the lab. They could see what had been going on from the outboard and on-board cameras, although the signal they received was about thirty seconds behind real time. "Commander Francis, please come in," Maria could hear on her headset. "Please come in."

"Hello, space centre. This is Commander Francis," she said, still trying to focus on Natasha, who had now drifted twenty metres away from the station and was still screaming down her com line.

"Maria, Maria! For God's sake, please help me, Commander Francis."

"This is Director Bernhard. What the hell is going on up there?"

"Director, we had an object strike the experimentation lab, which has created a breach in the outer hull right through to the inner hull. We were leaking oxygen before the automatic doors sealed the lab. Commander Kuzuhara was trying to repair the outer hull when an object struck her. She lost her tether, and she has a tear in her suit. She's drifting away from the station."

In her younger days, Akira Yamoto (surname was created by the orphanage), who liked to be called Aki, was a bit of a rebel, always running away from the orphanage on the outskirts of Hiroshima. Her ambition was to get a job in a big department store which sold fine clothes and jewellery. Her other passion, strangely enough, was science fiction 3D novels. Her favourites were an old English television drama called *Doctor Who* and old *Star Trek* episodes. The 3D novel had replaced books and Blu-ray discs about ten years earlier. These came in small boxes about the size of an old matchbox and were relatively cheap to buy, around five WDs (world dollars).

The world used one global currency, which avoided all the confusion of exchange rates and stopped the banks from exploiting every other currency and taking advantage of commission fees. There was a world bank based in Japan and sub-banks based in all the capitals of all the countries on the planet. There was even one at the South Pole.

The novel projected a 3D image about one metre above itself, and the images narrated the story or drama as if you were watching old movies at a cinema. They also projected the words on to the nearest flat surface for those hard of hearing. Aki had quite a sizeable collection of 3D novels, and she would spend much of her time at the orphanage just watching these novels. The other orphans and staff considered her a bit of a loner. Aki was now twenty years old and still living at the orphanage.

She was always in a rush. She never did anything slowly, as she felt it wasted time. In one of her ventures into Hiroshima, she met someone who was to change her life. She was looking through the window of one of the big clothing stores, gazing at a fashionable pair of shoes and hoping one day to be able to buy them. She was in a bit of a daydream as she swung around and away from the shop window, colliding with a burly man who was also in a rush, needing to get to an important meeting. Aki was sent flying, banging her head as she landed. The world suddenly became a blur. Faces were appearing and disappearing, and she was fading in and out of consciousness. Suddenly, there was a bright light. She thought she had died. Muffled voices were echoing in her ears. "Aki, Aki, Aki, are you awake?" the nurse asked in a soft tone.

Aki sat bolt upright shouting, "I'm sorry, God, for my life. I did not achieve anything! Forgive me."

The nurse spoke again. "Aki, are you ok?" She heard that more clearly this time.

"Where am I?" Aki asked.

The nurse said, "You're in the high-dependency ward of the Cherry Blossom Hospital in Hiroshima."

"What?" Aki said.

"Hospital, yes. You had a nasty fall. It was a bit touch-and-go for a while. You had lost quite a bit of blood from your head wound and have been unconscious for the last three days."

Aki screamed, "Three days! What are you talking about? I was looking through a shop window just a minute ago and then everything went black. I cannot afford to pay for hospital treatment. I live in an orphanage."

"Don't worry – everything has been taken care of," the nurse said. "A gentleman came in with you. He seemed extremely worried, and he has settled all the hospital bills. Here, he left a business card and asked us to make sure you contact him when you've recovered." The business card read in large bold type TADASHI KUZUHARA, PROFESSOR OF ASTRONOMY AND PHYSICS, HIROSHIMA UNIVERSITY.

Natasha was struggling to keep it together. Her suit was leaking oxygen, and she was in a blind panic. The distance between her and the station had now increased to about forty metres. "Maria," Director Bernhard bellowed down the com line, "keep talking to Commander Kuzuhara. She needs to remain focussed."

"Natasha, how are you doing? Try to stay calm. We are working on a solution to get you back."

"How are you going to do that? I've drifted too far away from the station," she said. "And I'm leaking air.

Maria had a thought. The suit also contained high-pressure jets. "Natasha," she called, "use the pressure jets!"

"What pressure jets?" Natasha said.

"This will teach you a lesson. You needed to pay more attention during training. Under your chest bag to your left, there's a hand control attached to your suit. It's about the size of a 3D novel box. There are two buttons, one for forward and one for back. Press the buttons gently or you'll lose all your air in one go. See if you can look at the buttons. You need to press the green one."

Natasha fumbled on the left of her suit with her heavy gloves and found something hard and small. She pulled it away from the suit to look at the buttons it was difficult to distinguish colours, and as she gently depressed one of the buttons, she found herself moving farther away from the station. "Oh, shit – wrong one." She pressed the other button and started to move back towards the station. Gently using short bursts, she moved ever closer to the station. She checked her oxygen gauge, and it showed only two minutes of air left.

Aki took the business card and read it again: PROFESSOR OF ASTRONOMY AND PHYSICS. "It's right next to the monorail station. Do you know where that is?" Aki asked the nurse.

"Yes," she said, "it's not far from the hospital. If you go out the main entrance and turn left, follow the path towards the tower in the distance. The university is about fifty metres past that tower."

Aki set off for the university. On her way, she passed the shop that had the fancy shoes in the window and could not resist one more look at those shoes. She must have only been there about twenty seconds when a voice behind her said, "Please turn around more slowly this time."

Aki obeyed the instruction implicitly and turned to see who had said that. Standing with his briefcase at his side was a man dressed in a smart grey suit and wearing a trilby hat. Aki asked, "Who are you?"

"I'm the man you collided with a few days ago."

"My God – and you have the cheek to tell me to mind where I'm going. I was in hospital for three days, you know, and I have a good mind to contact a lawyer."

"My dear, that's your choice, but before you make your decision, let me introduce myself. I'm Professor Kuzuhara."

Aki was speechless. In a sheepish voice, she finally uttered, "What ... what ... who?"

"Professor Kuzuhara. I called by the hospital this morning to see how you were but was informed that you were heading over to the university. May I accompany you on your journey?"

Aki stumbled over her response. "Of course, of course, please."

The professor had checked up on her background while she was incapacitated in hospital, so he knew a little bit about her history. "Akira ... May I call you that?"

"Aki will do."

"Well, Aki, I understand that you're living in the city orphanage."

Aki snapped back, "What's wrong with that?"

The professor said, "Nothing, nothing. I was merely stating a fact."

"Oh, OK, then."

Natasha had almost reached the station when the thirty-second audible warning sounded in her helmet. Her oxygen was almost exhausted. She needed to act fast. She depressed her pressure jet button firmly, which caused her to move rapidly towards the station. She had one chance to grab the tether handle. If she missed it, off into space she would fly.

Maria was watching Natasha on the outboard cameras. "Natasha, what are you doing? You're coming in too fast!" she screamed.

"Maria, my oxygen is depleted. It's now or never." Natasha thudded into the station and was about to bounce off when she managed to grab the tether handle. Struggling for breath, she pressed the airlock release button and crawled inside. The door sealed automatically behind her and flooded the compartment with oxygen. Natasha ripped her helmet off to get at the air. She gulped and gulped but was getting no air; she then realised she still had her internal helmet mask on, which she promptly removed. "Aaaaah," she gasped as the sweet air filled her lungs.

The professor and Aki arrived at the university quickly. "Aki, please follow me," he said. They went through the impressive front doors of the university. The doors and frame were removed from the building in Hiroshima that survived the nuclear bomb during the Second World War and formed part of the entrance to the main building. The rest of the university used the same concept as the Greenwich Millennium Village. A dome covered the entire university, and all power and water came from rainfall and sunshine. This kept the costs down for running the structure and would benefit the students with next to nothing fees. The university supplied its excess power and water back into the city's electric and utilities systems, earning the university enough money to pay all its professors and staff yearly.

Aki followed the professor to a small office with a secretary sitting outside. "Sit down," he said in a gentle but firm voice, Aki planted herself in the comfy chair opposite a huge plastic desk. Wood wasn't used anymore, as it was an ever-dwindling resource. The professor asked Aki what her plans were going forward concerning employment and her future career.

Natasha replied, "Well, I want to work in one of the big fashion stores as a salesperson."

"Aki, is that the limitation of your expectations?"

"Yes, what else is there for someone with no formal qualifications or formal training?"

"What would you think about undertaking a degree in space technology?"

"I'm not qualified enough, am I?" she replied.

"You have a flair for science fiction, and a lot of what's happening in the fiction world is migrating to the real world. Look at 3D novels. Only ten years ago, they were just a dream and appeared in many movies."

"Yes, but that technology was always around, with 3D imaging starting from 3D films."

"It doesn't matter," the professor said. "It happened, and the discovery was made by a technology student in his final year of his degree."

"Who was that, then?" Aki enquired.

"It was Takao Kuzuhara," the professor said.

"Any relation?" Aki asked.

"Well, actually it was my son. Amazing, eh?" the professor said.

Aki asked how she would apply for this space degree.

"You need to take an aptitude test and sit an entrance interview. You also need a sponsor and the backing of a university professor."

"Are you just doing this because you feel sorry for me?"

The professor got quite angry. "Silly girl!" he shouted. Who do you think you are? I'm a well-respected academic and professor. You would not have come to my attention if we hadn't bumped into each other. When you were unconscious in hospital, I did a little checking on your background and found out who your mother was."

Aki immediately responded, "Who? Who was she?"

"I'm sorry, Aki. I can't tell you that. I promised the authorities I wouldn't reveal that information. "All I can tell you was that she was a scientist."

"In what field?" Aki asked. "Sorry, I can't tell you that either," said the professor.

Maria screamed down the com line, "Natasha, Natasha, are you all right?"

"Yes, thank God I'm in the airlock and am enjoying the oxygen."

"I know you've just had a dreadful experience, but we still need to patch the lab – just had the director of WSOA on the com."

"Maria, you're bloody joking, aren't you? I saw my life flash before me out there in space. I'm not going out there again, thank you."

"Natasha, come back down to the toilet area. Let's have a coffee," Maria said.

Natasha made her way to the toilet block and into the kitchen area. "Maria, who the hell do the WSOA think they are?" Natasha asked.

"I know you're upset about this, but don't forget part of your obligation. We have a relief crew coming on board in three days, and the station must be fully functional when they arrive. I'd execute the repair myself but am not trained for outside lab activities, so you will have to try again. I know your suit is damaged but you can use mine, as I hopefully will not require it."

"OK. Let me have a couple of hours' rest and I'll give it another go. I understand my responsibilities, but you must cut me a bit of slack. I'm still shaken up from my ordeal today."

"Right," said Maria. "Let's give it another try in two hours, at four o'clock."

Aki was shocked and annoyed at the news that the professor knew her real mother and that he couldn't divulge her name or anything about her. What about her father? Maybe the professor could at least tell her that. "OK, Professor. Did you get any information on my father?"

"I'm afraid not," he said in a dismissive way.

"You're hiding something," Aki retorted.

"Not really. There's nothing much to find out, only that your mother had a one-night fling and here you are."

"Well, Aki, how about my offer for this space technology degree? Are you interested?"

"Well, I don't know," she said. "I still think it's above my capabilities."

"Nonsense, girl. If you're anything like your mother, it will be a breeze," said the professor.

Aki pondered for a while and then said, "Do I live on campus or do I stay at the orphanage?"

The professor outlined the course details. Should she pass the tests, she would be a sponsored student by the city council as their one-off help to the underprivileged, so her costs would be funded for the four-year degree and would require her to live on campus.

"OK, then, Professor. When do I start?" asked Aki.

The professor explained that the tests would take place on the Wednesday of next week and would last for about four hours. "Four hours – that's a lifetime."

It was a few minutes before four on the station, and Natasha was feeling quite the hero as she was climbing into the other OSL suit. She had braved the ordeals of outer space and survived. Her thoughts were interrupted as she heard Maria through the com line. "Natasha, are you ready yet? We said four o'clock."

"I know that," she said. She checked all her equipment: patch, adhesive, ultraviolet torch, additional line, multitool … *There's something else,* she thought. *Of course, where is that damned pressure jet control?* She groped around the top left of her suit and found the matchbox-sized control. "Must not forget that one," she muttered aloud.

"Natasha, what are you saying? Not getting cold feet, I hope."

"No, Maria, just making sure I know where the pressure jet control is." Natasha opened the door to the airlock and climbed in; the door automatically closed behind her. *Here we go again,* she thought. She opened the outer door, attached her line, and moved into the vacuum of space.

When Aki turned up at the university to take the tests, she was ushered into a small room with a single desk, chair, and keypad that was built into the plastic desk. The screen for the computer was built into the far wall. The professor popped his head in the door to wish her good luck. She sat down at the desk and awaited her instructions.

The wall suddenly burst into life, and a bright blue screen appeared: NAME, CANDIDATE NUMBER, AND SPONSOR were illuminated in bold type. Aki typed in her name, candidate number, and city council as sponsor. "Welcome," a voice echoed from the wall. "You will be given a set of multiple choice questions. Please take your time – think outside the box. Good luck."

Aki saw the first set of questions appear. There were a random set of shapes with a blank space for your choice. She thought, *this looks like a silhouette of a plate of premium sushi; the one missing is with the big prawn. Let's put that in there.* All the questions Aki answered were of this nature.

She ploughed through the paper, and in almost no time, the next thing she heard was, "OK, you have now finished the first part of the test. Now it's time to complete the final phase." The next set of questions that appeared on screen were of a hypothetical nature. The first was, "What is the first thing you would do if the sea level rose one hundred metres?" Aki thought that was a strange question. She would get to high ground and try to find out what caused it.

Again, the time passed quickly, and before she knew it, the test had ended. "Thank you, Miss Yamoto. You have finished all the tests. Please proceed to the interview room, left out of here, and to room one-hundred and one."

She knocked on the door and was told to come in. In the room was a panel of people. Two female professors flanked Professor Kuzuhara; one was called Kazuko Tonomi and was head of biological science; the other was called Tamiko Yazukara and was head of mechanical and electrical science.

"Aki, please take a seat," said Professor Kuzuhara. "We're going to ask you a series of questions. Please take your time. There is no time limit on your responses, although we would like to eat tonight. I can tell you, Aki, that you've passed all the aptitude tests."

"How can you possibly know that already? I have only just finished," Aki replied.

"Well, the test is directly linked to our main computer, so it was marking as you were answering. Now let us begin."

Professor Yazukara asked the first question. "Aki, if you were doing a spacewalk, hypothetically, what would you do if you became untethered from the space craft during your walk?"

Aki said, "Not sure, but I definitely would not panic, as the more movement you make, the further you would drift away. I would call on my com line to let my compatriots know that I was drifting and await a solution from them."

"Good, very good!" Professor Yazukara exclaimed. "Excellent response."

"Aki, conclusive answer, but what would you do if the food that you brought for the trip became contaminated?" asked Professor Tonomi.

"I'd check all the food supplies to see if any of the items were not contaminated. I would check our fluid supply, as you can go a couple of weeks without food but only three days without water. I'd then radio our situation to space control, as it would only take a week to ready another craft to resupply us."

"Very good," Professor Tonomi said.

The questioning continued for the next forty minutes, until finally Professor Kuzuhara said, "Well, Aki, one last question: "When can you start your course?"

Natasha started moving towards the experimentation lab, this time making sure to look all around her as she moved along the outside of the station. She made it to the second tether point without any incident and secured her line. "Maria, Maria, are you there?"

"I'm here," answered Maria.

"I've just secured myself to the second tether point and am proceeding to the tear in the experimentation lab," said Natasha.

"All right," Maria said.

Natasha reached the tear, although the object that struck them glanced off it left a small metallic fragment embedded in the lab. "Maria, this is going to take longer than I thought. We have an object embedded in the tear; I need to remove that first."

"Don't forget you only have two hours' of oxygen."

"OK." Natasha pulled her multi-space tool from her chest bag and clamped it onto the embedded object. She rested the arms from the tool on the space lab hull and started the electric motor. Slowly the object started to come loose from the hull. Natasha removed the object and placed it into her chest bag. She then proceeded to run a bead of adhesive around the edge of the patch and then placed it onto the hull. Once in place, she pulled out the ultraviolet torch to set the adhesive. She must have been so engrossed that she had forgotten the time.

Maria was crackling in her helmet com. "Natasha, Natasha, come in."

"What's up?" asked Natasha.

"You only have five minutes of oxygen left. Are you nearly done?"

"I need two more minutes to set the adhesive."

"Not a minute longer or you'll run out of air before you reach the hatch."

Natasha finished the repair ninety seconds later and made her way back to the airlock hatch. She activated the hatch unlock button, the door slid silently open, and she climbed in. The outer hatch closed automatically behind her, and she pressed the pressure and air equalisation button. Oxygen flooded into the compartment, and she removed her helmet. She was curious about the fragment that she had removed from the outer hull. It was a bit dirty. She gave the plate a rub and could make out some letters. "Sputn ...," was about all she could read. *What does that mean, I wonder?* she thought.

Aki responded to the professor's question. "When can you take me?" she asked.

"How about next Monday? It will give you time to say good-bye and sort out your affairs," the professor responded.

"OK, Monday it is," said Aki.

She got up from her chair and had started walking towards the exit door when Professor Yazukara called to her, "Aki, can I walk with you?"

"Sure, if you want," said Aki.

"I just wanted to congratulate you. Not many students pass the final interview. You did very well, one of the best I have seen," stated Professor Yazukara.

"Did I? Well, how about that?" Aki said with a sense of pride and achievement. "Life is looking up."

"I just wanted to also let you know I'll be your mentor during your four-year course, so if you need anything, you must let me know."

"OK, Prof. Hope it's OK for me to call you that."

Aki excelled in every aspect of her degree. She was eager to learn and liked to please. She breezed through her first three years, getting a distinction in each year. She was coming up to her last year. These were mainly practical exercises, putting the theory into practice. It involved underwater space walks, learning how to repair electronics, how to fly the space modules, what to do in certain dangerous situations, and so forth. It was on one of her final courses in electronics that she was to meet her future husband.

Natasha made her way to the toilet section of the lab to remove her OLS suit and slip back into her silicone paper one, Maria was waiting there for her with a latte, her favourite drink. "Natasha, fantastic job – the internal timinium repair system has sealed the experimental lab skin, and the oxygen levels have been replenished. Well done," Maria said in a relieved voice.

"Hopefully the rest of our assignment goes much smoother," said Natasha.

Maria had just remembered that they had not informed WSOA headquarters of the strange images of a roadway with white lines just south of the Azores. "Natasha, in all the excitement, we have not mentioned to WSOA the strange find that you spotted through the planetary scope yesterday evening," Maria said.

"The only problem is that if we tell them, then our assignment will continue until the observation has been fully investigated. Let's wait until we come back in two weeks. We can check again to see if it's still there," said Natasha.

Maria had reservations about withholding information from the WSOA, for if they found out, it would cost them their jobs. "All right, but we must reinvestigate this in two weeks when we come back aboard," Maria said, resigning herself to the fact Natasha was right; they would have to stay aboard until the phenomenon had been thoroughly investigated, and this would mean not seeing her husband or children for some time.

Aki was in her final year at university and ploughing her way through all the practical tests required to finalise her degree. She loved her electronics class, but that was more because her lecturer was a bit of a dish. He was the son of Professor Kuzuhara. Takao enjoyed his job as the lecturer for final year student electronics; of course, he was famous in his own right as the inventor of the 3D novel. He could have sat back and enjoyed life off the proceeds of his invention. However, Takao wasn't like your normal rich inventor; he wanted to give something back to education and to help students further their own ambitions. He never took a wage, only claiming expenses for driving back and forth to the university from Kure every day. Aki was one of the older students, as she started university at a late age. She was twenty-four now and so different from the girl who first emerged from the orphanage – much more refined, speaking with an intelligence that belied her humble beginnings. She still had a burning ambition to succeed but kept it more under control. She had turned into a beautiful young woman, with flowing dark locks, bright blue eyes (unusual for Japanese women, who normally have deep brown eyes), and a slim figure. Her skin was porcelain white, as with many Japanese people. She was going on her sixth date with him tonight and was just as excited as the first one because it was with the man she had fancied during her electronics classes, lecturer Takao Kuzuhara.

CHAPTER TWO

EARTH 2047

Maria and Natasha were travelling in one of the pods and nearing the space platform where the earth tether was. Natasha was looking forward to catching up with her father-in-law, Professor Kuzuhara, and Maria couldn't wait to see her husband and children. The com line crackled into life as they approached the platform. "Please ensure you have your harnesses on and your helmet oxygen lines open," a voice commanded. It came from the on-board computer. You needed to make sure you were strapped in, as the forces generated when the pod moved earthwards were quite high. The speed of the pods was around forty kilometres per hour whilst in space travelling down to the tether platform, but once connected to the tether and hitting the atmosphere, the speed increased to one hundred kilometres per hour to reach the earth in thirty minutes from space. The total journey time once on the tether was ten hours.

In Egypt, archaeologists were excavating the latest pharaoh's tomb, Ramses IX. The eighth was discovered in 2045. No one knew there was a ninth Ramses until they found the eighth's tomb in the Valley of the Kings underneath King Tutankhamen's tomb, which had been excavated by Howard Carter in the 1930s. When Ramses VIII's tomb had been excavated, the archaeologists discovered that there was a boy king who ruled for about ten months. He was twelve when he died, and he was called Ramses IX. During the excavation of the ninth's tomb, an unusual object was found in one of the organ jars. The head of the dig, Professor David Carter, a long-time removed relative of Howard Carter, had disturbed an organ jar, tipping it over, breaking it during the process.

Something caught his eye amongst the debris. It looked like a pair of spectacles, but that could not be possible. He picked up the object and gave it a clean with his hankie. It was definitely a pair of spectacles, and he took them to his mobile caravan to inspect them further. He called his team together for a meeting and asked who had put the spectacles in the organ jar, as it wasn't funny and was a joke in bad taste. His whole team looked perplexed and began pointing fingers at each other. One by one, they vehemently denied putting the spectacles into the organ jar. Professor Carter became quite agitated, as this had gone far enough, still his team denied any practical joking. Professor Carter suspended the dig. He put security guards at the tomb entrance and told his team that unless someone came forward and admitted to planning this joke, he would have to think about bringing in a new team of archaeologists. He gave them until the end of the day, saying that if no one came forward by then, the dig would be off limits to everybody.

The professor was deep in thought whilst reading papers in his caravan. When he heard a knock on his door, he opened the door to find his whole team waiting outside. They again professed their innocence. One of the team suggested to the professor that they could to get the object plutonium radiocarbon dated. They had the facilities here to do that – at least that would clear up the validity of the object. The professor was still not convinced, but he had known some members of his team for twenty years and they were the most insistent of the group. He agreed for them to plutonium radiocarbon date the object. It took twenty-four hours to complete, and his team called him to the mobile lab the next day. He was told to sit down, as he might be shocked by the results of the test. The oldest member of the team showed him the results, and he sat quietly for a while studying them. He read that the spectacles were made from a resin plastic and had a polarised tint with polished chrome temples. He tried to make sense of what he was reading. He thought resin plastic didn't appear until the late nineteenth century, and electrical chrome plating didn't appear until the early twenties. This just could not be. The new plutonium carbon dating process had put the spectacles at over 250,000 years old.

As the pods were nearing the end of their journey, Natasha and Maria were discussing the first things they were going to do upon arrival at the tether Earth point station. Maria said, "I'm going to find a fish and chip shop and have cod roe and chips."

Natasha said, "I'm going straight to a sushi bar and am going to order a huge portion of sashimi prawns."

The pods came to a sudden halt, the G-force was tremendous, making it feel as if one's stomach were falling to one's feet. Maria could never get used to that feeling. It happened every time she did the return trip from the station.

Natasha departed the pod first, followed by Maria. They were unusually met by WSOA security, who were to escort them back to the European base in London. The main headquarters for WSOA was in Houston, Texas, where the space shuttle launches were flown from back in the late nineties until the early noughties. There were several space centres around the world where space launches can take place: Houston, as previously mentioned; French

Guinea; Berlin; and several sites in Russia and China. There is currently only one earth tether, so all travel to the space stations is from England. There were several space stations in orbit around the earth. They were being used by several countries for research into many projects. For example, they were close to a breakthrough in finding a cure for incurable cancers. The low gravity and highly oxygenated stations provided better conditions to incubate and treat these diseases. Additionally, there were three underwater research stations based in deep-water seas: Deep Ocean One (DO1) was on the floor of the Pacific, in the shallowest part of the Marianas Trench; Deep Ocean Two (DO2) was on the floor of the Atlantic, in the Puerto Trench; the third (DO3) was on the Southern Ocean, in the South Sandwich Trench. Each station had around two hundred aquanauts on board at any one time. Part of the training for space was a six-month stint on one of these ocean stations. They were currently looking at alternative fuel and food sources. They had found billions of tons of frozen methane gases which could be converted into a cheap fuel source and were looking into the most economical way of mining it. New types of seaweed and fungi as well as unknown species of fish had been found, which could be used as alternatives to land-based and shallow ocean foods.

Maria and Natasha entered the London WSOA offices; these were based in the underground tunnels of the Bull and Bush underground station, which never opened to the public after being built in the 1950s. They were rushed in to see the station commander, General Graham Payton. "Please sit down," he said to Natasha and Maria. "Have you heard about a recent discovery in Egypt last week," he enquired.

"What recent discovery?" Natasha asked guardedly, thinking about the white lines and city they had found just south of the Azores.

Maria jumped in before Natasha could utter another sentence. "Well, General, it's like this ..."

"Like what?" he asked.

"Well, we have a little discovery of our own to report."

"Yes," said Natasha. "The space station got hit by an old satellite and gave us a few problems."

"What old satellite?"

"I don't know, but I did manage to retrieve a fragment that got embedded in the outer hull. Here, I have it with me. Look," she said. Maria was about to talk again, and Natasha looked at her, shaking her head as if to say, "No, Maria don't tell him yet."

The general studied the fragment. "Sputn ...," he said to himself. Of course, this was a part of the first space satellite launched by the Russians in 1957. "Sputnik," he said aloud. "My God, that disappeared about twenty years ago, and nobody had seen or heard from it since. We thought it had flown off into outer space, never to be seen again. If it is still flying around up there, we better warn the rest of the space community, as it could cause some major damage. You were very lucky, commanders. So, what was this other discovery?"

Natasha jumped in quickly. "Well, General, the new timinium compound works really well. It completely sealed the breach once I did the outside repair."

"Is that all?" said the general.

By this time, Maria was in line with Natasha's thinking. She said, "We did have a few other issues. Commander Kuzuhara became detached from the station, and we had a few tricky moments."

"Really?" the general said, clearly not entirely convinced of their stories. "Commander Kuzuhara, Commander Francis, what else happened up there? We could see from the on-board cameras quite a lot of activity from you both."

Aki and Takao Kuzuhara went out on the town for their sixth date. Dancing was first on the agenda, at the Hiroshima Palace, and then on to the best fish restaurant in Kure. They served the best prawn sashimi in Japan and had won many awards for their seafood sashimi. The restaurant was called *Kozakana*, which, when translated into English, meant "Little Fish". Whilst at the restaurant, Takao asked Aki what her plans were once she finished her degree. Aki replied, "I certainly will not be working in a department store," at which point Takao burst out laughing. He remembered the story his father had related to him about the collision he had with her and about her ambitions for the future – and generally about her dizzy approach to life. "What are you laughing about?" Aki snapped. "I was unconscious for three days."

"Aki, I'm not laughing about you, just the situation you got yourself into," he said.

"Well, it wasn't funny at the time, although I can smile about it now, as it has led me to you," she said with a gentle sigh.

"So, what are your plans?" Takao asked again.

"I want to make something of my degree," she said. "I'm considering joining the WSOA and training for a space assignment."

"But, Aki, that will mean leaving Japan and going to America."

"Does that worry you?" she asked.

"No, no. Should it?" said Takao.

They were playing cat and mouse with each other over their feelings. Unbeknown to Aki, this would be their last date for some time.

Maria asked the general about this discovery in Egypt to deflect any more questions to them about their discovery.

"Hmm, OK, then. Let's play your game, Commanders," retorted the general. "Professor Carter, who oversees the Ramses the ninth dig, has found something strange at the site. He has already communicated this find to all the big agencies around the world – CIA, MI6, IPA [formerly KGB], and the WSOA."

"Well, what is it?" Natasha asked impatiently.

"Apparently, and this has not been confirmed, but it was a pair of spectacles."

"So, what? Nothing unusual there." Said Maria

The general, obviously now feeling a little perturbed, snapped back at Maria, "Now listen here, Commander Francis – just shut your mouth and listen to what I have to say. Firstly, spectacles were never invented that early; secondly, the plutonium radiocarbon test put them at two hundred and fifty thousand-plus years old, which means they were made two hundred and forty thousand years before the Egyptian civilisation even existed."

"But what has this to do with the WSOA? We're looking at the future, not the past," said Maria. "We need to be worried about near-Earth objects, not a bloody pair of spectacles. So, one of the pharaohs was four-eyes."

This set Natasha off. She just couldn't stop giggling. "Four-eyes," she kept repeating.

The general absolutely exploded. "I have a good mind to suspend both of you and put you on gardening leave without pay. Fucking laugh about that then," he snorted.

"Sorry, General," Natasha said. We had a bad experience what with the collision on the lab, my drifting off into space, and to top it all, Atlantis."

Maria screamed, "Natasha, stop!"

Maria Francis, formerly Mara Smythe, formerly Mara Radich, had a similar upbringing to Natasha. She was adopted from her home country of Croatia. She was born near the Serbian border close to a city called Osijek. It changed hands several times during the Croat and Serbian conflict of the early nineties. It took several years after for people to get that conflict out of their systems. Hatred between these two small nations continued well into the noughties, even though the conflict had ended back in the nineties. Mara's father had a brother living in England, and her parents thought she would have a better life if she went and lived with him and his wife, Mary, who was from Angus in Scotland, as they were still relatively poor and not in good health. Mara was four years old at the time of her adoption. It was a huge wrench for her family, but they knew it would give her a better chance in life.

She came to England in 2011, just at the height of the austerity measures put in place by the government of the day to shore up the country's finances.

She lived in London with her adoptive mother and uncle. Mary was in her late forties when she met Drago, who was in his late forties. He was in England as an exchange university professor at the university in East Dulwich, teaching physics and mathematics; Mary was a university head chef. They met at the university Christmas party in 2009 and started dating shortly after. Mary's family didn't really approve of Drago. They thought he was only marrying Mary to stay in the country for good, but Mary and Drago knew differently. They were in love and wanted to be with each other for the rest of their lives.

They lived in a small flat in South Kensington, near Hyde Park. Mara's early years were spent going back and forth to Mary's family as her job didn't give her enough vacation. The little time she got only covered three weeks of Mara's school holiday. This meant that Mara was packed off to relatives, mainly in Scotland, during school breaks. She particularly liked to visit Mary's mother, Granny Mackie in Carnoustie, whose house by the sea allowed one to walk through the back gate and straight onto the beach. Mary had a brother called Tom who lived with Mary's mother, so her early years were spent growing up amongst adults.

General Payton asked Natasha to explain herself. Natasha said, "General, we observed a strange phenomenon through the planetary telescope yesterday evening."

"What did you mean by Atlantis?" asked the general.

"What Natasha means, sir, is we spotted a city and a road with white lines on it, just south of the Azores. It was about two miles under the ocean," said Maria.

"Why didn't you report this yesterday?" asked the general.

"In our defence, General, we had more pressing matters with the repair to our experimentation lab that it went completely out of our minds," said Natasha.

"General, what does all this have to do with the spectacles found in Egypt?" enquired Maria.

The general closed the doors to his office and said, "What I'm about to tell must go no further than this room. Do we understand each other, Commanders?"

"Yes, sir," they both said.

Mara's parents separated whilst she was still in her teens. It was quite a messy divorce, with Mara's uncle threatening to take her back to Croatia. This prompted her adoptive mother, Mary, to move them from house to house to avoid her former husband. They moved to Scotland and lived with Mara's adoptive grandmother in Carnoustie. In the process, Mara's adoptive mother changed their surname from Radich to Smythe, with Mara changing her first name to Maria to keep her uncle off the scent. She never saw her biological parents again.

In 2029, Maria went to Edinburgh University to study micro and marine biology and came out with a first-class honours degree. She also met her future husband, Adam Francis, at the university. He was studying mechanical engineering. Maria applied for a job with one of the big chemical companies after receiving her degree, and she had a successful career with the AMTChem chemical company, eventually ending up as director of their new chemical futures research centre. She had kept in touch with Adam, and they got married five years after she completed her degree. A couple of years later, they had their first child, Alana, followed two years later by their son, Sean.

Maria was now thirty-six and enjoying her life and her family. Even though she was a director of a research centre, she managed to maintain a balance between work and family. Maria came into work on her birthday and expected a routine day. When she arrived, the head of the chemical company she worked for was in the building doing his rounds. Maria rushed to her office to make sure her staff were aware of his visit. When she got to her office, there were some people in dark suits sitting at her conference desk. "What are you doing in my office?" she asked the group.

They were about to answer when a voice behind her said, "Maria glad you could make it." It was Phillippe Doucal, the head of the company, walking in behind her and closing the door as he did so.

"Maria, please sit down," one of the suits said.

"Who are you?" Maria asked. "And how do you know my name?"

The general asked Natasha and Maria to take a seat. He was much calmer now. "Commanders, the spectacles are just the tip of the iceberg. All our deep-sea research centres have been finding similar objects on the sea floor of varying kinds – plastic containers of food, modern calculators, bottled alcohol, modern porcelain, fountain pens ... As you well know, Natasha, from your time on DO1, I could go on and on."

"But, General, these objects could have fallen from ships and found their way into the trenches where our deep ocean centres are located," said Natasha.

"I know, and that's what we thought, until we found a piece of a space station and plutonium radiocarbon dated the food in the plastic containers and the ink in the fountain pens. All objects were over two hundred and fifty thousand years old," explained the general. "That's not the only discovery. Sputnik didn't just vanish mysteriously, as I said earlier. We believe its course was deliberately changed to take it out of our solar system."

"Who could have done that?" asked Maria. "Was it the Russians or Chinese?" asked Natasha.

"No, they were as baffled as we were," said the general.

"So what does this have to do with us, General?" Natasha asked again.

"We believe that the disappearance and reappearance of the sputnik satellite is somehow connected to all the objects being found. We also believe that the satellite hitting your lab was no coincidence. We are sure someone or something is trying to prevent us from looking into deep space and has been putting objects on Earth, like the spectacles, to keep us occupied while they attain their real objective, to possibly invade earth. Your lab is the only one that has a deep space telescope more powerful than anything we've built before, and that's the reason you've been targeted – to prevent your viewing further into space."

"General, that sounds a bit far-fetched and more like a science fiction movie," said Natasha.

"I need you back on the station in one week. Sorry, I know it cuts your vacation short, but this is too important to leave for another week. OK, commanders?"

"Yes, sir," replied Natasha and Maria.

Phillippe Doucal answered the question Maria had asked the suit. "Maria, I supplied them with all the information about you," he said.

"But why, Phillippe?" Maria asked.

"Maybe I'll let General Payton answer that one," he said. "Mrs Francis … or may I call you Maria?" the general said.

"Whatever," said Maria.

"We will be launching a new space station in twelve months and would like you to be one of the crew. This station will be for research on deep space and deep planetary oceans. You have the marine biology experience, and your pioneering work on new chemicals will be invaluable in our research," said the general.

"But I have a job here," quipped Maria, looking pensively towards Phillippe Doucal." Please say something, Phillippe," she pleaded.

"I'm sorry, Maria," he said. "My hands are tied. This order has come down from the very top. The prime minister has insisted that you become one of the team. If I did not agree, they would not renew our permits to produce chemicals."

Natasha and Maria left the general's office and headed straight for the train station to get back to their loved ones so as not to waste a minute of the week-long vacation. On the way there, Maria and Natasha looked at each other and broke into fits of laughter.

"Gardening leave," Natasha chortled. "Fucking laugh about, that then."

Maria chortled back. The general's seriousness and reaction to their questions was something he had never displayed before in all the time they had known him. They reached the station still giggling to one another.

"Maria, my train to Heathrow is about to leave. See you in a week's time. I'm meeting my father-in-law at the Holiday Inn by the airport," Natasha blurted out as she ran for her train.

"OK, Natasha," Maria replied. Maria walked in a more leisurely fashion, as her home was only twenty minutes on the tube back to Millennium Town. She got on at Charing Cross station, scanning her personal communication device at the entrance to the station which opened the doors. These devices were wrist mounted and carried all of the owner's details. The ticket cost was paid directly from the person's bank account.

The journey seemed to last forever, with the train stopping at every station. At last, it pulled into millennium station and she climbed down onto the platform. Even though it was after nine in the evening, the summer warmth was pleasant and the smell of the millennium gardens were intoxicating, with roses, jasmine, and other tropical plants. She made her way into the dome and took the escalator to the third level, where her apartment was located. She put her wrist device on the panel outside the door, and it clicked open.

"Mummy, Mummy!" shouted Alana and Sean, almost knocking her over in the rush to hug her. Adam, her husband, followed closely behind them.

"Hello, my darling," he said. "We all missed you terribly."

"I'm only going to be home for a week, so let's pack tonight and in the morning set off for Scotland to see my mother."

"What did you say, Maria? Only one week?"

"Sorry, darling. Just found out as we arrived back from the station today that we have to be back on board a week earlier than planned," said Maria with a sadness in her heart.

"But why? We had a plan for the whole two weeks. The kids will be devastated, and I'll miss you again," Adam retorted angrily.

"I am so sorry. It's a matter of national security, and I wasn't given a choice."

"What can be so important that you have to be back in a week? Don't they have a relief crew on board? Why can't they handle it?" Adam snapped back.

"I'm afraid they need my marine biology experience," said Maria.

After the meeting with the suits, Maria asked Phillippe Doucal for a private one-on-one. When the suits left Maria's office, Phillippe stayed behind to talk with Maria. "Well, Maria, what do you think?" asked Phillippe.

"To be honest, I'm fucking annoyed you didn't put up more of a fight."

"They threatened to close us down, and if I were you, I wouldn't mess with them. You have a family, if you know what I mean," Phillippe whispered, quietly peering over his shoulder as he said it.

"What the hell are you doing, Phillippe!" shouted Maria.

"Shush, shush. They might be still here," Phillippe said nervously, still looking over his shoulder. "They also want you as part of the team due to your work with the liquidized form of aluminium/titanium repair compound."

"What would the military want with that? It's for commercial use only and can't be turned into a weapon," said Maria.

"No, I know that, but just think of the applications if you were to use it for repairs to the space lab."

The next morning, Maria and Adam were up early to get the kids up and have some breakfast before setting off to visit Maria's mum in Scotland. The journey would normally take about nine hours by fossil fuel car, and if you were to drive with the UFV, it would be even longer. Today's journey would take about three hours in total, thirty minutes to the UFV terminus at Liverpool Street and then two hours by Fusion monorail to Dundee, then another thirty-minute drive to Carnoustie. The train left on time at 8.31 a.m. The Fusion monorail was a bit like the old car trains used to cross from Dover to Calais thirty-plus years ago, except the train was powered by an ion thruster drive; it was built back in 2035. This was designed to carry only UFV and was free to use, as it came as part of the package to owning one. The government permit needed, to drive more than ten miles with a fossil fuel vehicle was almost impossible to get. Having an ion thruster drive eliminated the need to run electric power in the mono lines. The obvious advantage was the speed it could travel, cutting down travel time between destinations.

The mono train arrived into Dundee station at precisely 10.30 a.m., unlike the old train services that were always delayed. The destination time was announced as 10.31 a.m., so the train arrived one minute earlier than expected.

"That was smooth and quick as usual," Adam said, trying to strike up a conversation, as Maria had not really said anything throughout the journey to Dundee.

"Yes, same procedure as always," Maria said. She just couldn't stop thinking about what the general had told them about these 250,000 years-plus objects.

Natasha just made it to her appointment with her father-in-law, Professor Kuzuhara. "Hello, Professor. I was a bit rushed, as we were summoned to the WSOA London branch before we could go on leave," said Natasha, breathing heavily because she'd run to the Holiday Inn from the station.

"Natasha, don't worry. We have all of two weeks together so no need to panic," said the professor.

"I'm sorry to say that we'll only have one week, as I'm required back on the lab in eight days' time."

"Why are they cutting your vacation short? From my dealings with the WSOA, it must be serious."

"I can't say, unfortunately, as we've been sworn to secrecy by our commanding officer," she answered.

"Is your commanding officer General Payton?" asked the professor.

"Yes, how did you know?"

"I knew him when he was just a lower grade officer working for the American government as the space specialist on their tactical development committees. He was assigned by NASA to advise the government on outer space threats like comets, asteroids, and other civilisations not of the earth."

What Natasha was also unaware of was that General Payton knew her mother. It was his initiative to encourage the professor to offer Natasha an opportunity to study for the space technology degree. General Payton met Natasha's mother during his secondment to the Japanese government in his early career. She was the technical expert on one of the space threats committees based around the world. With this one being in Japan, he was the liaison officer from NASA. They would often go out for evening meals. In those days, General Payton was a six-foot blue-eyed all-American blond football player type, a typical officer and a charming man. He was eager to see the sights of Hiroshima; they often ate at the Kozakana fish restaurant in the city, as it was the only one that served good sashimi. Tamiko would show Graham Payton areas of the city that the ordinary tourist would never find. There was a museum of antiquities based in the sewers of the city, and during a visit to this museum Graham Payton saw an object that was to become an obsession of his and spark his career into life.

In one of the display cabinets was on old watch, one of the digital types used in the early seventies until the early nineties, when eco technology watches became popular. The manufacturer's name was one he had never heard of: Mieko. He knew about the other Japanese manufacturers but not this one. Apparently, this watch was found after the nuclear bomb on the city during the Second World War and was treated as a sacred relic. Graham Payton, with Tamiko's help, asked the curator of the museum exactly where the relic was found. He stated that the nuclear bomb dropped on Hiroshima during World War Two had exploded above the harbour near a hospital and the ensuing water spray threw up this watch. The people of Hiroshima also hadn't heard of this make of watch, so it became a sacred relic, as it appeared after the bomb. The *shinseina udedoke*, as it was called in Japanese, was never to be removed from the museum because the people believed it to be a sign from the God of the sea, *Umi no kami*. Graham Payton was fascinated by this relic. Where did it come from? Why was it found in Japan? How could he get it out of the museum to exam it further? All these questions were racing through his mind.

"Graham san, Graham san," Tamiko uttered as she gently nudged him back to reality. "Graham san, are you with me?" she said repeatedly.

He finally said, "Sorry, Tamiko. I got lost in thought. What if this relic wasn't from this planet?"

"I think that's a bit far-fetched, don't you?" she replied.

"So, Professor, did he have any influence on your decision to offer me my space technology degree course?" Natasha asked.

"No, he was interested in your progress once on your degree, but that was only because he knew your mother and was a good friend of hers," said the professor. "Anyway, Natasha, let's not waste your vacation period talking about work. What shall we do tomorrow?"

"One second, Professor. You started the conversation on General Payton," snapped Natasha.

"I see you still have that short temper of yours," the professor quipped back, at which point Natasha burst into laughter.

"All right, Prof, how about we visit the Tower of London for starters? Then we can go on to Kew Gardens and have some lunch in the Tokyo Empire restaurant in Hammersmith."

Maria, Adam, and the children arrived at Granny Mary's cottage in good time, exactly thirty minutes after departing Dundee train station. Maria's mum was at the door to greet them, and she was now in her eightieth year and fit as a fiddle. She took long walks along the beach every morning and then tended her beautiful flower garden for a couple of hours before sitting down to her porridge and fruit breakfast. Her brother Tom was also living at the cottage. His wife had died and his family had long flown the nest, so he sold his business and moved in with Mary for company and the convenience of paying one set of household bills.

As soon as they got into the cottage, the children went with Granny Mary straight onto the beach. Maria's uncle had his golf clubs at the ready, and he was beckoning to Adam to follow him. Adam looked at Maria, at which point she nodded her approval. She knew they would be gone a couple of hours, what with the golf and a drink at the local pub, and it would give her time to digest what the general had told Natasha and her before their vacation.

Adam was a bit rusty on the golf course, as he had not played for a while; after he retired, he set up a consultancy business which kept him occupied most of the week. "Adam what does Maria actually do on this space station?" asked Tom.

"A good question, Tom. Maria does not tell me much, as the work is of world importance and not to be discussed."

"Oh, one of those types of jobs," said Tom. He knew the type of job Adam was talking about, as during his army career he worked for the Special Services and could never tell his family what was going on. "She seems to enjoy what she is doing and earns a good salary, I should imagine."

"Well, we've never wanted for anything, so I suppose you're right. I'm happy and so are the children," said Adam. "We'll only be staying about four days because I have arranged a surprise belated birthday party for Maria at my brother's house in the Lake District on Thursday."

Tom asked Adam if they had told Maria's mother, she had stocked up with food for the week.

Graham Payton related his story about this sacred relic, the *shinseina udedokei*, which he had seen in the underground museum, to his chief of staff, Admiral Mackenzie. "Well, admiral, what do you think?" he asked. "Do you think this artefact had been planted and is really a fake or do we think it's genuine?" the admiral asked Graham.

"I think that it is strange for a modern watch to be found in nineteen forty-five when this type didn't appear until the early seventies," replied Graham.

"Do you think the Japanese government would let us look at this artefact?" asked the admiral.

"It's a sacred relic, so it could be difficult to get hold of it. The people of Hiroshima would not support the Japanese government," said Graham.

"I'll have a word with the Japanese fleet admiral, Honju. He owes me a few favours."

Maria was still deep in thought when her mother came in with the children, their faces bright red from the sea winds. "Maria, Maria, Maria, wake up!" her mother yelled. By the time Maria responded, a few seconds had passed.

"Sorry, Mum. I was miles away."

"Shall we have some lunch? The children are asking for some cakes," she said in a proud voice, aware that the children loved her cakes and scones. Mary had even won prizes for them at the local summer fetes' and shows.

"Yeah, yeah, let's have some cakes and sandwiches!" shouted Alana and Sean excitedly.

"Mum, I'm afraid we're only going to be here a few days, until Thursday, when we'll be going to visit Adam's brother in the Lake District. Hope you didn't buy too much food," said Maria.

"No, not much," said Mary.

"Mum, now come on – I know you well enough. I can pay you for the extra food and take it with me to Adam's brother's place. I'm sure they'll use it up," said Maria.

"Why are you only staying a few days?" enquired Mary. "I thought you had two weeks' vacation."

"Unfortunately, a problem has arisen on the space lab and I should be back on board in eight days," said Maria.

"Maybe they will give you a longer break for your next leave on Earth," said Mary.

Admiral Mackenzie managed to get the *shinseina udedokei* on loan for a couple of days, which excited Graham Payton immensely. They tested the object, and it dated back to over 250,000 years old.

"Admiral, the carbon dating test has come back. The object is over two hundred and fifty thousand years old. What can that mean?" asked Graham.

"I think either the test was flawed or we have a mystery here," replied the admiral.

"That would put the artefact on the planet two hundred and forty-three years before the Egyptians even existed," retorted Graham excitedly, as if he had just solved the most difficult puzzle in the world.

Aki joined the WSOA after completing her space technology degree. She was going to start her training by spending the next six months on DO1 in the Marianas Trench. During that time, she would be trained in all aspects of space walking and how to service an orbiting space station. She kept in constant contact with Takao Kuzuhara, and they planned to get married when she finished her assignment. Part of her training was to go out onto the ocean floor, which at that point in the trench was four miles below sea level. They had to wear special deep-sea suits that could withstand the enormous pressure at that depth.

Whilst on one of her training exercises, she came across an unusual object. It was a plastic container of tomatoes, a type that she had never heard of, and the plastic container was strange because it had not deteriorated and had no paper label, just a picture of a weird-looking tomato. Her orders were to bring all objects back to the station for cataloguing. She questioned her superiors about those orders, but to no avail. If seen, these objects were to be brought back and catalogued. The mining operation for retrieving the vast quantities of frozen methane made much more sense to Aki, as the planet was running out of fossil fuels. The frozen gas was mined using specialist equipment because even at those depths, if the temperature of the frozen methane climbed by more than four degrees, it would explode.

During her time on DO1, she met a fellow aquanaut, Maria Francis, who was on a short visit to help with development of her latest breakthrough to produce a liquid form of titanium/aluminium compound. They were on the same rota for mealtimes. They were courteous and acknowledged one another but never really got to know each other, as Aki was in training mode and Maria in research mode.

Aki completed her six months on DO1 without much incident, although she did find all the procedures and paperwork a bit much and her attention to detail could be at times questionable. However, she just passed.

As planned, Aki went back to Japan and married Takao. It was the happiest day of Aki's troubled life, and it was a traditional Japanese wedding, with Aki wearing her ceremonial kimono and Takao in his samurai dress kit. They had a Western-style reception at the Kozakana fish restaurant, with several dignitaries from the world of science and the WSOA and General Graham Payton attending, as did all the professors from Hiroshima University.

Aki's mother was also at the wedding. Professor Tamiko Yazukara gave birth to Aki out of wedlock, something that in those days in Japan was a complete taboo. She had no choice but to send Aki to the local orphanage to protect her family's honour and safeguard her career on the space technology committee. The decision to send Aki to the orphanage broke Tamiko's heart. She struggled to come to terms with it, but her family pushed her to that point. It was a matter of honour. It would bring shame on the family and would affect careers and opportunities for her siblings, aunts, and uncles if she kept the baby. During her time on the space technology degree, Aki learned that Professor Yazukara was her mother. It was one of the reasons the professor wanted to mentor her, and it was during one of their weekly sessions that the professor revealed her identity. The professor never revealed who her father was; she was sworn to secrecy by Aki's unknown father's organisation.

Aki settled back down to life in Hiroshima, Japan, working for the WSOA in an office-based job. She gave birth to her daughter, Natasha, twelve months after she married Takao. She was extremely contented for the first time in her life. Takao was still teaching at the university, and her father-in-law, Professor Kuzuhara, was also there. Life just could not get any better. She frequently had her mother over to visit, as she was still teaching at Hiroshima University. Professor Tamiko Yazukara was so happy she could now formerly recognise Aki as her daughter.

She enjoyed her visits to see Aki and her grand-daughter, Natasha. It was during one of her visits to see Aki that Tamiko experienced several dizzy spells. She was babysitting for Aki so Takao could take her out for the evening. Natasha was now eight years old and a child so full of life, always dragging Grandma Tamiko all over the place. They were playing their usual game of hide-and-seek. Tamiko was hiding in the cloakroom downstairs when she suddenly blacked out. The next thing she remembered when coming to was Natasha and Aki standing over her. Natasha was crying and repeatedly saying, "Mummy, Grandma's dead. She's dead."

Tamiko was rushed to Cherry Blossom Hospital for tests. She had a small growth on her left cerebral lobe, which meant she had a brain tumour. That was the reason she suddenly blacked out – the pressure of the growth cut off the oxygen supply temporarily to that part of the brain until the growth shrank back. The rushing around when playing with her grand-daughter caused the growth to swell.

Tamiko had the very best treatment to try to cure the cancer. Unfortunately, it had been there for quite a few years and had gone past the point of no return in terms of a permanent cure. She was given a few months' respite with the new specialist gene therapy treatment; however, this was only a temporary solution. Tamiko lived for another seven months before the cancer beat her. She died peacefully in her sleep whilst staying with Aki. Natasha cried constantly for her grandma.

Her death deeply affected Aki. She had just found her mother and only had a few years with her. Her entire attitude changed, and she was back to that rebellious teenager of her late teens. She didn't seem to care about anything. Takao, her husband, tried to console her daily, but even he couldn't break through to her.

This period of mourning was also affecting Aki's work. The WSOA were on the brink of firing her. General Payton intervened to prevent her dismissal. He came over to Japan to meet with Aki. He had a proposal for her to consider. Aki arrived at work one morning and was immediately ushered in to see General Payton. "Take a seat," said the general.

"What do you need to see me for?" Aki snapped.

"Now, Aki, I know what you have been going through. Professor Yazukara was a close friend of mine, and I miss her too. You aren't the only one in mourning," said the general. This took Aki a bit by surprise, as the general wasn't normally a sympathetic man. "Look, Aki, you must snap out of this lethargy, as it's not only affecting your work. You have a family to consider," continued the general.

"General, I'm struggling with the whole situation. To find my mother and then lose her after a few years has been very hard for me. I spent all those years at the orphanage with no future, no parents, and I had so much pent-up anger that is starting to surface again. I'm sorry if I have caused you too much trouble."

"Let's not worry about that for the moment. I have a proposal for you. In about twelve months, we're going to launch a very special space station. It will be for research and for looking into deep space to detect asteroids or comet threats."

"What does that have to do with me?" asked Aki.

"I'm looking for a couple of astronauts to man the station on a three-monthly cycle, and you're top of my list. What do you think?" asked the general.

Maria and Adam's time at her mums went by quickly. It seemed like only yesterday they were saying hello, and now Adam was packing the car for the five-hour drive to Adam's brother in the Lake District.

"Mum, we had a really wonderful time. Thanks for having us over," said Maria.

"It was nice to see you; hope your next visit isn't too far away," replied Mary.

"On my next vacation, we'll come and spend a week with you."

"That would be lovely, Maria." Said Mary

Adam and the children said their goodbyes to Mary and Tom. Maria hugged her, as she might not see her for a few months, and they jumped into their UFV and buckled up. The journey was going to take five hours, as they planned to stop a couple of times for coffee breaks. Their journey would take them through Edinburgh

"That was short and sweet," said Adam.

"I know. Wish it could have been longer but we must see your brother before I go back to the space station," said Maria.

Adam and Maria chatted more on the journey to his brother's than they had on the journey from London to see Maria's mother. Adam was enquiring more about Maria's work, and she was happy to share some details. "Adam, did you know there are two near-Earth objects that are going to pass by the earth at the end of July and end of August?" asked Maria.

"Yes, I was aware of that, but there's no panic, because like the last two asteroids, they will miss the earth," he said.

"Well, we cannot always be sure, but you're right. They're supposed to pass by rather than strike Earth."

"What else do you get up to on the space station?" asked Adam.

"I can't really say, but you can rest assured that I'm always thinking of coming home and spending time with you and the children," replied Maria.

After the long drive, Adam, Maria, and the children pulled up in the driveway of his brother Gerald's cottage. It was now three in the afternoon, and the sun was shining. Gerald, Valerie, and the children were standing by the front door to greet them.

"Hello, brov! Nice to see you again – come in!" Gerald shouted from the doorway of the cottage. The children ran to each other, embracing and hugging one another, as they didn't often see each other. Lauren was also there, home from her second year at university. She was studying anthropology, and her speciality was ancient civilisations.

"Lauren, I have a puzzle for you to solve. I'll talk to you about it later," said Maria.

"Sounds intriguing, aunty Maria," replied Lauren.

"You must be tired after that five-hour drive," said Gerald's wife, Valerie. "Let's go through to the garden and have some bread and jam and a nice cup of tea. I made the jam myself from our abundant supply of fruit. This one is called manora. It's a combination of mangos and oranges."

"I could really do with a nice cuppa," replied Adam.

"Let me give you hand," Maria said to Valerie.

"That would be lovely. We can have a catch-up. You need to tell me every detail of your exciting job," said Valerie.

Aki was a little shocked that the general was not there to dismiss her but offer her another job; she was half expecting to lose her job with the WSOA, so his question about a specialist position took her by surprise.

"I don't know, General. I want to stay closer to my husband and daughter since my mother's passing," replied Aki.

"You will get two weeks back on Earth, every three months. The pay is the best we offer in the whole of the WSOA, except mine, of course," the general said.

"Do I have time to think about this?"

"Of course, you do. Take a two-week break from work and give me your answer then," the general said.

"OK, thanks, sir," replied Aki.

Aki went straight home to Takao and Natasha and hugged them both tightly.

"What's that for?" asked Takao.

"I've just realised how much grief I'm causing you and Natasha," said Aki. "I've been given two weeks' leave with pay to decide upon a new job offer. They're looking for a couple of astronauts to run a new space station."

"How will that work, Aki?" asked Takao.

"I'd be on the station for three months and then back on Earth for two weeks. The general has asked me to take the position; that's why I have two weeks off to decide."

"Only you can make the decision. I'll always support whatever decision you make – you know that." Replied Takao

Maria's fortieth birthday party at her brothers-in-law was a complete surprise for her. "Adam, you managed to keep that a secret," she said.

"I know. It was very difficult because the children also knew."

Maria's best friend, Stephanie, and Stephanie's parents travelled all the way from Essex to be there. Adam's mum had also made the journey from Japan. Adam's dad had been in the army and had met his mum when on secondment to the Japanese army back in 1990. His mum was in her eighty-sixth year and as fit as a fiddle. His dad had passed away at fifty-one years of age.

"Aunty Maria, do you want to have that discussion you mentioned when you arrived yesterday morning?" asked Lauren.

"That would be a good idea. Let's go into the conservatory, and I'll ask your opinion on something that we found recently," replied Maria.

"I'm going to say no to the general's offer, Takao," said Aki.

"Why?" asked Takao.

"I want to spend more time with both of you. Don't you realise you are now my only family since the death of my mother?"

"Don't forget my father. He's still your relative, and you must stop worrying about us. It's important that you have a goal in life outside of just family," stated Takao.

"No, I've made my mind up, and no one will change it. My goal in life is to dedicate my time to both of you."

"I know that look. I don't think I'll try to change your mind."

"Well, Aunty Maria, what is it?" asked Lauren.

"Have you heard about some of the deep-sea finds that have been found on the ocean floor recently," enquired Maria.

"I don't think so."

"What I'm about to tell you is top secret. Can you keep this to yourself?" asked Maria.

"Of course, I can."

"No, I mean it, Lauren. This is not a topic for one of your university projects," snapped Maria.

"What side of the bed did you get out of this morning?" said Lauren

"I'm sorry. This has me so rattled and having to keep it from everyone is driving me potty." replied Maria

"No, I'm sorry. I realise that you're under pressure having to spend every three months away in space. Let's start again," said Lauren.

"When I was doing my training on Deep Ocean One, the teams kept finding everyday objects like plastic containers of food, pens, plates – you know, the normal things that might fall off ships during their voyages – but when these objects were carbon dated, they were over two hundred and fifty thousand years old. What do you think?" asked Maria

"I think, aunty Maria, that these objects seem to be modern-day items that have somehow been contaminated with undersea radiation, causing a false reading on the plutonium radiocarbon dating," said Lauren.

"What about the modern spectacles found in the tomb of Ramesses the ninth? They weren't in contact with any radiation."

"That one is a bit of an anomaly," said Lauren.

Maria and Lauren were in deep conversation when Adam's brother, Gerald, walked in. "What are you two whispering about?" he asked.

"Dad, it's rude to interrupt people's private conversations," said Lauren.

"What is so important that Maria's missing cutting her birthday cake? Forty's an important milestone in your life," stated Gerald.

"Not to worry, Lauren," Maria said. "We can continue this discussion later."

"Come on, old girl. Time to cut your cake and make a wish," Gerald said in a sarcastic tone.

"I'm coming. Stop fussing. It's only another birthday. Nothing special, you know; in fact, I'm going to ban all future ones," replied Maria with a laugh.

"OK, General," said Aki, before coming off the tele-link with General Payton.

"Well, what was his reaction when you turned down the job?" asked Takao.

"He was very calm and asked me to take a little longer to think about it. He explained that it was an opportunity of a lifetime, with good pay as well," replied Aki.

"What did you say to that?" asked Takao.

"I still turned down the job and told him that I wouldn't change my mind."

"You should have taken more time to consider it. Did you tell him why you were turning down his offer?"

"I told him I needed to spend more time with my family and I would look to get a teaching post at the university."

"All right. You know I will support you, whatever you decide to do. Shall I speak with my father and see if any vacancies exist at the university?" asked Takao.

"Oh, by the way, the general also fired me, so I don't have a job at present. So yes, a word in your father's ear would be very useful now."

Professor Kuzuhara was pleased to have Aki working at the university. It meant that he would see more of her. Despite being her father-in-law, he found her personable and liked working with her.

Aki was again back to being that sophisticated and smooth person before her mother died. She was settling back into working life and enjoying her time working with the professor and teaching new students.

One day when Aki arrived at the university and parked in her named space, she was strolling along without a care in the world when she suddenly noticed Professor Kuzuhara standing at the main entrance and beckoning to her. *Strange*, she thought, *I wonder why he's looking so agitated.*

"Aki, Aki!" the professor shouted across the car park. "You must come – I need to speak with you!"

"What is it, Professor. Why the panic?" asked Aki as she approached him.

"Come on. Let's go to my office," said the professor in a shaky voice.

"What's the matter? You look as white as a sheet," she said, following him into his office.

"Please take a seat. I have some terrible news for you."

Aki, being her bubbly self, said, "Don't tell me I have to take on extra classes and will need to work during the summer break."

"No, I'm afraid it is worse than that. Takao and Natasha have been involved in a car accident. It happened when Takao was taking Natasha to school."

Aki turned white. "What accident? Are they, all right? Please tell me they are all right, Professor, please!" screamed Aki.

Maria did her training on DO1, where she bumped into Aki during lunch breaks; they had time to exchange pleasantries but not much more than that. Maria had decided to take up the general's offer to man the space station. She had lost complete faith in the company she was working for and thought a new opportunity would reinvigorate her enthusiasm for researching novel ideas. She was getting a bit stale in her old job. She had to spend six months on DO1 to undertake astronaut and technical training to prepare her for the space laboratory and a further six months at NASA. She was a dedicated trainee, as she realised any errors up there could be your last.

She noted that Aki was blasé about all her training, as if she didn't care how she achieved a pass. Maria was to specialise in researching new materials for earthbound uses. She was to develop her new liquid aluminium/ titanium compound for use on the station. It was at one of their dinner time discussions that Maria got to know a little bit more about Aki. She was so laid back about the training because she was going into a desk job back in Hiroshima and additionally getting married. All she could think about and talk about was Takao and getting married. Poor girl was completely besotted with her fiancé – her concentration was poor at the best of times. In one of their training sessions on the centrifuge, she didn't buckle her seat belt correctly, and as the centrifuge slowed to a halt, she flew out of her seat and was glued to the windshield. If it were not so serious, you'd think you were watching some slapstick comedy programme. She looked a real picture stuck on the windshield, arms and legs flailing all over the place. Maria passed her training with flying colours, and Aki just scraped through. She was glad to leave DO1, as you did not see sunlight for six months, and she was looking forward to seeing her husband and children.

Aki's husband and daughter had been killed instantly in the accident. A car went through a red light on the main street in Hiroshima and ploughed into the side of their car, where the protection was at its weakest. You couldn't have hit the car in a more vulnerable spot. The driver of the other car was never found. Police found the vehicle to be empty. A witness saw a man in a dark suit running away from the scene. Witnesses on the street remarked how the driver seemed to be waiting for a car to cross the junction before it accelerated from a standing stop to hit Takao's car, almost like a hit-and-run in a gangster movie.

Aki and Professor Kuzuhara got to the hospital as quickly as they could, only to be ushered into a separate room and asked to wait while they checked on her family's progress. A few minutes later, a sombre-looking doctor came into the room. "I'm sorry to inform you that Mr

Kuzuhara was pronounced dead on arrival at the hospital. The little girl was still barely alive through some miracle, but she died minutes after arriving here," the doctor said in a calm voice.

At this point, Aki screamed and then fainted. When she came to, her father-in-law was standing over her. "Professor, where are Takao and Natasha? Why have they not come to see me?" asked Aki.

"Aki, I'm so sorry, but they won't be coming," said the professor, at which point Aki screamed again and again, sobbing violently as she was screaming.

"Why, why? Why my little girl and my darling husband!"

The professor hugged her close to try to calm her down. "I know. The loss for me is my son and grand-daughter and my friend – your mother, Tamiko – in such a short space of time, but we must be strong and not let their memories die."

Maria's visit to her mother's and her brothers-in-law went by so quickly. They were travelling back on the UFV shuttle to the Liverpool Street station, which was still another hour away.

"I'm not really looking forward to going back onto the space lab. I know it may not seem like it, but I'd rather be at home with you all," Maria told Adam.

"I know that your job is important to you, but at least we can talk once a week by video link," said Adam.

"I'm hoping to be back on Earth in three weeks. I'm going to push the general for that," replied Maria.

Maria and her family arrived back into the UFV terminus at Liverpool Street within the scheduled time, and they drove home to Millennium Town. Maria immediately started to pack for her morning return to the space lab. Adam got the children ready for bed. They were tired and overexcited about the trip they had just been on.

"Maria, you won't forget to mention to the general about a longer break next time, will you?" asked Adam.

"No, of course not. I want a longer break as well, you know," said Maria.

Natasha was having dinner with her father-in-law, Professor Kuzuhara, on her last evening before returning to the space lab. "Professor, I've had a wonderful time with you in London this week. Takao and Natasha would have loved it," said Natasha in a happy, reflective mood.

"I know they would have, but it's been several years now since we lost them. We must think of the future, as we cannot change that," said the professor.

"I know, I know, Prof," Natasha said.

The next morning, Natasha and Maria met at the earth tether terminus to journey back to the space lab.

"Hi, Natasha. How did your holiday go?" asked Maria.

"Great. Had an enjoyable time with the professor," answered Natasha. "How did yours go?"

"I didn't want to come back because I enjoyed it so much. I wonder how the general got on with his investigations into these everyday objects appearing all over the place."

"I'm sure if something had cropped up, we would have heard about it by now," said Natasha.

They went through security check-in and were met on the other side by the general himself, which was a bit of a surprise, as he seldom left his office, let alone the building. "Hello, commanders. Hope you had a good break. The space lab has been fully restored, and all systems have been upgraded. I'd like to speak with you," added the general. It was most unusual that he joined them in the pod to travel back to the orbiting platform.

"Why, General, I didn't think you cared for babysitting us back to work," said Natasha sardonically.

"Now don't get smart, commander. If you think I like travelling in these suicide bubbles, you've got another thing coming," snapped the general.

"Sorry sir," said Maria. "Why are you travelling with us? It must be important."

"I wanted to speak with you both in private because the office has prying ears. The WSOA wants you to continue studying the oncoming meteors, but I also want you to undertake a special task for me."

"I still don't understand why can't we discuss this in your office," said Natasha.

"As you may be aware, all WSOA offices are monitored and I'm operating out of their remit," replied the general.

"I don't understand, General. Why would that be a problem to talk openly in your office – anyway, these pods must also be monitored," said Maria.

"Not this one. I had the communication lines temporarily cut because I needed to talk with you in private." Just as he started to explain why he needed to talk with them, a voice came over the pod speaker.

"Please fasten your harnesses and put on your oxygen mask." This was an automated message.

"Shit, I'll have to travel with you up to the platform and then come back down when you get out!" screamed the general. "*Anyway*, let me tell you why I need to speak with you in private. I believe someone is manipulating us what with all these artefacts appearing and the disappearance and reappearance of the sputnik satellite."

"Don't you think that all this is just a coincidence?" asked Natasha.

"No, commander. Take the sputnik satellite, for instance. How could that disappear completely out of our solar system for twenty-two years and then suddenly reappear. Most of the everyday objects were found on the ocean floor, except two that I know of."

"Which two were they, General?" asked Maria.

"The watch in the sewer museum in Japan and the spectacles in the tomb of Ramses the ninth. It's as if somebody wanted us to find them," he responded.

"Isn't that a good thing, then, General, if somebody is trying to warn us? What are they trying to tell us?" said Maria.

"I don't know, which is what's bothering me. It's instinct. You know all of us military types have it. We can smell danger, and I don't like what I'm smelling. I also believe that someone has infiltrated the WSOA."

Tamiko and Graham Payton became more than close friends during the time he was stationed in Japan. They became lovers and spent many evenings together reflecting on the world and generally enjoying each other's company. Tamiko was a little bit older than Graham, by about six years, so Graham respected her opinions, as he had always been taught as a boy and in the military to respect authority, and age usually meant authority to him.

Their relationship would have gone on for many more years except for two things happening simultaneously. Graham was recalled to the States because they had a new job for him. Their government, in conjunction with others around the world, were creating a new organisation called World Space & Oceanic Agency, and they wanted him to head it.

The other reason was a little more complicated. Tamiko told Graham she was pregnant. He was over the moon. He could propose to Tamiko and take her and his unborn child back to the States with him. With the new job offer, things couldn't be any better for him. He excitedly told Tamiko about his new job and said that he wanted to marry her. She didn't take the news as he was expecting. In fact, she seemed a little down.

"Tamiko, this is the happiest day of my life. Come on – give me a smile and marry me," said Graham, with the excitement of a little boy who had just got the keys to the sweet shop.

"Graham san, I cannot marry you even if I wanted to" she said.

"For heaven's sake, why not, Tamiko?" Graham said with some confusion in his voice. "Graham san, I love you very much, and if the circumstances were different, I would not hesitate to say yes, but you know my family think I have brought shame on them by bearing a child out of wedlock. It's the worst crime I could commit in my family's eyes," said a tearful Tamiko.

That was the last time Graham would see Tamiko. When the baby was born, Tamiko was made to give it up to the local orphanage in Hiroshima, as no family would be allowed to adopt it because of the circumstance of its birth.

CHAPTER THREE

ASTEROID

The general was still talking about the security breach at the WSOA as the pod finally reached the orbiting platform. He was convinced that the infiltrator was not an agent of a foreign government but someone off-world.

"What do you mean by *off-world*, General?" enquired Natasha.

"I believe we're being studied by forces not of this world," said the general.

"Come on. You don't believe in all that UFO and alien nonsense, do you?" remarked Maria.

"Commander, it's not nonsense, believe you me. There are things I could tell you about that are in storage around the world that would blow your socks off. Did you know that we have asteroids that are not from this solar system and when cut open they contained communication and monitoring devices?"

"I don't know what to say about that, General," said Natasha.

"Commanders, I'm relying on you to support my request. I want you to continue monitoring the world oceans and additionally monitor remote regions of the planet," commanded the general.

"What are we supposed to be looking for?" enquired Maria,

"The same as you have already found. Anything unusual, like the city you found under the sea, but I want you to report any findings only to me. Is that understood?" The general was quite firm on that command, which meant he was deadly serious about it.

"General, we'll do our best, but if everything is being monitored, the WSOA will know what we're up to," replied Natasha.

"I have set up a secure line for you to contact me directly, and it's is not monitored by the WSOA."

"You're the head of the WSOA. Why do you need to work in secrecy?" asked Natasha.

"I told you before that I think we've been infiltrated. I can't risk these people finding out what I'm up to. I need to flush them out, and you're the bait, I'm afraid."

"What do you mean by *bait*? We have nothing to hide. Our work is not top secret and who can we influence from up here," asked Maria.

"Commanders, you have the only long-range deep space telescope in the world. Whoever it is will try to stop you from using it to find out what else is on our ocean floor. You've already been hit by the lost sputnik satellite, and there are other missing satellites which you aren't aware of that may well reappear and collide with you."

"Is it safe for us to go back to the space lab?" asked Natasha.

"Not to worry. Whilst you were away, we enhanced the structural integrity so the panels are much harder to penetrate. We have also installed a new device we've been testing, an electronic shield which will deflect most objects unless they are bigger than the space lab."

"Whoa, what have we here – science fiction technology?" quipped Maria.

"I told you we have off-world technology and have reverse engineered it for our own use, so aliens and UFOs aren't such a myth now, eh?" the general responded, gloating.

The pod finally reached the space platform. "Hang on, General. How are you going to get back? We will now fly to the space lab; you'll have to travel with us and then come back again," said Natasha.

"If you look above you, you'll see another pod on the tether. We'll connect with it, and you'll use it to fly over to the space lab. I'll stay in this one and return to Earth."

At that point, there was a slight clunk as the two pods came together. This was also new; it was installed to allow off-loading of supplies to save time required on round trips to the space lab and could be a standby pod should the first one fail. Natasha and Maria climbed up to the new pod and strapped themselves in for the trip to the space lab.

Lauren had thought long and hard about what her aunty Maria spoke about when she visited last week. How could everyday items be over 250,000 years old and be so well preserved if they were not deposited quite recently? Then she remembered about the "bog man" who had lain in a peat bog for six thousand years and was perfectly preserved, with little or no decay when extricated. Maybe objects lying in deep water and are cut off from oxygen and untouched by sunlight stayed well preserved, but that did not account for the spectacles in Egypt or the watch in Japan. *Hmm, there must be some logic behind this somehow,* she thought. Then she came up with a most radical thought.

Perhaps I'm looking at this from the wrong angle. The Egyptians had complex mathematics and knew how to move huge pieces of stone by simple engineering methods, such as pulleys, blocks, tackles, and simple cranes. The city of Atlantis was supposed to be far ahead of its time. Even with all this past knowledge, it took us hundreds of years to get back to the same level as the ancient Egyptians and Atlanteans. Where am I going with this? Maybe we get to a certain level of technology and then along comes a huge natural disaster and we have to start again. Look at the dinosaurs completely wiped out. Look at the great flood of Noah, humans wiped out to very few people. Maybe we're coming to the next huge natural disaster and are being warned of its coming by finding these old objects which are really from our past and not being placed there by some off-world agents!! I must tell Aunty Maria.

Commanders Francis and Kuzuhara docked with the space lab without any incident. They opened the docking hatch and climbed in.

"Maria, do you notice the lighting in here?" asked Natasha. "It's not the bright white light we had when we left; it's more a blue light. Don't like it, although it makes everything so sharp, as if each object was outlined in dark pencil line."

"Natasha, let's get down to the rest area and grab a coffee before we start work," replied Maria.

The general descended back to Earth in the pod. Down the tether, he was deep in thought. *They just do not understand, my commanders, that there is a lot at stake: my job, my life, the life of all the people on our planet. Something or someone is manipulating our organisation to keep us away from the truth. I still don't believe these objects are as old as the plutonium radiocarbon dating is showing. I must speak with Professor Carter, as his object didn't appear on the ocean floor.*

The pod came to sudden halt. *Good God, that was quick. I've reached Earth.*

The general alighted from the pod to be met by his chief of staff and a couple of soldiers. "Hello, Colonel, to what do I owe the pleasure?"

"General, sir, we're here to escort you to Heathrow Airport. You're expected in Houston tomorrow," said Colonel Mackenzie.

"Colonel, I'm quite capable of organising a flight to the states. I haven't seen any standing orders for me to go to Houston. What are you talking about?" General Payton retorted.

"This is not a request; it's an order from the admiral. You are to be sent immediately to Houston the minute we find you," said the colonel.

Maria and Natasha went down to the lounge area of the space lab to make coffee and have a snack before starting their shifts.

"Natasha, do you want a biscuit with your coffee?" asked Maria.

"That would be lovely. Thanks, Maria."

"Oh, my God!" Maria shouted.

"What is it, Maria? Are you OK!" Natasha called across the lounge.

"Come and look at this!"

Natasha rushed over to see what Maria was looking at. Maria was pointing to one of the food lockers. Natasha peered in and screeched, "Oh my God, there's enough food in there for an entire year on the space lab!"

"Natasha, let's go check the other essentials."

It was the same with the oxygen, water, and working suits. There were even twelve OLS suits. The station had been kitted out for an extended stay, almost as if they were an old castle under siege.

"I don't like the look of this. It's as if we aren't going to return to Earth for quite a while. We need to speak with General Payton," Natasha said in a pensive voice.

Meanwhile, the general was on board his flight to Houston. *I wonder what could be so important,* he thought. *I hope they haven't found out about my communication blackouts … or maybe they have a question about the amount of supplies I have put on board the space lab.*

"Drink, sir? Which meal option would you like?" enquired the flight attendant, bringing the general back to reality. "Sir, you need to make a drink and meal choice now or it will be too late. The flight time is exactly two hours. With the new ion drives, the flight times to most destinations on the planet are no longer than three hours.

"Give me a whisky and lemonade, and I'll take the beef salad. Thank you," replied the general. No sooner had he finished his meal than the fasten harness signs were coming on in the cabin. That meant they were ten minutes from docking.

Maria and Natasha continued checking the manifest and found that every essential item on the space lab had been replenished to levels that would last two astronauts at least fifteen months, thirty if they rationed their supplies and only had half the daily requirements. The oxygen tanks would last twelve months, eighteen with recycling and scrubbing.

"I think the general has loaded us up because maybe he's planning to come on board for an extended period. We even have treble the supply of Kevlar patches," said Maria.

"If we stripped the oxygen tanks out of the escape craft, that would give us enough air for two years on board," said Natasha.

"Where are you going with this? I don't want to stay on board for more than our allotted three-month period.

It would be a nightmare to be on board for a year or any longer," stated Maria.

"I was just saying that if you needed to extend your stay past a year, those were the alternatives. I don't want to stay past my three months either. Let's go down to main control and see what new goodies we've installed."

The commanders made their way to the control room. What was immediately apparent was the new panel that had been installed. It was light blue in colour and had an array of eight buttons on it. Natasha went over to look at the panel and then realised what it was for, with the first button legend reading "defensive laser".

"Maria, come and look at this!" she shouted.

Being a United States citizen, the general went through passport control quickly. The admiral himself met him on the other side. *This must be serious,* he thought, *if the admiral is meeting me personally.*

"Hi, Graham. How are you? Glad, you could make it," greeted the admiral.

"It is not as if I had a lot of choice, did I?" replied the general.

"No, I suppose not, but you're here now. Let's go and get a beer; we can have a chat before we go into the United Nations council meeting."

In the UFV on the way to the bar, the general had to ask the admiral straight out, "What's the panic that caused you to rush me over from London? Where's the fire?"

"We have plenty of time for that. How are you? How are Commanders Francis and Kuzuhara coping on the space lab? My intelligence tells me that you have stocked the old girl up to the hilt with latest technology and supplies."

"I've done that to make sure our astronauts can survive up there for longer should we have any re-supply problems from here. It's just a backup."

"And the defensive lasers? They don't need those as backup, do they? What are they going to target?" asked the admiral.

"During their last tour of duty, a rogue satellite hit them, so I installed our latest defensive shield and defensive lasers," said the general.

"Graham, you're not still going on about the off-world threat, are you? I hope you haven't contaminated our astronauts. If you have, I'll have them removed from the space lab," said the admiral with a snort. "I have made sure that you had everything you needed. Graham, why are you doing things behind my back? I even had commander Kuzuhara's family removed from the equation so you got your girl onto the space lab."

That statement by the admiral made Graham sick with shock and anger. "You did what!" screamed Graham. "You had my daughter's family murdered, you fucking bastard! That was my grand-daughter; she was only eight years old!"

"Now, Graham, stop your bleating. She doesn't know you're her father, and you never actually had any contact with the family. You got what you wanted: Commander Kuzuhara on the space lab. It was the only way she would go up there."

"How did you know she was going to turn my job offer down? Only I knew that." Graham snorted.

"Son, I have all communications monitored. There is nothing going on in this organisation that I don't know about," barked the admiral. "Let's go and have that beer. I'll brief you about the council meeting on the way there."

Natasha continued studying the new panel in the main control room and started reading it aloud: "Defensive lasers, targeting scanners, ram scoop out, ram scoop in, offensive missile armed, offensive missile launch, shield on and shield off. My God, Maria, we're like a flying weapons platform! I didn't sign up for this. What the hell is going on?"

"Calm down. We can't do anything about this yet until we contact the general," said Maria calmly.

"If we're armed to the teeth, we'll become a target for something or someone trying to knock us out of orbit!"

Suddenly, the video phone was ringing in the experimentation lab. "You get that; it could be the general. I'll continue looking at our new modifications," said Natasha.

Maria moved up to the experimentation lab, half expecting it to be locked down. When she got there, the phone was still ringing. She grabbed the receiver and pressed the RECEIVE button. As a picture appeared on the screen, it wasn't who she was expecting.

The general and the admiral climbed into their chauffeur-driven vehicle. The general was still upset about the admiral's actions concerning commander Kuzuhara's family.

"Now, come on, Graham. I can't change what I did. You have every right to be upset, but we have more important things to discuss," said the admiral.

"Like what?" snapped Graham.

"Like the meeting, we are going to. It's about the objects that are hundreds of thousands of years old and the concern over the incoming asteroids and the satellite disappearances," replied the admiral.

"What do they want to discuss?" Graham asked, trying to show that he was interested, although this had now indeed piqued his interest, as he was familiar with the topic. The United Nations headquarters was now based in Houston, and they were both expected to attend the Security Council meeting.

The meeting was a drab affair. There were no answers, just questions. Where were the objects coming from? Why did some of the old satellites disappear? Where were they? How close were these asteroids going to pass the earth? However, one person there was of interest to Graham, and that was Professor David Carter. He went over to speak with him.

"Hello, Professor Carter. My name is Graham Payton, head of the WSOA. How are you?"

"I'm fine. How do you do? enjoying the meeting?"

"No, not really. You?"

"Me neither," Professor Carter said.

"David ... May I call you that? Could we go somewhere to have a chat?" asked Graham.

"OK, let's go to one of the small conference rooms allocated for our use," said Professor Carter. "What do you want to talk about, Graham?" he was asking a few minutes later.

"The spectacles you found in your dig ... Were they carbon dated to over two hundred and fifty thousand years old? Had any aging taken place?"

The person on the other end of the video phone was Maria's niece Lauren. "Hi, aunty Maria. Bet you weren't expecting me," quipped Lauren.

"Not really. What can I do for you?"

"I called because there's something I can do for you. Remember the discussion we had about these objects?" asked Lauren.

"Shush. Not so loud. Someone may be listening," whispered Maria.

"Well, I did some research and concluded. You may not like where I ended up, but it's my theory. I believe your objects are real things left over from the last time humans reached a level of technology and then an extinction event took place, say a comet or volcanic action, which wiped out that society."

"Very interesting, Lauren. Did you come to that conclusion all by yourself?"

"Look, aunty, there's no need to be sarcastic. Think about it – first the Atlanteans, then the Egyptians, then the Babylonians and all those advanced societies? Why did it take us so long to catch back up with where they advanced to?"

"Lauren, sorry, but I'm a bit stressed now. No excuse, I know, but accept my apologies. I think that seems to be the only plausible explanation rather than some aliens planting the objects, as my boss thinks," said Maria.

"Well, I must dash. Going out with some friends to the local night club. Hope you get to the bottom of your puzzle. Bye-bye.

"Bye, Lauren. Thanks, and don't forget this is not to be discussed with anyone, even your parents," said Maria.

"To be honest with you, Graham, I was a bit sceptical until I read about the other items you have been finding on the ocean floor," said the professor.

"Wait a minute – where did you read about these items? They were supposed to be kept secret and a statement has never been released to the press," replied Graham.

"Admiral Mackenzie contacted me after we informed the WSOA of our find. He sent me a document of all the finds that you made on the ocean floor to see if I could shed any light on them," said the professor.

"Do you think the find you made in Egypt was genuine or was it planted?"

"No, I think it was genuine, because the seal on the organ jar had not been broken or tampered with. I tried to blame my team for planting it because I was in shock, until they plutonium radiocarbon dated it."

"Graham, are you coming back to the meeting!" called Admiral Mackenzie.

"Just coming, Admiral," said Graham.

The Security Council continued to discuss these strange finds; there were professors from all fields of archaeology, theology, and even from the fields of biology and physics. They could not agree on the validity of these objects. In fact, they couldn't even agree with scientists from their own fields of expertise about these objects. However, they were all of one voice about plutonium radiocarbon dating each item again, but at one institute to guarantee consistency of testing. All the items were to be gathered and sent to Edinburgh University, where they had the latest and best plutonium radiocarbon dating equipment. They also had a new piece of equipment to test the materials in each object down to the molecular level to see if any materials were present that were not known. Admiral Mackenzie insisted that his security team be present at the university whilst the objects were there to ensure nothing went missing.

Maria made her way back to the main control room to help Natasha establish what had actually been added to the space lab manifest. "Have you found any more surprises and delight features, Natasha?" enquired Maria.

"Maria, it's not a laughing matter. This puts a whole new complexion on our reason and purpose for being up here."

"Look, we have two objectives: one is to check the rest of the oceans and planet for any other unusual objects, sites, cities; and the other is to keep monitoring the incoming asteroids," Maria said in an authoritarian voice.

"Enough of all this intrigue. Did you find any more added technology and figured out why we have this strange bluish glow to our lighting? I've found one more added technology and am not sure what it is."

"Show me where it is, Natasha," Maria said.

Natasha pointed towards a strange black box that had been installed above the main control panel. It was about one hundred millimetres square and about fifty millimetres deep. There was what looked like a small door inset into the top of it, and it had no obvious keyhole or button to open it.

Maria was feeling around the box when up came a small-lit panel with the words "Input Code" in a white light. "I wonder what that means," remarked Maria. Natasha came over, looked at the box, and started tapping the screen. Suddenly, another message appeared in the inset panel: "First code accepted. Input last code."

"Tap the screen now and let's see what happens," commanded Natasha. When Maria touched the screen, a new message appeared: "Second code accepted." The door to the box opened in a slow and controlled manner.

All the objects found on the ocean floor, plus the watch and spectacles, were transported to Edinburgh University, and testing was begun immediately. All the objects' carbon dating was in line with the original testing; however, the molecular material testing threw up some interesting results. There were materials that were well known, like the plastic in the spectacles, and there were materials that were of unknown origin. The glass in the spectacles was not made of sand or plastic; it was a type of crystal not found in the elements table and certainly not found on our planet at present.

Some of the food containers were opened to test the contents again the carbon dating was in line with the original testing, but the chemical make-up of the tomatoes in the plastic-type containers was strange. The shape of the tomatoes had never been seen before. They were long and elongated, more like a broad bean pod, but they were tomatoes, red in colour with seeds in the middle. The liquid they were in wasn't tomato juice but a luminous green jelly. The jelly wasn't strange, but the chemical make-up was. There was no animal content in the jelly, no thickening agents, no salt, no preservatives of any kind, but the tomatoes were perfectly preserved. They even smelled fresh as if picked the same day. Most of the containers of food had this green luminous jelly which preserved the contents perfectly. Even with containers that had been punctured, the food was perfectly preserved inside. They found some other material on the outside of these plastic-type containers, like a sand of some kind. Again, this sand-type material wasn't found anywhere on our planet, but this latest discovery set alarm bells ringing. The material was known to Edinburgh University, as they had tested the meteorites that contained communication and monitoring devices, and this sand-like substance was what the meteorites were made of.

Maria was stunned by what was in the box as the lid opened. Inside were two buttons, one with a red top and one with a blue top. There was a label for each one. The blue button's label read "Disarm station," and the red button label read "Only to be pressed as a last resort – see instruction book." Sure enough, there was a small instruction book inside the box, and it was coated in plastic laminate and consisted of three pages.

Natasha wandered over to Maria. "Maria, what is it? It looks as if you've seen a ghost," she said excitedly. Maria moved aside to let Natasha look inside the box. "What the fuck does 'as a last resort' mean?" snapped Natasha. "I understand the other button and am going to press it because we aren't a flying weapons platform."

"No, no, don't do that!" screamed Maria. Before she got the last word out, Natasha depressed the blue button.

There were a lot of mechanical noises and then silence. Then the lighting in the space lab returned to a normal white colour.

"Do not touch the other button, as I have just read what it does!" shouted Maria.

"It can't be that bad, Maria. What does it do?"

"If you had pressed that, we would have five minutes to exit the station. That's a station self-destruct button," replied Maria.

"What? The bastards have us wired as a flying bomb. You know what this station would do if it made landfall. It would hit the earth like a nuclear bomb!"

The findings from Edinburgh University were reported back to the United Nations Security Council and the admiral. The last finding regarding the sand-like material on the outside of the plastic-like containers is of interest to the WSOA. The Security Council reconvened to discuss the findings. Admiral Mackenzie gave the council members details of the asteroids that had come from outside of the solar system. Each one had been found on or near a strategic military base and on WSOA and NASA sites. No asteroids had turned up anywhere else in the world. The secretary general asked the scientific community at the meeting to give some rational explanation to these asteroids and how they had managed to land on the planet without any explosion or noise and without anybody seeing them.

Professor Carter was the first scientist to respond to the question. "I think that we're making more of this than we need to," he said.

This caused uproar in the chamber, with finger-pointing and accusations being thrown around liberally. "What do you know about space rocks, Professor? You're just a relic digger wielding a trowel!" shouted one of the biologists.

"We have conclusive evidence that the elements in these meteorites didn't originate from Earth!" exclaimed one of the biologists.

"What conclusive evidence? Just because we have not seen some of the elements before does not mean they are alien. Look at some of the discoveries made in the Amazon over the past decades – strange creatures, new plants, new elements, and new insect life. Are you saying they came from space too?" retorted Professor Carter.

The noise in the chamber grew into a crescendo before the secretary general started banging his gavel and shouting. "People, people, please let's have some calm. We still need to discuss this like civilised human beings." The chamber became silent.

General Payton stood up and spoke passionately about the threat posed by these objects and asteroids. "We must not treat this lightly. Last week someone or something launched the sputnik satellite at our space lab. Fortunately, it glanced off. This was not an accident, as this satellite had left the solar system twenty years earlier."

"Surely you must be mistaken, General," said the leader of the astronomy and physicist's community. "Could it have just disappeared out of site behind, say, Saturn or Neptune for that time?"

"No, not possible. We would have detected it. Don't forget that these satellites give off a distinctive signal that we can track even if it had gone as far as Pluto. No, we can say it left the solar system, as did several other old satellites, for we could find no signal from any of them," said the general. "I'm afraid, and it is only my opinion."

"Stop, General!" hollered Admiral Mackenzie. "We don't want to hear your alien theory again."

"Sorry, Admiral, but I will have my say. I believe we're being monitored and investigated by someone or something outside our solar system with a prelude of invading our planet. Why go to all the trouble of placing these objects on the earth if you aren't trying to distract us from their real intent?"

Maria was still getting over the shock of Natasha pressing the blue button when an alarm sounded. It was not one they recognised. It was almost like a nuclear air raid warning sound from the old movies. "Natasha, what's this alarm? I've never heard it before," said Maria.

"I don't know but look on the main control panel. There's a part of the main panel flashing, and there's some writing in that panel," replied Natasha.

Maria moved over to the panel and read out the message: "Incoming object being tracked on station sensors ensure self-defence mode is turned on."

"I'm going to press the blue button again, just in case the sputnik satellite is going to strike us again," she said.

No sooner had Maria pressed the blue button Natasha noticed something out of one of the observation windows – a large object moving towards them. "There's a big silver object coming towards us at some speed; it looks to be on a collision course with us!" screeched Natasha.

Maria moved rapidly to the observation window. The object must have been about two hundred metres away from them, coming in fast, and then suddenly the station shuddered and three bright lights from the station moved towards the object. There was a blinding flash, and when Maria's eyes adjusted, the object had disappeared.

"Natasha, are you OK?" called Maria.

"Yes, I'm fine. What the hell was that?"

"I think it looked like an old satellite, but where did it come from and why was it on a collision course with us?"

General Payton's video phone bleeper was sounding in his pocket. *Who can that be? I gave orders that I was not to be disturbed,* he thought. He took the device out of his pocket to see who was calling him.

"Who is it, General?" asked the admiral when he recognised the sound coming from the general's device.

"I don't know. Do you mind if I step out of the meeting and check? It could be important," said the general.

He went into an ante-room at the United Nations building and held the device up to his face. He was immediately concerned when he recognised the caller.

"General, Commander Francis calling. Will you please connect?" demanded Maria.

"Commander, what's happened? You wouldn't have called me unless it was important."

"We've been targeted again. An old satellite suddenly came out of nowhere and was on a collision course with us. Fortunately, the station defence system eliminated it," said Maria.

"OK, commanders, please keep your station defences on standby. Don't turn them off. I don't think this will be the last attempt to knock you out of orbit. I must get this information back to the Security Council. Talk with you later. Over and out."

He rushed back to the Security Council meeting, as he walked in, the debate was continuing about Edinburgh

University's finds. "Ladies and gentlemen," he bellowed as loud as he could, "I have some very important news. Please listen carefully. I've just received a message from Commanders Francis and Kuzuhara, who are on board our space lab. They've been targeted again. An old satellite was on a collision course with them until the station defences stopped it!" shouted the general.

The general secretary of the UN said in a stunned voice, "What? You have armed defences on a research station? Who gave you permission to do this? You've broken the agreement of all nations not to station weapons platforms in space."

"I don't think this is the time to debate the whys and where fors with regards to the arming of the space lab. We have far more important things to worry about," said the general.

The space station alarm sounded again only five hours after the first warning alarm. "Quick, Maria, brace yourself. I think we're about to be hit again!" exclaimed Natasha.

Maria looked out the window and saw a drone supply ship flying towards the Russian and Chinese space lab for cancer research. The Chinese and Russians used these ships because they didn't require a pilot and could be launched from the back of a commercial airliner flying at thirty-eight thousand feet. They were small and light, able to carry minimal supplies, so they would be used more regularly. Once their cargo was deposited, they flew into the lower atmosphere and were picked up by a military transport plane. This was what made them so cheap to operate, as they were reusable.

"Oh, my God, the station defences have locked onto the Russian/Chinese drone ship. I can't see anything else out there. Can you find the abort button!" shouted Maria.

Natasha rushed to the main control panel, searching it up and down, "I found a big red button but don't know what it does," she panted. She was about to depress it when the station shuddered and three white lights streaked away from underneath them. "Sorry, I wasn't quick enough."

Maria rushed to the observation window and saw the three white lights bypass the drone ship and impact with something on the other side of it. Again, there was a blinding flash and then nothing. "It looks like our defences have just prevented the Russian/Chinese station from being hit. I'll let the general know," said Maria.

The general had taken another call on his video phone and then rushed back to the Security Council chamber. "Ladies and gentlemen, I have just received another call from our space lab. The defence systems have just prevented another collision, not with our lab but with the

Russian/Chinese one. Looks as though we're all being targeted."

"I think we need to call a world state of emergency!" barked the admiral.

"All of you please calm down; let's not start a world panic. We need to assess what's going on. These collisions could just be rogue asteroids and just coincidentally two appeared in a matter of hours," the UN general secretary announced.

"These aren't rogue asteroids. Our commanders in the space lab said the first one was a silvery object and looked like an old satellite. They couldn't see the second object because it was too far away," stated the general.

"I suggest we wait to see if there are further incidents up in space before we make a decision," said the secretary general.

The meeting broke into several factions to discuss the recent discoveries and the events in space.

"I'm telling you that this is outrageous, the Americans arming their space lab. It's as if they were expecting trouble and didn't let the rest of the community know what was going on!" shouted the Swedish professor of biology, Marcus Tromby.

"Let's not get overexcited about what they did to their space lab. I think it was a godsend, as they have prevented both stations from being struck, but more importantly, who is using our old satellites as missiles?" asked professor of archaeology, David Carter.

Maria and Natasha were still on edge waiting for the station alarm to start ringing again. "Phew, it's been several hours since the last warning klaxon," sighed Maria.

"Thank God," replied Natasha. "Let's go and have a coffee."

"Excellent idea. We need to relax. The station seems to be able to cope with any event or projectile."

They had both just sat down to drink their coffees when the station alarm started ringing again. "Oh, my God, Maria, not again. Let's get up to the observation window and see what it is this time."

They reached the observation window in quick time, and Maria looked out. She could make out a huge object coming towards them. As the station moved and the sunlight lit up the object, she could clearly see what it was. The old Hubble Space telescope was moving towards them. It had also disappeared into space several years earlier. The station defence again sent three bright lights speeding towards it. There was a blinding flash, and as previously happened, Maria wasn't expecting to see anything left. "Natasha, those missiles didn't destroy the object moving towards us. It's the old Hubble telescope. It's too massive to destroy with missiles, and it's still coming towards us!" cried Maria in absolute terror.

The general and admiral joined one of the discussion groups talking about possible alien invasion of the planet. Professor Wang Chen from the University of Beijing and a world authority on alien technology, as she had been part of the Chinese governments, classified "Yellow Book Project", like the American Area 51 phenomena. She had seen many strange objects and even taken apart extra-terrestrial craft that had landed or crashed in China. She was also part of the team investigating the hollow meteors with listening devices in them. "I believe we're being assessed and our planet is being assessed for possible colonisation from outside our solar system," stated the professor.

"What brought you to that conclusion, Professor?" asked the admiral, still sceptical about the whole affair.

"Admiral, these aren't isolated instances," said Professor Wang Chen. "All of our nations have been experiencing contact of some sort with off-world intelligences. Look at some of the carvings and drawings on Mayan temples, depicting people in space helmets. Your government have found crashed craft and even some alien life forms."

"Who told you that!" shouted the admiral.

"Come now, Admiral, let's not be coy. We all know what you've found. Anyway, enough of the past; we need to find out who is targeting us."

"So, Professor, what do you make of the objects that have been found under the ocean and in Japan and Egypt?" asked General Payton.

"I'm not sure what to make of them. I would assume, like other people, that they're just everyday objects fallen off ships, but the plutonium radiocarbon dating seems to defy that. Additionally, if they are objects from off-world, they must be from a world that's like ours, for the pens, mobiles, and food are exactly like we use and eat today but have unknown manufacturers' names on them."

Maria was still screaming when the station interior lights turned green. "What the hell is happening now?" She didn't get all the words out before two bright green lasers came from the station and hit the Hubble telescope, totally disintegrating it into minute particles.

"Wow, that was close. What other surprise and delight features do we have for the next object?" replied Natasha.

"So, Natasha is not so unhappy about the weapons platform now," said Maria.

"Look, we're armed to the teeth and obviously, someone knew that and is targeting us."

"I still don't like it. I'm scared to death having all these weapons on board; that's why we're being singled out," said Natasha.

"What about the meteor attack on the Chinese/ Russian station? They have no weapons on board."

"I can't explain that one," replied Natasha. "Maria, you get some sleep. I'll take the first watch."

"OK, I'll take three hours, not a minute longer, and then you must come and wake me." Maria went to the sleeping section of the station full of trepidation about what may happen next or, more to the point, what Natasha may start fiddling with on the new control panel.

Maria had only been asleep for about an hour when she was awakened by the alarm klaxon from the main control room. She jumped out of her compartment and pulled on her working suit; she then rushed up to the main control room.

"Natasha, Natasha, what's happening? Why is the alarm sounding again?" shouted Maria so she could be heard above the sound of the klaxon.

"There's another object heading our way. Looks like a small meteorite, about the size of a melon, and it is coming in fast. I don't think our defence system will get it." As she finished speaking, the meteorite impacted with the space lab. The structure juddered, and then there was nothing. "Maria, we're still in one piece. I don't understand it."

"I don't know why that is. We should, at minimum, have a gaping hole somewhere or should have been knocked out of orbit," replied Maria.

The UN meeting broke up without any conclusive action being decided upon, it was agreed that the situation with the objects being found should continue to be monitored and catalogued. With respect to space labs, the UN wanted the WSOA to get a sample of what was trying to impact with them to ensure these were not just coincidences.

"I just cannot understand these people. We're being monitored and targeted for invasion. Why can they not see that?" said the general.

"Now, Graham, let's be careful what we're saying or we will be removed from our positions and labelled as cranks," said the admiral as their car sped back to WSOA headquarters. "Have you had any more communication from your commanders on the space lab? We need to know what's going on up there."

"No, not since the object was stopped from hitting the Russian/Chinese station," said Graham.

"You need to get in contact with them and give me a full report. I want every detail so we can make our own assessment of what's happening up there – and don't leave out anything. Do we understand each other?" demanded the admiral.

"Yes, sir, you will get all the facts," snapped Graham.

"Now, son, there's no need to get uppity. All we want are the facts. I agree something does not smell right, but we have to follow protocol and report everything that happens."

"There's a voice coming out of the main control panel. Look at the top right; a panel is flashing," said Natasha.

Maria walked over to the panel and saw a message in the panel. It read "Input security code." Maria touched the panel and then heard a familiar voice.

"Hello, come in, Commanders Francis and Kuzuhara. It's General Payton here."

Maria touched the panel again and then said, "Hello, General. It's Commander Francis here. How can we help?"

"Listen carefully, ladies. The UN council have not made any concrete decisions on what to do about the objects or the attacks on your station. Has anything else happened since your last report?"

Natasha jumped in before Maria could say something. "General, we have been targeted again. A small meteorite about the size of a melon came at us too fast for our defences to handle. It hit us but nothing happened."

"Commanders, something did happen. The station defence system decided that it wasn't a big enough threat to destroy it so it allowed the force field to deal with it. The meteorite would have bounced off you like a tennis ball on a hard court. I need you to continue monitoring our planet for any other anomalies and report back only on this secure line. I can't even trust the admiral."

"OK, General. If we encounter any more problems or spot something on the planet, we'll let you know," said Maria. Natasha burst into fits of laughter after Maria had finished speaking with the general.

"This is no laughing matter," snapped Maria. "What's wrong with you? First you moan about us being a weapons platform and then you start laughing at the events that have just happened."

"Sorry, Maria. I'm not laughing at the situation. It's just ... have you looked in a mirror lately?"

"What do you mean? This isn't a fashion parade, you know," retorted Maria.

"You've put your lab suit on back to front, and you have all the pockets and poppers at the back. The ones lower down make it look like you're showing your bum crack," said Natasha, giggling uncontrollably.

Maria peered over her shoulder and then suddenly burst into fits of laughter. Oh, I see what you mean." She giggled.

They would have continued laughing but for the sound of the warning klaxon. "Not again!" screamed Natasha.

Maria rushed to the observation window and could see several small meteorites heading their way. They were not as big as the melon-sized one that bounced off them earlier; they were closer to the size of tennis balls. "Natasha, brace yourself," shouted Maria, trying to be heard above the sound of the klaxon. "We're about to be hit by at least fifty or sixty meteorites." The station juddered slightly; the meteorites bounced off. Maria was still peering out of the observation window when she saw an extremely bright light coming from the direction of the Russian/ Chinese station. When the glare had died down, all she could see was empty space. Then a face suddenly appeared in front of her. It was one of the Russian cosmonauts. "Come quick! I think the Russian/Chinese station has been destroyed!"

Natasha hurried over to the observation window and recoiled in horror as one of the cosmonauts was floating past their observation window without an OLS suit on. "Oh, my God. What a horrible way to go," she said.

"Natasha, we must focus our long-range scope back towards the William 6 and Mona 3, as we haven't looked at them for a few weeks," said Maria.

Natasha and Maria headed off to the experimentation lab to where the controls for the LRT were located. "All right, let's look at our big asteroids that are due to pass by the earth, William 6 in two weeks and Mona 3 in six weeks. They'll pass about fifty thousand miles the other side of the moon so at least three hundred thousand miles wide of the earth."

"What is that?" asked Maria excitedly.

"What is it what?" said Natasha.

"I think there's another object behind Mona 3. It looks like another asteroid."

"Another asteroid. That's not possible. Scientists have been tracking these objects for the last twenty years and surely would have noticed another asteroid, hang about there are small objects in front of William 6," said Natasha.

"So, that's why we're being bombarded by objects. The magnetic field of the big asteroid is throwing out objects in all directions, a bit like firing grapeshot from one of the old naval cannons."

"I think we'd better call the general," replied Natasha.

Back in Admiral Mackenzie's office, the general and admiral were on a three-way video link with the Russian and Chinese military leaders.

"Boris and Chen, I'm sorry to hear that. What do you think blew up your space lab? We haven't heard from our team recently," said the admiral.

"I'm not sure, but our last message from them was about your station being hit by meteorites and then a big explosion – then nothing," said Boris.

"General, contact your team and let's get some more information for our friends," ordered the admiral.

"All right, Admiral. I'll go and contact them immediately." The general went to the office set aside for him when he was in the States, and just as he closed the door, his video phone started ringing. "Hello, General Payton here," he said. Just as he finished speaking, a picture came up on his screen. It was Commander Kuzuhara from the space lab.

"General, we have some tragic news. The Russian and Chinese space lab has been destroyed by a meteorite, and there's another asteroid heading for a near-Earth collision," said Natasha, trying to get all the words out in one go.

"Slow down. I know about the other space lab's destruction. What was the other thing you said?"

Maria came into view and said, "General, Commander Francis here. What Natasha is trying to tell you is that we have spotted a third asteroid heading our way. It's been hidden behind Mona 3 until now and it's as big as Mona 3."

"I must inform the Security Council and the admiral of this. I was right about us being infiltrated, although not by someone off-world but by one of the admiral's secret agents," said the general.

"Why would he do that? You're all part of the same organisation," said Natasha.

"I'm not sure, but we must only communicate on this secure video link until we have the answer. Over and out."

The general returned to the admiral's office to hear the admiral saying to the Russian and Chinese military leaders, "We have a protective shield around our station, and that's what probably saved it. I thought General Payton was being a bit paranoid about aliens and all, but it looks like we owe him a great debt for adding the additional safety features to the space lab. "Ah, General, come in and sit down," said the admiral.

"I got hold of our team on our space lab, and they have given me some more details," the general said. "Gentlemen, your station was hit by a small meteorite and has been totally destroyed. Additionally, the team has discovered another asteroid behind Mona 3, which will pass the earth a month after Mona 3. Don't you find it strange that all of a sudden we now have three asteroids heading our way?"

"I don't think so. After all, look what happened to Jupiter in the noughties when a huge asteroid ploughed into the big gas giant and that broke into several large fragments," said the admiral.

"Maybe that's what has happened here. Our asteroids were originally one big mass that has broken up," said Field Marshall Boris Ivanov from the video link.

"Our space lab team said that running in front of our big asteroid is a trail of smaller debris which have been hitting our space labs," replied the general. "This still does not account for the bombardment of our space stations by our missing satellites. I still think we're dealing with an off-world presence."

Maria was still studying the asteroids when she noticed something strange. "Hey, Natasha, you've not been fiddling with these controls, have you?" she asked.

"No, I have not. Why do you think that everything that goes wrong on the station is to do with me?" said Natasha.

"You didn't stop to think of any implications or effects when you pushed the blue button in the main control room. Anyway, this is more important. If you didn't touch the controls, it looks like William 6 is slowing down."

Natasha rushed over to the telescope controls. "How do you come to that conclusion? Let me look." A moment later, she said, "I think you're right. The asteroid should have been in line with Jupiter by now."

"That cannot be possible. This asteroid has been travelling at a constant speed, as has the one behind it.

Let me look at Mona 3. My God, that has slowed down as well. What's going on?"

Back on Earth, the three superpowers were now pooling their resources. They all agreed that something was not right with the destruction of the Russian/Chinese space lab and the objects that should not exist being found on the planet. "I believe we're being manipulated by another civilisation. All these things happening at once can't be a coincidence," stated General Payton over the video link to the Russian and Chinese military leaders.

"What do we need to do? How do we find out what or who is behind these strange events? The carbon dating of the objects being found proves they have been on our planet at least two hundred and fifty thousand years," said the Chinese people's military leader, Chen Wai.

Maria and Natasha had been monitoring the incoming asteroids for the last week now, and strange things had been happening with them. All of them seemed to have slowed down. "Natasha, they have slowed down even more; William 6 is just coming in line with the moon. It should pass by within the next twenty minutes at current velocity," said Maria.

"You keep watching and I'll record all the telemetry," said Natasha.

"Oh, my God!" shouted Maria.

"What is it?"

"William 6 has come to a complete stop just within the moon's orbit, which means it's only a few miles from the surface, not fifty thousand miles as originally predicted."

"What does that mean?" asked Natasha.

"I think we'd better contact the general, as all earthbound telescopes have been tracking these asteroids," replied Maria.

"Wait a moment – let me have another look before we contact the general. Oh, shit! William 6 has started moving again. That's strange. It's changed direction and is now heading towards Earth!"

General Payton's secure line phone was sounding in his earpiece. He moved from his office to a blackout room next door. "Hello? General Payton here."

"General, you must warn the Security Council that William 6 is now heading towards the earth. At its present speed and trajectory, it will reach you in about ten hours; it's going to strike somewhere in the mid-Atlantic," said Maria.

"How can that be possible, Commander? It was going to pass the other side of the moon by fifty thousand miles. Have you been drinking or something?" said the general, somewhat perturbed. "Please don't communicate this information to anyone else. We need to assess this information."

"I think this information will be out by the time you tell someone. Most of the scientific community have been tracking these asteroids, and they will spot its change of direction," stated Maria.

"OK, I'll let the Security Council know immediately and try to make what plans we have in the time scale," said the general.

"Another thing: we can do nothing for our families from here. Can you please get my father-in-law and Maria's husband and children to a safe location? You owe us one."

"I'll do my best, but you realise the entire world will be in a state of panic," said the general.

"Now, General, I don't want to hear any excuses. Just get our families to safety," snapped Maria.

"Will do. Over and out," said the general.

Most of the world's telescopes had now noticed the fact that William 6 was earthward bound. The video links and communications networks were completely jam-packed with the news about the asteroids. Maria's husband, Adam, had just put on the morning news and was watching reports about William 6. "Oh, my God, how could our scientists have been so wrong? I must contact Maria," he said quietly to himself.

Adam got the children up and gave them breakfast; he had turned off the news broadcasts so as not to alarm them. "Alana and Sean, time to get ready. Come on, kids. I'm going to contact Mummy. You want to talk with her, don't you?"

"Mummy!" both children said in unison.

"Come on, Sean. Hurry up or we'll miss Mummy!" exclaimed Alana, unable to contain her excitement.

The children quickly dressed themselves and joined their dad around the video link machine. Adam pressed the communications button, but all he got was a crackling in the speakers and lines on the screen. "Come on, Daddy! We want to talk with Mummy," both children were shouting.

Adam thought to himself that there must be complete panic around the world and everyone was trying to use the satellite communication video links. He was about to let the children down slowly when there was banging on their apartment door.

"Just a minute," Adam called. He rushed to the door and opened it. He was confronted by two men in uniform.

"Is your name Adam Francis?" one of the uniforms barked.

"Yes, what do you want?" he asked nervously.

"We have been sent by General Payton on request of your wife to take you and your children to a safe place. Get some stuff together."

"You have ten minutes and then we must leave," said the other uniformed man.

"Kids, get your overnight bags. We're going on a short trip!" shouted Adam. As a family, they were well organised and each always had a bag packed at the ready in case they needed to go somewhere at short notice. Adam grabbed his and Maria's bags, gathered up the children, and left the apartment with the uniforms.

Professor Kuzuhara was just wrapping up his last lecture when two military officers came into his lecture theatre. "Are you Professor Tadashi Kuzuhara?" one of the soldiers asked politely.

"Yes, who wants to know?"

"Professor, we have been sent by your daughter-in-law, Commander Kuzuhara. We need to move you to a safe location."

"You have ten minutes to gather what you need," ordered the other soldier.

"Wait a moment. You cannot just burst in here and expect me to jump. I'm not one of your toy soldiers, you know, and how do I know my daughter-in-law sent you?" snapped the professor.

"Look, sir, we don't have much time. When we get to the safe location, you can speak with her on the secure link. Please hurry. It's a matter of national security."

The professor went to his rooms in the university followed by the soldiers and gathered a few important things from his humble abode. The soldiers loaded him into a military vehicle and sped off in the direction of the airport. They passed many checkpoints and people running around aimlessly. The professor was put aboard a military six-seater ion drive jet. As soon as the door closed, the plane took off.

Back on Earth, Adam's brother, Gerald, had been watching the news with his eldest daughter, Lauren.

"Dad, I spoke with aunty Maria a couple of weeks ago about some archaeological matters," said Lauren.

"Shush a minute, Lauren. They're talking about William 6, the asteroid that was supposed to pass by the earth by at least three hundred thousand miles," said Gerald in a dismissive way.

"I spoke with aunty Maria about William 6, and she agreed it would pass harmlessly by," said Lauren with an air of confidence.

"Well, I'm afraid your aunty got it wrong. The asteroid is now heading towards Earth and is going to strike somewhere in the mid-Atlantic. That means there will be one heck of a Tsunami, which will cause widespread flooding. Just in case the floodwaters reach us here, I'm going to load our pleasure cruiser moored at the lake with supplies and water and we'll board it the night before the asteroid strikes," stated Gerald in a defiant voice.

Gerald had had the pleasure cruiser named *Lily Rose* moved up from its Thames mooring when he opted out of the business rat race. He used to use it for entertaining his business clients, and it had all the comforts of home. This boat could sleep up to sixteen people and could carry enough fuel and supplies to be at sea for around three months. It was ninety feet from stem to stern, with a beam of twenty feet, and it carried jet skis and small rubber dinghies, scuba diving equipment, and even a mini-sub. Additionally, it had the latest satellite navigation systems on board, flare cannons, and a pulse cannon to disable electrical systems. This was to deter pirates from trying to board, almost like a floating hotel battleship. The cost for shipping it up from London used up half his money made from the business, but he felt it was worth every penny, as the boat was a prized possession, probably valued in today's market at around 170 million WD. It was moored at Lake Windermere so he could use it for pleasure days out instead of flying off to exotic holidays as he did in the past when he had his business.

Adam and his family arrived at the London headquarters of the WSOA around fifteen minutes after they were collected, and General Payton himself met them. "Hello, Mr Francis. Welcome to the WSOA. Hello, Alana and Sean. I have heard so much about you from your mother," said the general.

"Why have we been brought here?" asked Adam.

"For your own safety. People have gone completely mad due to the incoming asteroid, and obviously, we want our space commanders only worrying about up there and not down here," said the general.

Professor Kuzuhara landed at the Maplin Sands airstrip two hours after departing Hiroshima and was immediately whisked to the London WSOA offices to meet with General Payton. His first question upon seeing the general was, "When can I speak with my daughter-in-law?"

"Soon. We'll link with the space lab so Commanders Kuzuhara and Francis can both speak with their families," replied the general.

"General, may I speak with you in private for a moment?" asked the professor.

"Sure, let's go to my office." The general led the professor down the hallway to an office with a huge metal reinforced door. "Come in," beckoned the general. "What do you want to speak about that is so private?"

"Have you told her yet?" asked the professor.

"Have I told who what?" replied the general, at which point the professor grew furious.

"General, stop playing games. Have you told Natasha that you're her father?"

The general reeled back in absolute horror. How could he know this? "I don't know what you're talking about," he said angrily.

"Tamiko told me everything. She had to take time off from the university to have the baby, and she told me it was yours. I was sworn to secrecy, but in the circumstances, I think you should tell her," said the professor in a pleading voice.

"I can't. It will compromise my decision making and affect her ability to think rationally. She has enough to deal with now," replied the general with a hint of sadness in his voice.

"The world is going to end, and even now you can't bring yourself to tell your only daughter that she still has a father. Shame on you," said the professor.

Back on the space lab, Maria and Natasha were watching as William 6 started to approach the earth. At its present velocity, it would hit in thirty minutes.

"Hello, is that General Payton?" Maria and Natasha said in unison, talking into the secure link video.

"Yes, it's the general, and I have a massive surprise for you both. OK, you can speak now," said the general to Adam and the professor. "*Konnichiwa*, Natasha and Maria," said the professor in his humblest voice.

"Prof, is that you!" shouted Natasha in absolute delight.

"Are Adam and the children there?" asked Maria.

"I'm here, my darling. How are you?" said Adam.

"We're here, Mummy!" shouted Alana and Sean.

After warmly greeting them, Maria said, "General, we really appreciate you getting our families to safety. How safe are they going to be where you're based?"

"We're going to be in an underground bunker four hundred feet below us, so we'll be safe from the initial blast. Who knows what the after effects will be once William 6 makes planetfall."

Gerald and his family were now on board his pleasure cruiser, *Lily Rose*. He her loaded up with three months' supply for sixteen people and was awaiting the asteroid impact.

"Dad, do you think we'll be safe from the shock wave once the asteroid hits the earth?" asked Lauren.

"I think we stand a better chance on the lake, as it is surrounded by high hills and any shock wave will push us along the lake," said Gerald. What Gerald didn't appreciate was that the shock wave would be superheated. Anything within a one-thousand-mile radius would be scorched or vaporised, depending where the asteroid made planetfall. It would also depend on what was in the content of the shock wave that they got.

Back on board the space lab, Maria and Natasha were monitoring William 6 as it entered the Earth's atmosphere. It was travelling at 250,000 miles per hour. Something was unusual about this asteroid. Normal asteroids at this point would start to break up, but all that happened was William 6 started to glow and again the object seemed as if it was slowing down. William 6 was heading towards the Azores, which was grave news for Earth, as this impact would throw debris and dust into the atmosphere, block out the sun, and send a superheated shock wave around the globe.

Five minutes from impact, William 6 suddenly slowed to almost five miles per hour. It was now directly over the Azores. It started to lower itself onto the Azores, eventually coming to a halt as it settled on top of the island chain.

"Natasha, William 6 hasn't impacted at speed with the Azores. It seems to have landed rather than crashed!" exclaimed Maria with absolute delight in her voice.

"That's strange," said Natasha. "General, calling General Payton!" shouted Natasha into the secure com line.

"Commander Kuzuhara, no need to scream. I can hear you," said the general. "What news do you have regarding William 6?"

"The asteroid has landed on the Azores," said Maria.

CHAPTER FOUR

REUNION

Maria and Natasha were working in the experimentation lab analysing the vapour trail of William 6. The asteroid burned with an orange and green flame. The orange flame indicated that it had a high iron and nickel content, in addition to something else. They checked the spectrometer for the constituent make-up of the green flame and were shocked with their findings; this asteroid also had a high content of malachite, which was the ore that copper was refined from. This was unusual, as no other asteroid had been found with Malachite in its make-up. The asteroid was sitting on top of Corvo Island in the Azores. It didn't have enough weight to destroy the island, but something was happening – Corvo island appeared to be sinking.

The UN ships were now at the Azores, where William 6 was sitting nicely on top of the island in the Azores chain. It was still glowing and was giving off immense heat. If one were to get closer than a quarter of a mile, he or she would be severely burnt. The asteroid was about six miles long and about three miles wide. Strangely, it was only about two miles deep. It hadn't broken up in the atmosphere as most asteroids would. The reason it hadn't broken apart was that it seemed to be under its own power and landed on the island like a rocket coming from space, although no flames were coming from it, so it wasn't rocket powered. General Payton was with the admiral on the American carrier the *Enterprise III*, named after a famous ship.

"I told you, Admiral, that we're being studied. How can an asteroid be under its own power? God help those people on the island when it landed," said the general.

"Now, General, let's not get ahead of ourselves. I think it's mere coincidence that this asteroid soft-landed on the Azores," replied the admiral.

"Soft-landed. More like guided, precise and pre-planned," retorted the general.

"Graham, I don't want you spreading rumours. We have enough panic in the world at the moment."

"But, Admiral ..."

"Enough, General Payton. This is the last word we are going to have on the subject."

"Yes, sir," said the general.

Gerald and his family were settling down on board *Lily Rose*. Their cruiser had moored on Lake Windermere the night before William 6 was due to impact on the earth.

"Let's put the news reports on," said Lauren.

"I think it's best we get some sleep. Could be a rough day tomorrow, and the asteroid is not due to impact the earth until 11 a.m. GMT," said Valerie.

"I agree with your mum. It's after eleven. Let's go to bed and set our alarms for no later than 8 a.m. so we can prepare," said Gerald.

The next morning, the sun was up at four. Gerald didn't manage a wink of sleep all through the night, as he was worried for his family. He was making himself a cup of tea around five when he heard a noise in the kitchen. "Who's there?" He was trembling as he said it.

"Don't worry, Dad. It's only me. I couldn't sleep," said Lauren.

"Me neither," said Gerald.

"The asteroid is due to make landfall in a few hours," stated Lauren.

Gerald was about to reply when an almighty bang came from the bow of the boat.

"What the hell was that? It can't be the asteroid already. It's not due for at least six hours!" Lauren cried.

"Calm down, number one daughter. It's probably the anchor chain. I programmed its release for five am to allow us drift further down the lake. For obvious reasons, I wanted to ensure we were moored in the middle," Gerald said in his calmest voice. Gerald went to put on his satellite audio/video screen to check on the latest news.

"We have the latest from Commander Francis on board the space lab," the newscaster was saying. "Commander, where did you say the asteroid would make landfall?"

"We predict that on its current trajectory, it will impact with the Azores Island Chain at around 11 a.m. GMT," said commander Francis."

"Lauren, come quick. It's your aunty Maria on the video screen," called Gerald.

"Where? Let me see. Oh, you're right. Hi, Aunty Maria!" she shouted at the screen while waving frantically.

"Lauren, don't be silly. She can't hear you or see you. It's a recording from earlier today," said Gerald, laughing so loudly he could wake up a hibernating bear.

It had been eight days since William 6 landed on the Island of Corvo. The island was sinking, as confirmed by the space lab, and the rate was alarming: about 150 millimetres per day. William 6 was still emitting a level of heat that made landing on the island impossible. It wasn't as hot as when it landed but could still give a nasty burn if one got too close. The four hundred or so people living on the island were almost certainly killed, although there had been several unconfirmed reports that some inhabitants managed to get into ships and leave as the asteroid landed.

Maria and Natasha were still studying William 6 from the space lab. Still photos were taken of William 6 and the rest of the planet as a matter of course. This would allow one to see any changes to the oceans or land masses and was primarily used to monitor the rainforest areas of the world. Unfortunately, they were still being harvested, even though the need for timber was no longer necessary because more plastics were being used. This was an ideal way to inform the countries affected if their rainforests were still being harvested, as the photographs would over time show the green area shrinking. It was while studying these photographs that Natasha noticed something strange. "Hey, Maria, come and look at these pictures of the Isle of Wight, off the coast of Southern England," she called across the lab.

Maria floated across to Natasha and picked up the picture in question. "Nope, cannot see what you're talking about."

"Oh, you're a numpty. You need to compare the picture you're holding, taken seven days ago, with this one I'm holding," Natasha said in a sarcastic tone.

"Oh, why did you not say?" Maria studied both pictures but was still struggling to see what Natasha was talking about. "Sorry, Natasha, but I still can't see what you've spotted."

"Let me show you. Look at the west end of the island, at what they call the Needles, in the first picture. Now look at them in the second picture."

"Oh, my God yes. I see what you mean now. Some of the rock stacks are much lower in the water than in the first picture. What can this mean?"

"It means that either the water level is rising or the Needles are sinking," replied Natasha.

All over the world, land masses appeared to be sinking and, incredibly, at the same rate as the Island of Corvo: 150 millimetres per day, albeit it a day later than Corvo. At this pace, certain low-lying land masses would be under water and the Maldives will have almost completely disappeared. Fortunately, the earth tether anchored off the east coast of England was on a floating platform, so it was unaffected. The UN science division started working on the problem of how to either stop or cope with the rising water levels.

"Hello, is that General Payton? It's Major Sian Campton from DO3. Come in, please."

"General Payton here. What can I do for you, Major?"

"We seem to be having problems with our depth readings. We've been monitoring the ocean depth since

William 6 landed on Corvo, which was eight days ago," said Major Campton.

"What is the issue, Major? We have far more worrying problems on land at the moment," said the general dismissively.

"General, we have less ocean above us than eight days ago, around twelve hundred millimetres less. We thought you ought to know," said the major.

"That cannot be. Our sea levels have risen by twelve hundred millimetres in the last eight days. You should have more water above you, not less. Check your readings again and confirm them with DO1 and DO2. Then get back to me."

"Yes, sir, will come back to you in the next few hours," answered the major.

"Natasha, I'm going to contact my brother-in-law Gerald!" called Maria from across the lab.

"What for?"

"I think I should warn him to get to his cruiser and stay on it because the water levels are rising fast and he lives by a lake that feeds into the sea," she said.

"Hello, Gerald. Come in. It's Maria here."

"Hi, aunty Maria. It's Lauren here."

"Lauren, thank heavens I got hold of you. I need to speak with your dad," said Maria.

"OK, aunty. I'll get him. Dad, it's aunty Maria!" she called out across the living room.

"Lauren, no need to shout. I can hear you," replied Gerald.

"Hi, Maria. How are you?" asked Gerald.

"Let's skip the pleasantries, Gerald. You need to stock up your cruiser and get on board ASAP, as the water levels are rising fast," demanded Maria.

"I know the water levels in the lake have risen by at least two feet," said Gerald.

"I need a favour from you. If you get the chance, would you sail up to Scotland and pick up my mother from Carnoustie?" Maria asked in a pleading voice.

"Maria, I'm one step ahead of you. I have been stocking up my cruiser over the last week now and have enough supplies on board to be at sea for a year. Regarding your mother, we're currently landlocked so no can do, but if we do get the chance, I'll contact her and let her know we're coming."

"Oh, thank you. Bye."

"Deep Ocean Three here, Major Campton. Are you there, General?" asked the major.

"Yes, I'm here, Major. What news do you have for me?" asked the general. "I've spoken with DO1 and DO2. They are reporting the same drop in depth. We appear, for all intents and purposes, to be rising up, and the water level is getting less above us," said the major.

"I want you to give me daily updates of the changing depth, Major," barked the general.

"OK, sir. Will do about the same time as today," replied the major. "Absolutely, Major. Over and out."

The UN task force were picking up survivors from Corvo Island on the neighbouring islands, as a few boats had managed to escape during the asteroid's decent to the island.

"Admiral, we must speak with these survivors. They can give us a clearer indication of what happened," said the general.

"I agree. We must find out how many survived and what the conditions were like on the island," said the admiral.

"I also mean we can find out how the asteroid landed or crashed."

"I know what you mean, General, but we have had that discussion already, remember? Not another word about aliens and the like," retorted the admiral.

"Yes, sir, I understand," said the general. The general and admiral managed to speak with the mayor from Corvo, and he was quite clear that William 6 landed. He believed it slowed right down to about two miles per hour, the admiral asked him how he knew that, as the heat would have vaporised him if he was that close. The mayor explained that he was watching from a boat out at sea, as they had been on a fishing trip with several other boats from the island at the time. That's why there were rumours of survivors, a hundred people were on a fishing trip at the time the asteroid landed.

Maria and Natasha were watching Mona 3 and the other asteroid that had come into view, named Maria 2, after Commander Francis, who discovered it, and because the two also represented the diameter in miles of the new asteroid. Mona 3 had also changed trajectory and was now on a collision course with the earth. No one was sure where it would strike, but on its present course, it would hit the South Pole.

"Natasha, I've been monitoring the ocean depths with our telescope, and they are definitely rising," said Maria.

"That makes sense. So, the rising water levels aren't because the land is sinking but the ocean floor is moving up," said Natasha.

"I wondered what triggered the ocean floor to start moving. There are no earthquakes anywhere because of it. Could it be William 6 that has caused this?"

"The ocean floor moving does not seem possible, as it isn't in line with the earth's tectonic plates."

"I suppose that is one consolation. If it were on the tectonic plate boundaries, then we would have massive volcanic disruption and huge tsunamis all over the world," said Natasha.

"I'm starting to worry for our families. There will be worldwide panic once people realise that the rising water levels are due to the sea floor rising. It will leave them with no safe dry land shortly."

"Perhaps we can convince the general to let our families come aboard the space lab. We have enough supplies and oxygen for six people. If we use it right, it will last at least one year," said Natasha.

"Maybe that's what the general had in mind. Why would he stock up the space lab and add defensive capabilities?"

Mona 3 was due to impact with the earth in three weeks. If it hit the Antarctic, then the ice and snow would melt, causing more flooding around the world. At present, the asteroid seemed to have slowed down, just like William 6.

"General, this is Commander Francis here. Is this still a secure line?" asked Maria.

"General Payton here. Yes, it is a secure line. Only you and I are on this call. What else do you have to report?"

"The sea-bed is definitely rising. We believe William 6 has triggered the movement. It's like a counterbalance weight sitting on top of Corvo. The island is like a trigger, as in Egyptian pyramids, where you push a stone and the sand actuates a door. William 6 is actuating a trigger to make the sea-bed rise."

"It's a bit implausible and more like a movie special effect, don't you think?"

"No more far-fetched than thinking we're being invaded by aliens."

"OK, Commanders, you've made your point. What else do you want?" asked the general.

"We need a favour," said Natasha and Maria in unison.

"What sort of favour?" asked the general, as if he was expecting them to want to come home.

"Well, the space lab is stocked with enough supplies and oxygen for six people to last at least one year," said Maria.

"Yes, I know that. What's your point?"

"We want our families to come aboard. That way we can continue monitoring the situation without any distractions," said Natasha.

"We could take them with us on board one of our naval carriers," said the general.

"No, that wouldn't help us. We would still be worrying about their safety, and I don't trust the admiral, if the truth be known; you don't have enough room to cover all the military personnel, let alone civilians."

"We'll make special provision for them," stated the general.

"I'm sorry, General, but we both feel the safest place for them is with us up here," said Maria. "What do you think the rest of the military will do once they find you've taken civilians aboard your ships?"

"It will be difficult to get your families to the earth tether platform. It's guarded by the admiral's troops," replied the general.

"You still owe us. Please find a way and let us know immediately when you get them on the tether."

"Ok I'll do my best."

Back on Earth, Gerald was continuing to stock up *Lily Rose*, his pleasure cruiser, as he might need to add another person to the crew: his sister-in-law's mum.

"Dad, how much stuff are we going to put on the cruiser? We have already filled up two of the guest rooms with food and water," said Lauren.

"We need to make sure we're stocked up with at least one year's worth of supplies to cover us five and potentially another six people," replied Gerald.

"Why another six people? We need to look after ourselves. Fuck the other people," said, his wife.

"Now, Valerie, enough of that. I'm banking on my brother and his family joining us. The more the merrier, as we'll need as much help as possible once we're on the water," said Gerald.

"Dad, what are you expecting to happen when we get seaborne?" asked Lauren.

"It's going to get quite messy once people realise they have nowhere to go; dry land will disappear fast, and we may need to fight off boarders."

"General Major Campton here from DO3. The water above us is decreasing each day. It's been twelve days since the William 6 landed on Corvo. We have moved up one point eight metres in twelve days."

"So, the space lab findings are confirmed. They indicated that the seabed was rising," said the general.

"General, I don't want to alarm you, but if we move up too far, DO1 will explode because of the air pressure in our system to help maintain our structural integrity due to our extreme depth," said the major.

"Can you not reduce the pressure in your systems as you are rising?" asked the general.

"Not without compromising our structural integrity. How much do we reduce it by, if you know what I mean," Major Campton said?

"Send your data to the space lab; they have sophisticated software and computer on board. They've been calculating the depth changes. Perhaps they can give you a sequencing program."

"OK, sir, we'll contact Commanders Francis and Kuzuhara. Many thanks, General," said the major.

Maria and Natasha were still tracking Mona 3 and the new asteroid, Maria 2.

"Hey, Natasha, although Mona 3 has slowed down, the new asteroid has not. It's still travelling at speed and on its current course will strike somewhere in the Northern Hemisphere," said Maria.

"Is Mona 3 still headed for the Antarctic?"

"Yes, its present course will put it right on top of the Antarctic mountain ranges," replied Maria.

"We're receiving a message from Sian on DO3. Hey, how are you, Sian? Missing all the fun up here and on the surface?" asked Natasha.

"Not really, Natasha. We're at risk of DO3 exploding due to our air pressure," said the major solemnly.

"How can we help?"

"The general said you're monitoring the change in depth daily. If you can give us a daily sequencing forecast of the depth changes, we can program our air system to reduce the pressure as we move up, therefore reducing the risk to our structural integrity," said the major.

"We can do that, Sian, but what about DO1/2?" enquired Natasha.

"Not to worry. We'll send DO1/2 your findings so they can do the same," said the major.

"Good luck up there. We heard about the attacks on the space lab and the destruction of the Russian/Chinese station. You keep safe and we'll see you soon hopefully," said the major.

"Thanks, Sian. Keep safe yourself," said Maria.

It had now been twenty-one days since William 6 landed on Corvo, and the River Leven that flowed out from Windermere had risen by three metres. Gerald was guiding *Lily Rose* down river towards the sea estuary at Arrad Foot. It was slow going, as the water depth varied and there were some tight turns on the River Leven.

"We'll reach Arrad Foot in about two hours, just before we lose the daylight," said Gerald to his family.

"Dad, are you going to sail to Scotland to pick up aunty Maria's mum?" asked Jade.

"Of course. Your aunt asked me, and I said we would," replied Gerald.

They reached Arrad Foot in ninety minutes, a little earlier than Gerald predicted. As they drew level with the town, a small speedboat came out to meet them. Gerald scanned them with his infrared scope. There were five people on board, all carrying machine pistols.

"Dad, look. A boat is coming out to greet us," said Lauren, waving frantically at them.

"Valerie, get the kids back inside. This is an armed boarding party, and they don't look friendly!" shouted Gerald.

"Come on, kids. You heard what your dad said. Get back inside quickly," ordered Valerie.

Gerald fired a warning shot at them from the bow flare cannon, but all they did was motor past the flare and continue coming at them at full speed. "I gave them the chance to back off. They leave me no choice," he said to himself. He aimed the pulse cannon at the speeding boat and sent an electromagnetic pulse towards the boat. The speedboat immediately slowed down as her engines burnt out. What happened next completely shocked him. The speedboat burst into flames and exploded twenty seconds later. Those on board stood no chance.

The children were crying, and Valerie was in shock. "Those poor people," she said.

Gerald answered, "It was them or us, my darling, I'm sorry for them," he said.

General Payton called his London headquarters adjutant, Colonel Richard Cropel, into his office. "Colonel, I have a special mission for you," he said.

"Oh, good. You want me to take out the admiral's men so you can get to the earth tether," he said excitedly.

"Not exactly. I want you to distract them and draw them away from the tether, as I need to get there. I want no bloodshed unless it's absolutely necessary."

"All right, sir, but why do we need to draw them away? Can't you just order them to leave? After all, we are on the same side, are we not?" asked the colonel.

"This is a need-to-know mission only, and I'm afraid you don't need to know at this stage," barked the general.

"OK, sir. We'll let you know when we have drawn them away."

"Take this communicator with you. It's a secure channel. I don't want the admiral to get wind of what we're up to. Signal me once you achieve your objective. I'll be close by."

The general got Maria and Natasha's families together and explained what his plan was. He told them that both Maria and Natasha wanted them up with them on the space lab and he was going to try to get them there. He had already let Maria and Natasha know his plan and what time they would be on the platform.

"General, what about the children? They will be frightened, and to be honest, so will I," said Adam, Maria's husband.

"Additionally, we have not been trained to use the equipment. How will we dock with the space station once we get there?" asked professor Kuzuhara.

"Don't worry. Commander Francis will meet us on the tether platform in space. She will pilot you to the space lab," said the general. "Let's go – my special force is going ahead of us to clear the way."

The general and the families jumped aboard a military personnel carrier with six heavily armed soldiers. They sped off in the direction of the river to be loaded on board a naval ion-powered antigravity landing craft. This craft could achieve incredible speeds and was more heavily armoured than a battleship of old. It could withstand high-speed impacts without suffering any remedial damage. It would get to the earth tether in twenty minutes.

Maria was about forty minutes away from the earth tether platform. She had been travelling for about nine hours in the pod.

"Commander Francis, come in. Are you there?" asked Natasha.

"Natasha, we need to keep communication silence. What part of 'no communication until we have collected the package' did you not understand?" replied Maria angrily.

"Oops, sorry. Over and out."

"Admiral, we have just picked up a communication from Commander Francis. She is heading towards the earth tether platform. Was that scheduled?"

The admiral was furious. "They're trying to get back to Earth, and we need them to stay up there. Contact her immediately!" he screamed.

"Commander Francis, it's Houston control here. Come in, come in, come in!" shouted the space room controller. "I'm getting no reply sir," said the controller.

"Give me that fucking communicator," he ordered.

"Commander Francis, I know you can hear me. Come in. Why have you left the space lab!" shouted the admiral.

The speakers suddenly crackled to life. "Hello, come in. It's Commander Kuzuhara here. Houston, do you read me?"

The admiral grabbed the communicator again. "Hello, Commander Kuzuhara. Why are you travelling back to the earth tether platform?" he snapped.

"I'm not. I'm calling you from the space lab," said Natasha.

"Then why is Commander Francis travelling to the earth tether?" asked the admiral.

"Oh, she is going to collect some additional supplies sent up by the general. We understand that we can't take any leave anytime soon, and we requested a few more special food items," said Natasha.

"I wasn't aware of any special request. I'll contact the general to confirm. Please ensure you stay up there and continue monitoring the asteroids," ordered the admiral.

"Of course, we will, sir. We know you're all relying on us. We have sent data to DO1/2/3 to help them with their ascent," said Natasha.

"Why is Commander Francis not replying to our hails?" asked the admiral.

"We have had some trouble with the communication devices on the pods. I think the communicators are on the blink," replied Natasha sheepishly.

"OK, over and out," said the admiral. "Get me Payton on the video link," he shouted at his orderly.

Gerald and the *Lily Rose* cruiser were now heading out to the open sea, coming into Morecambe Bay and motoring towards Whitehaven.

"Hello? Who is this calling?" said Mary, Maria's mother.

"Hello, Mary. This is Gerald, Maria's brother-in-law. I was asked to call you about being picked up," said Gerald.

"Picked up? Do you know our house is five feet underwater, with it rising day by day?" said Mary.

"Not a problem. We're in a seagoing cruiser. It will take us another day's sailing to be with you. We're doing thirty knots," said Gerald.

"Oh, that's fantastic. We look forward to seeing you. I'll have some cakes and scones ready when you get here."

Gerald had to use the underwater depth finder due to some rocks and pinnacles being covered by water, which slowed them down a bit. "*Lily Rose* could do fifty knots in open seas."

"General, the platform is clear. Unfortunately, we got into a firefight with the admiral's men and we have two wounded men down," said the colonel.

"How about the admiral's men?" asked the general.

"I'm afraid none of them made it. We had no choice. They wouldn't leave the tether point."

"OK, we don't have time for recriminations. Set up a defence perimeter. We're coming through," said the general.

The ion drive antigravity landing craft docked with the earth tether platform, and the general and the families climbed up to the pod docking area. The general got the families and himself into the eight-person pod. "Strap yourselves in and put on the oxygen masks," he said. "Colonel, get back to headquarters and make sure no one gets in. I'll be back in a few hours."

"Sir, you're not staying up there," said the colonel.

"No, I'll be needed down here as the situation gets worse," said the general. "Now, people, this is going to accelerate quite quickly. Just breathe normally or you will get cramps. Professor Kuzuhara, I have a letter here for Commander Kuzuhara. Please make sure she gets it only when you're docked and on board the space lab."

"All right, General. I hope the content is what we spoke about in your office a few days ago," said the professor.

"All right, everyone. Strap in and let's go," said the general, at which point he pressurised the cabin and pulled the throttle back to start the pod. The pod moved off quite gently at first and then accelerated up to one hundred kilometres. They were now in the clouds and still travelling upwards. The professor looked up through the glass canopy and could see the darkness of space.

"General Payton, come in," said the admiral at the video link.

"General Payton here. What can I do for you, Admiral?"

"I understand that you've sent extra food supplies up to the space lab. Is this true?" asked the admiral.

"Yes, that's right. They may need to stay longer than their allotted time, and they asked me for extra food rations," said the general.

"Hmm, is that so? Where are you taking this call from?"

"I'm in one of the pods travelling up with the extra supplies," replied the general.

"That's strange. My men haven't informed me that you were at the earth tether. In fact, we're having trouble contacting them," said the admiral.

"I didn't see any of your men at the platform."

"That's not possible. I posted six marines to guard the entrance. Are you sure you didn't see them?"

"No, never saw anyone. Anyway, must break off, as we're entering the ionosphere," said the general as he terminated the link.

"Get my plane ready," ordered the admiral. "I don't trust that bastard. He's up to something. I'll fly to London, get in contact with the Abraham Lincoln Carrier that's moored in the channel. I want it ready and in the Thames Estuary when I arrive."

Lily Rose was now out in the Irish Sea and heading up the coast towards the Orkney Isles. "We need to stay clear of any coastal ports or we may have the same problem as at Arrad Foot," said Gerald.

Gerald sailed *Lily Rose* around the outside of the Orkneys to avoid any contact with the local fishermen. He was making valuable time and would be off the coast of Carnoustie by midday tomorrow, as he had planned.

He made another video call to Mary. "Hi, Mary, it's Gerald here. We'll be with you by noon tomorrow. How are you coping?"

"Hello, Gerald. We're all right. The water level is now just above our ground-floor windows. I moved all our non-perishable foods up here with us. Thought you may need to top up your supplies."

"Good idea. That would help greatly. Don't suppose you have some baking yeast? We have lots of flour but have run out of yeast and have been baking flat breads. What I wouldn't give to have a proper loaf of bread."

"You're in luck," said Mary. As you may be aware, I do a lot of baking so have lots of dried yeast which you are very welcome to. Another thing: my brother Tom will need to come with us. He's living with me now."

"No problem. We can accommodate him; it will give us another person to help repel boarders."

"What? You're taking in lodgers?" asked Mary.

"Sorry. Not boarders as in hotel guests but boarders as in people trying to get on our vessel and take it over," said Gerald with a wry smile on his face.

"See you tomorrow, then. Bye for now, Gerald," said Mary.

"God, we're like bloody Noah's Ark. How many more strays are we going to take on board?" said Val.

"Darling, as I said before, we have room for sixteen people, and with Mary and Tom, that will bring our complement up to seven. Besides, Mary is a great cook and will be a useful addition to our crew."

It was getting dark and, *Lily Rose* was sailing by GPS and infrared scanning. Gerald had set the cruiser on autopilot so they could all get some sleep, as it would be another risk to the ship and a nerve-racking time picking up Mary and her brother, Tom, with the need to get in close to the shore.

Maria was just docking with the space platform as the pod from Earth arrived. She opened the secure channel and said, "Hello, Earth pod 2. Come in."

"Earth pod 2 here. Hello, Commander Francis. We have the package you requested. Please dock with us to collect," replied the general.

Maria went through the docking procedures, which took another ten minutes for the two pods to connect with each other. As the connecting doors slid open, she was greeted with a wild shriek of "Mummy" from her children.

She hugged them and then said, "Please calm down, everyone, and move from your seats one at a time and come through to Pod 1 and strap yourself in." Everyone moved one by one to Pod 1 in silence without question. Adam seemed impressed with the way Maria handled the operation. He had never seen her at work before.

"General, are you coming, sir?" asked Maria.

"No, Commander. I need to get back to Earth and coordinate operations from there. Look after yourself and remember not to let anyone else board the station. Keep your station defences on."

"Good luck down there. You need to get on a ship of sorts, as the water levels are still rising," said Maria in a more consoling voice. She climbed back into Pod 1 and closed the airlocks connecting her to Pod 2; she then went through another ten-minute procedure to undock from Pod 2.

"All right, now ensure you have your oxygen masks on," ordered Maria. "We're now going to embark on a ten-hour flight back to the space lab."

"Hello, darling. Thanks for bringing us up to join you," said Adam.

"Whilst we're travelling to the space lab, all of you will address me as Commander. This is normal protocol, as I'm your lifeline up here in space," said Maria.

In unison, the whole group chorused, "Yes, Commander."

General Payton prepared himself for the return journey to Earth knowing he was going to face some real problems once the admiral got to England. He needed to find a way to explain the killing of the admiral's marines and why he travelled up to the platform just to deliver a package of food. The pod jolted to a halt, and he was back on the ground. Waiting for him was Colonel Cropel.

"Sir, the admiral's plane will be touching down in about thirty minutes. How do you want to handle this?" asked the colonel.

"Just leave it to me. Make sure you have the squad on standby. We may need to make a quick exit. What did you do with the bodies of the marines?"

"They have been dumped at sea and weighted down. No one will find them," said the colonel.

"I'm not happy about dumping our marines at sea. They were human beings, you know, probably with families," barked the general.

The general headed back to his London office whilst the colonel went back to the barracks to prepare the one hundred soldiers in his squad. Just as he got back to the office, the admiral's plane touched down on the Maplin Sands runway. He immediately opened the video link to the general. "This is the admiral. Come in, General Payton."

"General Payton here. What can I do for you, Admiral?" he said.

"Send me a car. I've just landed at Maplin. I want to have a meeting with you," said the admiral in a strangely calm voice.

"All right, sir. We'll send a heli-jet; it will be with you in fifteen minutes," said the general. The colonel was listening in on the conversation and was preparing his own surprise for the admiral. He planned to shoot down the heli-jet so that it didn't reach its destination.

Gerald and his cruiser, *Lily Rose*, were now off the coast of the Scottish golfing town of Carnoustie. He had asked Mary to signal him by torch when she could see their ship.

"Dad, I can see a small light coming from that pink house!" screamed Lauren excitedly.

Gerald trained his long-range scope on the windows and could see someone waving at them frantically. "That must be Mary," he said to himself. He continued scanning all around to make sure there were no other boats nearby. "OK, team, looks like the water level is sufficient for us to get close by with *Lily Rose*, although we'll need to use the launch to take them out. Don't want to hit a submerged pylon," he said to the rest of his family. "Right, Val and Lauren, when we get in close, you take the launch to the bedroom window and help load our passengers and any food items they have."

"We'll do that, but this is the last pickup we make," said Val.

"I understand. I'll continue to watch for any other boats. Don't want to repeat the issues we had at Arrad Foot," replied Gerald. Val and Lauren positioned the launch right next to the upper floor window.

"Mary and Tom, are you ready?" asked Val.

"Yes, we're right here," said Mary. Mary passed out a couple of boxes of tinned food, some meagre belongings, and a small brown suitcase.

"Mary, you climb out first but be careful. Don't want you slipping into the water now," said Lauren.

"Now you, Tom," said Val. "Gerald, we're fully loaded and are on our way back to you" said Val.

Just as they left Mary's cottage, three fishing boats appeared from behind the other houses. They were not as quick as the *Lily Rose* launch but would be able to catch them as they were unloading their passengers. Gerald fired a warning shot from the bow flare cannon and waited to see what the fishing boats would do.

Pod 1 was close to docking with the space lab. "Just a few more bursts on the manoeuvring jets and we'll be there," said Maria.

"Commander, will there be enough suits for us when we're on board?" asked the professor.

"Yes, Professor. We have ten suits to spare, enough for all of you," replied Maria.

After a gentle bump, the pod had docked and been clamped to the space lab. The two airlocks equalised the pressure, and the doors automatically opened.

"Right, team, please climb through one at a time," said Maria. "Children, you first, then the professor, then Adam. I'll follow up last."

As the professor came into the space lab, Natasha gave him a big hug. "You're my only family in the entire world. Couldn't afford to lose you," said Natasha excitedly.

"I love you too, daughter-in-law," said the professor.

The automatic airlocks closed, and the space lab was a sealed environment again. "Natasha, please go and switch on the station defence system," ordered Maria.

"What for? We're safe now," said Natasha.

"The general felt we should. He asked us to do so to make sure no one can board us. Plus, we don't know if we're going to be hit again by rogue objects, do we? By the way, that wasn't a request; that was an order. We have our families on board now, so maximum protection is required."

"OK, sir," said Natasha sarcastically.

"Now, ladies, let's not start bickering. We're with you now and are very glad you brought us up here," said the professor.

"Is there anything we can do to help while we're here?" asked Adam.

"I'll give you a quick tour of the station and assign you your sleeping quarters. I would ask you all, however tempting it might be, not to touch any of the controls, especially you, Adam. Is that clear?" asked Maria.

"Yes, sir, Commander," they all said in unison again.

This made Maria laugh. "Team, we aren't on the pod now. Mummy or Maria or darling will be fine whilst on the space lab," she said, chuckling to herself.

The lighting on the space lab suddenly turned an unusual colour, much brighter and bluer than before. "Mummy, why have the lights changed?" asked Alana.

"Well spotted, darling. They have changed in brightness and colour because we have put on the automated station defences," said Maria.

The heli-jet was just about to land on the WSOA headquarters roof when an object streaked towards it trailing white smoke. The pilot saw it and shouted, "Everyone out! It's a rocket-propelled projectile." He had barely finished what he was saying when the object penetrated the outer skin of the heli-jet and exploded. No one survived the impact. The general heard the explosion and rushed to his office windows in time to see burning debris falling past.

"Oh, my God, what has that idiot done now? He has fired on the admiral's Heli-jet. He's become a liability," said the general. "Colonel, come in!" screeched the general.

"Colonel Cropel here," he said.

"What the hell have you done?" the general shouted.

"General, take it easy. I've made sure there will be no recriminations. The admiral didn't make it," said the colonel, laughing as he said it.

"You're a traitor and a liability to our organisation. First you kill the admiral's marines when I gave you orders that no one was to be harmed and now you take it upon yourself to act without my orders. I'll have your head for this. You're relieved of command," said the general.

"Just as I expected. I knew he was hiding something," said the admiral as his car sped towards the London headquarters of the WSOA.

The fishing boats slowed down on seeing the flare, and they hailed the *Lily Rose*. "Ahoy there. Who are you and why are you taking goods from Mary's cottage?" asked the skipper of the *Dundee Angel*.

"Hi, I'm Gerald the brother of Mary's son-in-law. Her daughter, Maria, asked us to pick Mary and her brother Tom up and get them to safety," replied Gerald.

All the fishing boats had now slowed to a stop. "We're doing the same, rounding up all the people we can find. Where are, you headed?" asked the skipper.

"Not sure yet. We'll contact the space lab and ask for advice."

"If you get any good advice, please pass it on, as we have no idea where it is safe now. Our call sign is *Dundee Angel* on 376 Ghz," said the skipper of the Rose.

"Will do. Good luck on your mission. Hope you can rescue many lost souls," said Gerald.

"Come in, Maria," he said into the video link.

"Commander Francis here," said Maria.

"Do you have to be so formal, lass?" asked Mary.

"Mum, thank God you're safe," said Maria.

"Yes, Gerald has just picked us up. We're on board a luxury floating hotel. Do you know they even have a cinema?"

"Mum, enough of that. Will you put Gerald on the video link, please?" asked Maria.

"Gerald here."

"Thank you so much for picking up my mum. We're in your debt," said Maria.

"Do you have any updates for us, like what direction we should head?" asked Gerald.

"I'd head east towards the Philippines, as the water levels are rising. Keep away from the south because Mona 3 is going to strike the Antarctic in three days, which could cause a Tsunami of huge proportions."

"Then east it is. Keep us posted. We need to speak at least once a week," replied Gerald. He steered the boat towards the Philippines, a journey that would take them about six days.

The admiral arrived at the WSOA in time to see the burning wreckage of the heli-jet. "What does he think he is playing at? I'm no fool. I thought there may be problems with us going by heli-jet, but not these sorts of problems," quoted the admiral to his chief of staff on board the *Abraham Lincoln*.

"Captain, send me a squad of marines. Tell them to meet me at the WSOA headquarters in London. I expect them here in ten minutes. Use the heli-jets," ordered the admiral.

"Yes, Commander," said the captain of the *Abraham Lincoln*.

Professor Kuzuhara handed Natasha the letter the general had given him. "Here, Natasha. This is for you, a letter from the general," said the professor.

"I'll read it later. Can't be that important. If it were, the general would have called us," said Natasha.

"I think this is important and something he wanted to tell you alone, maybe," answered the professor.

"OK, Prof, I'll take it back to my sleeping quarters and take a read just to get you to stop nagging me," replied Natasha mischievously. Natasha made her way back to her sleeping quarters, passing Maria on the way.

"Where are you off to? We have work to do, you know," said Maria.

"Oh, I got a private letter from the general, and the professor said I should read it now."

"Don't be too long," Maria said.

Natasha climbed onto her bed in the sleeping compartment and opened the letter from the general. She began to read:

Dearest Akira,

Please do not be alarmed. I am not going to fire you or anything. I thought you should know something very important. As you're aware, I was a very close friend of your mother's – and her passing affected me greatly. She was a wonderful person and was absolutely devastated that she had to give you up once you were born, but that was what life was like back then, saving face.

I was a little more than just a close friend. We were lovers and planning to get married, but her family absolutely forbade it, as she was pregnant with you. Being pregnant out of marriage was a complete taboo. It was only after she refused to see me anymore that I learned the reason why. I spent many years trying to find out which orphanage you had been sent to, but it was hopeless, for they had given you a different name. I was beside myself trying to find you. What I'm trying to say is that I'm your father and have been trying to tell you for a long time now. I was so sad when I heard that my granddaughter Natasha had been killed in an accident. I would have liked to have met her, and I am sad that you lost your husband and daughter at the same time.

I wanted you to know this, as we may not see each other again due to what I had to do to get you and Commander Francis's family on to the space lab. I know you think that I am not a warm and caring person, but you are wrong to assume that. I have been manipulating your career the minute I found out who you were: the university degree, the recruitment into the WSOA, and even making sure the wedding venue was kept clear for you to marry Takao.

Please don't worry. You and the professor
are safe now that you're on the space lab. Keep
the defence perimeter up and don't let anybody
board, even me.

I love you with all my heart,
Graham Payton

Natasha burst into fits of hysteria. She could not control
her crying. "Why, why?" was all she kept saying to herself.
"Why did he not tell me sooner?" She was still sobbing
when the intercom sparked into life.

"Natasha, Natasha, come in, please. We need you
up here in the main control room!" shouted Maria on
the com.

"OK, Maria, I'm coming. Give me a few minutes. I'm
a little upset now," she sobbed.

"What, for heaven's sake, is wrong now?" said Maria
quite dismissively.

The admiral and his men burst into General Payton's
office with guns raised. The general was sitting behind his
desk and quite calm. "Admiral, nice to see you're all right,"
said the general in a calm voice.

"Don't give me that fucking smug look, General.
What are you up to and where are my marines that were
stationed at the tether!" screamed the admiral.

"Admiral, I don't know where your men are. I'm sorry."

"Then why did you go up to the space platform?" asked the admiral.

"To deliver Commander Francis's and Commander Kuzuhara's families to them," said the general.

"What? We have civilians on the space lab? What the fuck were you thinking!"

"Admiral, this will ensure that they stay up there and monitor the planet and asteroids, a workable solution, if I say so myself," said the general sarcastically.

"Captain, I want you to take a squad to the earth tether and get a pod up to that station. Remove those civilians. If they resist, shoot them and dump them out the airlock. No, no, forget that. Just shoot them and dump them out of the airlock," ordered the admiral. "As for you, General, you will face a court martial for this. Marines, take him back to the *Abraham Lincoln*."

Mona 3 slowed down and landed on the highest mountain peak in the Antarctic, Vinson Massif. As with William 6 onto the Island of Corvo, Mona 3 landed on the peak and settled. The weight of a three-mile-wide and two-mile-deep asteroid started to push the peak down.

From the space lab, Maria was taking readings and noted that the whole Antarctic land mass was starting to sink slowly at first, then more rapidly as Mona 3's weight pushed down on the Vinson Massif peak. "Natasha, the readings are showing the Antarctic sinking by two metres since this time yesterday," she said.

"At that rate, it will not take long for the habitable plains to be underwater," said the professor before Natasha could respond.

"We better get these results to the general," said Natasha.

"I'll let WSOA know," Maria said. "Hello, General, are you there?" Maria said into the video link.

"No, but I am," said the admiral.

"Hello, sir. Just wanted to report some crucial data," said Maria.

"Well, commander, what is it?" snapped the admiral.

"Mona 3 has landed on Vinson Massif peak in the Antarctic, and it has caused the land mass to start sinking," said Maria.

"What is the rate of sink?" asked the admiral.

"About two metres per day now."

"God, that is not good!" screeched the admiral. "Another thing, Commander: we understand that you have your families on board the space lab. Is that true?" asked the admiral.

"Yes, sir, that's true. We wanted them up here with us so that we could remain focussed on our jobs at hand," said Natasha.

"Commanders, I'm sending up a pod to collect them. They should not be up there with you. General Payton is going to face a court martial over this. Do you understand?" barked the admiral.

"Yes, sir. Over and out," Natasha and Maria said in unison.

"Maria, let's keep the station defences on. That's why the general told us to be careful and keep them on. We may need to repel boarders, as they say in the movies," said Natasha. "Do you have a minute? I need to talk with you in private."

"Of course. Let's go to the main control room," replied Maria. They both made their excuses and made their way to the main control room.

"Well, let's have it. What's the problem this time?" asked Maria in her sternest voice.

"The professor gave me a letter from the general when he came on board. Here, read this." Natasha handed Maria the letter.

"Hmm. My God, is that true?" mumbled Maria to herself whilst reading the content. "The general is your father! I wondered who your fairy godmother was and why you were not taken off the training programs. If any others had made the blunders you made, they wouldn't have made it on this station."

"That's a bit unfair. I worked bloody hard to get here," said Natasha.

"I know. I was only joking. So therefore, the general fortified the space lab. He knew this day was coming. Thank God for that. Does the professor know?"

"I'm sure he is fully aware of the fact that the general was my father; early on, he said he was part of a secret organisation and he couldn't tell me his name," stated Natasha.

"Knowing this information and with the admiral knowing this too, the pod coming to us from Earth is not to take our families back but to get rid of them. I never trusted that bastard. The general was right to keep him out of the loop."

Gerald and the *Lily Rose* were off the coast of the Philippines and contemplating what to do. "Dad, let's go ashore. I've always wanted to visit the Philippine Islands," said Lauren.

"No, not yet. I want to speak with your aunty Maria or my brother before we do anything," said Gerald.

"Hello, Maria, are you there?" Gerald shouted into the video link.

"HI, brov. It's Adam here. How are you doing?"

"What the fuck are you doing on the space lab? Sorry. Excuse my language, but I just got a bit of a shock, that's all."

"Maria managed to get me and the kids and Professor Kuzuhara up here to keep us safe from the rising water," said Adam.

"You're a lucky bastard. It's not much fun down here. The water levels are rising fast – many people have drowned already. We have seen so many bodies in the water. The sharks are having a field day."

"What can we do for you, brov?" asked Adam.

"I want to speak with Maria," he said.

"Maria here. What can we do to help?" she asked.

"We have reached the Philippine Islands and wondering about going ashore."

Natasha butted in, saying, "Absolutely not. You will get boarded. We're reading news reports of mass hysteria now and lots of people fighting over ships and boats. Stay on board is my advice."

"I agree with Natasha. Don't go ashore under any circumstance," Maria concurred.

The space lab alarm klaxon started sounding, and the lights started to flicker.

"Maria, what's that noise and why are the lights flashing!" shouted Adam to be heard above the din.

"Natasha, get to the observation port and find out what it is," Maria demanded. "I hope it's not another object heading for us."

"OK, you go and check to make sure we're still armed," Natasha said.

"Adam, this warning klaxon is tracking an incoming object and is letting us know. Go and strap yourselves, the kids, and the professor in. Natasha, what is it? Can you see anything from the observation port?"

"Yes, it looks like one of the pods from Earth," replied Natasha. She had just finished confirming to Maria what she saw when the intercom crackled into life.

"Come in, Commander Francis," they heard coming over the communications system.

"It's Commander Francis here. Who's calling?" asked Maria.

"It's Captain Alun Spiros Morgen of the admiral's staff," he replied,

"What can we do for you, Captain?"

"We have been instructed to come aboard and take your civilians back to Earth," said the captain.

"On whose authority?" asked Natasha.

"The admiral is concerned that your families will interrupt your mission," said the captain.

"What's happened to General Payton?"

"He has been arrested for treason. Allowing you to take your families on to the space lab is totally against all the rules, so drop your force field to allow us entry."

"I'm sorry, Captain. You have had a wasted journey. We suggest you turn around and head back to the earth tether."

"Sorry, Commander, but we have been asked to use force should you not comply," said the captain.

"I'm warning you for your own sake that once the station defence is on, we have no control over what it might do should you attempt to enter the station."

"Maria, they're disembarking from the pod eight marines in space suits; they're armed with laser rifles!" screamed Natasha.

"Captain, for God's sake turn back, please. We don't want to hurt anyone. Don't fire your lasers at the station, as it will respond automatically!"

Unfortunately, one of the marines was a little trigger-happy and opened fire on the docking hatch. The beam deflected away as it hit the defence shield. The station defence sent out a single beam which totally disintegrated the marine.

"Captain, I warned you. Get your men back to the pod and don't attempt that again!" cried Maria.

"Commanders, this means war. We'll be back but with a space shuttle full of troops. You had your chance," said the captain.

"Did you hear that, General? Your team has killed one of the marines!" cried the admiral at General Payton.

The admiral was back on board the *Abraham Lincoln* carrier in his office with the general, who was handcuffed and sitting on the opposite side of the admiral's big wooden desk.

"I'm sorry for the marine, but you, of all people, should know that once the defence system is up, it will repel anything, even a shuttle full of troops," he said.

"I want you to tell the commanders to turn off the space lab defences!" barked the admiral.

"I'll not do that. I heard your orders: shoot all the civilians and dump them out of the airlock. You've already murdered some of my family. I'm not going to let you murder the rest," said the general defiantly.

"We'll have you executed. We can, you know, because you've committed treason," said the admiral.

"I don't think I've committed treason. Having their families aboard has not stopped them continuing with the prime objectives. In fact, I think it will improve their work efforts," said the general.

"How so!" exclaimed the admiral.

"They have much more to lose now if they don't keep on their toes and the space lab gets destroyed. They will not only lose their lives but those of their families as well. I think that's enough incentive, don't you?"

"Trooper, take the general down to the brig. We'll keep him there, as he might be useful in the future."

The incident with the marines had deeply shocked Maria into reality; the space lab was like a flying fortress. Nothing seemed to be able to penetrate its defence mechanisms.

Natasha was studying the last of the three asteroids, Maria 2. It had not changed course or slowed down. It was due to strike the earth at the Arctic. She noted on closer inspection that it looked completely different to the other two asteroids which had landed on Earth. "Hey, Maria, look at your namesake and tell me what you think," she said.

Maria floated over to the LRT to take a closer look at the incoming object. "You're right. It's completely different. It appears to be perfectly spherical. It looks metallic and has a completely smooth surface, almost like a big ball bearing. The asteroid is not slowing down like the others. If it hits the Arctic at that speed, it will melt a lot of ice and create an enormous tidal wave that will sweep the planet."

"When do you think, it will hit the Arctic?" asked Professor Kuzuhara.

"At its current speed, in about five days," said Maria.

"We should warn my brother to get as far south as he can," said Adam.

"Now, guys, this is still a space lab with a chain of command. We need to inform the admiral and the general to get out of the Northern Hemisphere," stated Maria.

"Admiral, its Commander Kuzuhara here. Come in, please."

Admiral Mackenzie here. What information do you have for me, Commander?"

"Just wanted to warn you to get out of the Northern Hemisphere, as Maria 2 is going to strike the Arctic in five days," said Natasha.

"Have you warned DO1/2/3 yet?" asked the admiral.

"No, not yet, sir. They aren't so much at risk as you are."

"I'm glad you're still doing your jobs. You had me worried for a bit," said the admiral.

"Sir, we only wanted to make sure our families were safe. This was all it was about, and we were not going to let it undermine our jobs. We know our obligations."

"Shame about the marine who died," said the admiral.

"Were also sorry we did warn the captain not to make any hostile moves against the lab. We had no control on what actions the lab took when attacked," said Natasha.

"You can keep your families up there with you, but if I find that you aren't performing your duties, I'll send up a shuttle. Is that clear?" snapped the admiral.

"Very clear, sir. What about the general?"

"I'm still not sure what to do with him. He broke the rules and is aware of the consequences of his actions. I'm still undecided."

"OK, sir. Over and out," said Natasha.

Once off the video link, the admiral took a completely different tone. "Captain, I want you to take a heli-jet and move the general to our Antarctic base," he ordered. "I still don't trust those commanders in the space lab."

"Yes, sir, why do you not trust them? They are giving us the information we need, and they did warn me not to approach the station," said the captain.

"They are hiding something. Why do they want us to move to the Southern Hemisphere? Wait, I know why – so we leave our northern bases unprotected, especially the earth tether. They're going to try to sneak back to Earth."

The captain collected the general and took him on board the heli-jet. "Where are you taking me? Captain," asked the general.

"South Pole base, sir," said the captain.

"Why?"

"Admiral's orders."

"Hello, Gerald. Come in," said Maria over the video link.

"Any news?" he asked.

"Yes, get to the Southern Hemisphere as fast as you can. Maria 2 is going to strike the Arctic in five days, and this will create a shock wave and tsunami of gigantic proportions. You don't want to get caught in that."

"It will take us four days even at full speed to get down to the Southern Hemisphere," said Gerald.

"I would set off immediately. The water levels are rising fast with the ocean floor rising and the land masses sinking simultaneously," said Maria.

"Thanks, Maria. We'll leave the Philippines straight away. Stay safe."

"And you." Replied Maria

All over the world, water levels had forced people to higher ground. Unfortunately, the higher ground had also been sinking. With both the ocean floor rising and the land masses sinking, most of the world was flooding. Maria 2 was now hours away from striking the Arctic, and there was panic everywhere. The admiral's carrier fleet was still stationed in the channel. The earth tether platform was now twenty metres above its original position, and there were no visible landmarks for miles. London was underwater. In fact, most of the south-east corner of the UK had gone. There were bodies in the water everywhere. The UK government had moved to Scotland to the base camp at the summit of Ben Nevis to await the inevitable mayhem that would ensue once Maria 2 made planetfall. DO3 was still operating and were working with the space lab to ensure they corrected the air pressure in line with their ascent; however, DO1 and DO2 had been destroyed. They were unable to make the necessary corrections in time.

The general was locked in a secure facility at the South Pole to await his fate. Maria and Natasha continued monitoring the incoming asteroid and the depth changes in the world's oceans, whilst their families were secure and settled into life on the space lab. Adam's brother, Gerald, had reached as far south as he could possibly get. The *Lily Rose* was now moored close to the Antarctic land mass. Everyone was awaiting Maria 2 to strike the Arctic. The Antarctic land mass appeared to have stopped sinking, which was a relief for the troops stationed there, especially for the imprisoned general. Maria 2 was closing in on the Arctic when it suddenly stopped dead above the polar ice.

"Maria, the asteroid has come to a dead stop above the Arctic!" exclaimed Natasha.

"That's impossible. It was moving at such a speed that it must have hit the Arctic ice by now," said Maria.

"Come and look. The ball bearing is hovering above the polar ice."

Sure enough, the ball bearing–like asteroid was just hanging there. No movement, just hanging in the air about five hundred metres above the ice.

"What next?" asked Maria. Before she could say anything else, what happened next shocked her. The asteroid started to glow orange.

CHAPTER FIVE

NEW BEGINNING

The admiral received reports about the asteroid from the space lab. "Just as I thought; they were trying to get me to move the fleet away from the earth tether," he said. "Nothing's happened. The asteroid has stopped like the others."

Maria was still observing the hovering asteroid and noticed the colour change from an orange glow to a bright white glow; she measured the temperature of the white glow to be at somewhere near three thousand degrees Celsius. "Oh, my God, the temperature of Maria 2 has reached three thousand degrees Celsius and the polar ice is melting fast!" she cried across the lab.

"Admiral, you need to get out of the Northern Hemisphere. The polar ice is melting fast, and the water displacement will cause a huge tidal wave," said Natasha over the video link.

"I think we have time. We know the asteroid didn't impact the ice and is just hovering above it," said the admiral.

"But, sir, if you don't leave now, you will never outrun the wave!" shouted Maria

"Stop your panic. We're quite safe. Just keep monitoring the asteroid commanders. That's an order, by the way," ordered the admiral.

Maria 2 started to descend. It dropped into the Arctic Ocean to about a mile in depth. It then exploded. The explosion created a shock wave of intense heat which moved out from the Arctic at over three thousand miles per hour. Just like a nuclear bomb, the heatwave was at over two thousand degrees centigrade and incinerated anything within a one-thousand-mile radius. Most life was obliterated within this area. The admiral and his fleet was totally destroyed, most of Europe was devastated, and the ensuing winds from the explosion wiped out more life within a two-thousand-mile radius.

This wasn't the end of the devastation. Just behind the winds, a huge amount of water was travelling out from the epicentre. As it hit the continental shelf, it rose up to a mile and a half in height. Due to the sinking land masses, this amount of water swept inland for hundreds of miles, destroying any remaining life in the top half of the world. The movement of such a mass of water caused the planet to wobble on its axis. This caused earthquakes and tremors around the rest of the planet. Many big cities were destroyed in the Southern Hemisphere, and the loss of life was unimaginable. The only surviving people all lived in the Southern Hemisphere.

Three days prior to Maria 2 exploding, the *Lily Rose* hailed the *Dundee Angel*. "Come in, *Dundee Angel*. It's Gerald on the *Lily Rose*. Can you hear us?"

"We hear you loud and clear, *Lily Rose*. What news do you have for us?" asked the skipper.

"Get as far away from the Northern Hemisphere as you can. Another asteroid is heading for the Arctic, and it is not slowing down," said Gerald.

"That will take us three days at three-quarter speed," said the skipper.

"If you don't move now, the shock wave will incinerate you."

"Where are you getting all your information from?"

"My sister-in-law is one of the commanders on the space lab, and she hasn't been wrong yet," said Gerald.

"I'll get together all ships that can make the journey and join you in three days," said the skipper.

The general was still incarcerated at the South Pole station. He was contemplating what would happen to him when his cell door burst open. *This is it. I suppose the admiral has ordered my execution.* He shut his eyes and awaited the burst of gunfire. Then suddenly he heard a voice saying, "General, are you awake, sir? Come on, sir, please wake up!" shouted the captain. The general opened his eyes, and standing in front of him at attention with a full salute was Captain Alun Spiros Morgen.

"Yes, Captain, what can I do for you?" he asked.

"General, you're now in command. The whole of the admiral's fleet and the admiral himself has been destroyed. Maria 2 exploded and has destroyed the top half of the world."

"Oh, my God, just what I feared. We're systematically being wiped out by some unknown force," said the general.

"What do you mean, sir?" asked the captain.

"This has to do with the unusual objects found on the ocean floor, the attacks on the space lab, and the guided asteroids," said the general. "Do we still have a communications link with the space lab from here?"

"Yes, sir, we have a communications link with the space lab DO3 in the South Sandwich Trench and any ships still afloat from our fleets."

"Open a com channel to the space lab. I want to speak with my daughter," said the general.

"Daughter?" said the captain in a confused voice.

"Yes, you heard – my daughter, Commander Kuzuhara."

The water levels around the world were continuing to rise, the ocean floor was still rising, and the additional water from the Maria 2 explosion had flooded almost all the world's land masses, except Corvo Island and the Antarctic continent, which had started to rise out of the water a week before Maria 2 hit. From the space lab, the only visible land masses were the Antarctic land mass, Corvo Island, and parts of Greece which had not been sinking. In fact, it looked from space that the land mass had risen out of the water by at least fifty metres.

Natasha was observing the earth from the LRT and taking readings of the water levels to feed back to DO3 when she noticed that the Antarctic land mass wasn't sitting in its usual position. "Maria, can you come down to the LRT? I've noticed something strange with the land position of the Antarctic land mass!" she bellowed over the com line.

"Maria here. I'll be with you shortly. Just finishing my breakfast duties for our guests," she said. Maria soon made her way to the LRT, as Natasha sounded quite excited by her findings. Maria reached the LRT in quick time and remembered to stand back because Natasha's arms always flailed when she was excited.

"OK, Natasha, what have you found that has made you so excited?" she asked.

"Look through the LRT at the Antarctic and then check its position relative to the magnetic pole."

Maria moved over to the LRT and looked through the viewer. She centred the scope on a fixed point on the Antarctic mass and overlaid the magnetic poles. "You're right – the Antarctic has moved further north by at least five hundred miles," noted Maria.

"You know what that means," said Natasha.

"Yes, the weather conditions will be much warmer, and the ice will melt and further increase the sea levels."

"No, not just that. The earth has moved on its axis. The explosion and ensuing tsunami not only caused the earth to wobble but moved it several degrees off its axis."

"Come in, *Lily Rose*. It's the *Dundee Angel* here. Captain Duncan Ross, are you reading me? Over," he said.

"*Lily Rose* here. Over," said Gerald.

"Hi, Gerald. We have made it down past the tip of South America. Where are you?" asked Captain Ross.

"We are anchored just off the Antarctic in the Weddell Sea, just off Halley research station."

"We're about another day's sailing from you," said Captain Ross.

"How many of you made it – and did you manage to get any supplies?" asked Gerald, knowing that they may need to share food and water with them.

"Just myself and two other ships. We have fifty people, including crews, on the three ships. We have enough fuel, food, water, and other supplies to manage for a couple of more weeks. What's your situation with supplies?" asked the captain.

Before Gerald could reply, his wife, Valerie, put the link on mute and said, "For God's sake, Gerald, don't tell them what we have or they will try and take it from us. There are fifty of them versus us seven."

"We have adequate supplies for a few weeks," said Gerald, returning to the captain.

"That is a bit of a white lie, Gerald. You have enough supplies to last sixteen people for at least another year," stated Mary, Maria's mother.

"I know, Mary, and we'll share them when the time comes. We're not savages, you know, but I agree with Val – let's not be too open yet."

"All right. We'll need to use our fishing nets to get food from the sea, and hopefully the Antarctic Island has some running water or we'll melt snow," said Captain Ross.

"Hello, are you there, Maria? It's Major Sian Campton here."

"Commander Francis here. What can I do for you, Major?" asked Maria.

"Why so formal?"

"Just keeping to WSOA protocols, Major."

"Maria, for God's sake, there's not a WSOA left to have any formal protocols. Most of the world is gone and we must stick to protocols. Give me a break."

"Anyway, what can I do for you?" asked Maria.

"We need updated water level change readings. We must keep adjusting the pressure or we'll explode like DO1 and DO2 did," said Sian defiantly.

"OK, I'll ask Natasha to supply the latest depth changes. How are you managing down there and how are your supplies and crew holding up?"

"We lost several crew members who were outside the station working when Maria 2 exploded. They fell into crevices that had opened up," said Sian.

"How many did you lose?"

"Twenty people. We lost my second in command, Captain David Smith. You remember him, the dishy one, in his squad. We have about twelve months of supplies left, although we're harvesting seafood as well so we can probably last indefinitely."

"I'm sorry to hear that but glad you have enough food, for I think that's going to be a major problem for all of us going forward. I'll make sure Natasha sends you that information. Over and out," said Maria.

"Maria, how's our food and water situation on board the space lab?" asked the professor.

"We have enough food and water to support us six for at least twelve months. Our problem is going to be oxygen. We're using it faster than we predicted and only have nine months left by our calculations."

"Hello, come in. It's General Payton here. Are you receiving me?"

"God, it's like a bloody commercial radio station up here," said Adam. "Hi, General, it's Adam Francis here. Glad to know you're still with us". Before he could reply, Natasha moved Adam out of the viewing screen and plonked herself in front of the link.

"Hello, Father. Thank God, you're all right. Where are you?" asked Natasha,

This caught the general by surprise, and he stuttered his reply. "I'm in the Antarctic," he said.

"Where in the Antarctic? It's a bloody big place, you know," said Natasha.

The general burst into laughter. "My God, here you are dictating to me. Who do you think you are, Commander?"

"Your daughter," said Natasha.

"Indeed. How are things? How are the families holding up? I hope you have enough supplies up there. You should. I gave you everything we had left in the stores on Earth."

"We have enough supplies for twelve months. Our problem is going to be oxygen; we only have nine months' supplies left," said Natasha.

"You could take out the oxygen tanks from the pods and one of the escape ships. That would give you at least another couple of months," stated the general.

"Yeah, we have thought about that one. We'll strip out the tanks from both pods but leave them on the two escape ships, as we may need both to leave the space lab."

"Natasha, may I speak with the general? I need to ask him a favour," said Maria.

"One minute, Dad. Commander Francis would like to speak with you."

"How can I help?" asked the general.

"Firstly, General, I'm glad you're safe. Secondly, my brother-in-law is in the Antarctic with my mother and his family on board a pleasure cruiser called *Lily Rose*. If you get the chance, can you please take him under your protection?" Maria asked.

"I need to check our situation first, as I've only just taken command of this station. I don't know what men and equipment I have. Give me their call sign and I'll contact them. That's all I can promise at this stage, Commander."

"All right, sir. That's all I ask. Over and out."

"Hello, *Lily Rose* calling. Is anyone up there?" called Gerald. This call came in on their secure audio only network.

"My, we're popular today," said Maria.

"Hi, Maria. It's Gerald here. We made it to the Antarctic and are anchored just off Halley research station in the Weddell Sea. I thought we should let you know that everyone is safe."

"Thank you for picking up my mother. I owe you one. Did you have any problems getting from the Lake District?"

"No, not really, but we did encounter a small fleet of fishing boats in Scotland, and they are about to join us. Should be with us in about twenty hours," said Gerald.

"I have just spoken to General Payton. He also made it. He is in the Antarctic; you may want to link up with him for safety. I've given him your call sign so be prepared for him to contact you."

"Captain, what men, supplies, and equipment do we have left at our disposal?" asked the general,

"We have forty men at this base here in McMurdo and a supply depo with fuel, food, water, and armaments to restock several large warships," said Captain Morgen. "We also have a small twelve-thousand-ton Kansas Class cutter and resupply vessel in addition to a former coast guard ship called the *Niagara*, with a two-thirds crew complement of one hundred and twenty men."

"Are there any other naval ships in the other oceans?" asked the general.

"We have tried calling on all frequencies, but, no ship has responded," said the captain.

"I want you to make sure our ship is stocked with enough supplies to last two years on the water for a crew complement of two hundred and twenty people and that it is fully armed with everything we've got and then some."

"Sir, for two hundred and twenty people? But we only have one hundred and sixty service personnel, including the ships complement."

"I'm expecting to find other survivors and want to make sure our ship is able to cope with additional people on board," answered the general. Today I learned that another ship is docked in the Weddell Bay with seven people on board and an additional three ships with fifty people on board will join them later today."

If viewing the planet Earth from space, one would be hard pressed to find any land mass of any significance. Only the Antarctic continent and Corvo Island would be seen. It had been several months now since Maria 2 exploded. The ocean floor was now visible through the water, and some of the land masses had dropped into deeper water and were no longer visible. At its present rate of ascension, the sea floor in some areas of the world would be above water in a few weeks. DO3 was now only in one hundred metres of water and no longer in danger of exploding. There seemed to be fewer bodies floating on the ocean surface, as most would have either sunk or been eaten by the sea life. A few ship trails could be seen from space, but not more than a handful. These events had been devastating to the earth's population, both animal life and plant life. Only about five thousand people were left alive on the planet. It wasn't known what animal life remained, if any, and what sea life was still in the oceans. Both William 6 and Mona 3 had cooled down so they could be approached if it was necessary to analyse where they came from.

Life on the space lab had become routine: breakfast, exercise, lunch, exercise, tea, exercise, evening meal, and exercise. They all needed to keep exercising to stop their muscles from atrophying or they would not be able to step back on the earth. They had been scanning deep space to make sure no more objects were heading towards them. They had had a few scares with small meteorites getting too close, causing the space lab to go on alert and destroy them, but other than that, it had been very quiet.

Maria's brother-in-law and the fishing ship community from Scotland were now moored in Ross Bay, close to the

McMurdo base. The fishing ships had been trawling to keep food supplies up. They had been netting some most unusual fish. These fish must have come up from the deep oceans. Some species had never been seen before. The best eating ones were the big deep-sea halibut – or at least they looked like halibut, except they had green flesh. There about fifteen hundred researchers and scientists and soldiers spread around Antarctica, with another thirty-five hundred people scattered around the Southern Hemisphere and on board a handful of ships and on DO3.

General Payton had contacted all the groups except the one based in what was left of Australia, whose size was five hundred strong. He was planning to get everyone to Antarctica. The weather had changed dramatically on Antarctica because the continent had shifted further north by at least five hundred miles. More of the surface had now become normal land, and it was no longer frozen. The sun stayed out much longer, and this created plant growth. Some trees had started to spring up. They must have been under the ice in suspended animation. Grasses and flowers are growing in abundance, and freshwater lakes were starting to form. The soldiers from the general's teams were helping construct living accommodations from the supplies stored at McMurdo base. These would house the incoming people rescued from around the Southern Hemisphere.

Gerald and his family and guests had decided to make *Lily Rose* their permanent home. The people from the three Scottish fishing trawlers were the first to take up residence in their new homes. The homes were sparsely furnished but had heating, sleeping, and cooking facilities. Each unit could house up to ten people, so sharing was essential, not a choice. The soldiers and engineering teams had built around two hundred new homes of the five hundred that would be required, fifty of which were already occupied. The general was due back shortly with another overcrowded ship. The *Niagara* was due to dock in the next hour. She had three hundred people, including a crew of fifty personnel, on board, which is 120 more than it was built to carry. All the decks were full, and down below, people were sleeping in the galley, restaurants, and mess halls.

The soldier on watch, over the still functioning radar, had picked up another vessel making its way to the McMurdo base. He could see the *Niagara* on screen and another blip, which indicated a much larger vessel. It was about two hours behind the *Niagara* from their base. The soldier made his way to Captain Morgen's office.

"Captain, sir, I have picked up on radar another vessel heading our way. It looks to be a much larger ship than the *Niagara*," stated the soldier.

"How long before it reaches us?" asked the captain.

"On its present course and at its current speed, in six hours.

"I'll radio the general and let him know. He may be able to send Niagara's heli-jet to see what ship it is. I want you to keep tracking the ship," said the captain.

"Yes, sir," said the soldier.

The general sent the heli-jet from the *Niagara* towards the oncoming ship. It took them around forty minutes to reach it. The pilot sent a message back to the Niagara. "General, this is a big ship. Looks like one of the old cruise liners. She can carry at least fifteen hundred people. When they were popular, they could carry one thousand passengers and five hundred crew. Would be a useful addition to our fleet. We could pick up the rest of the survivors in that."

"Excellent work, Lieutenant. Try contacting them with your shortwave radio."

"Come in, approaching ship. This is Lieutenant Stuart here from the McMurdo base," he said.

Before he could speak again, machine gun fire was whistling past their windshield.

"Shit, let's get out of here before they knock us out of the sky," said the lieutenant to the pilot.

The heli-jet made a sharp banking turn away from the cruise liner. As they were banking away, the lieutenant noticed that the ship had a five-inch gun mounted on the bow. "Come in, General Payton."

"General Payton here. What have you to report, Lieutenant?"

"Sir, the ship started firing at us so we're coming back. They also have a five-inch gun mounted on her bow. She is heavily armed. Must have come under fire from at least fifty machine guns."

"OK, Stuart, get yourself back here. I'll inform the base," barked the general.

"On our way back," he said.

"Come in, Captain Morgen. It's General Payton here."

"Captain Morgen here. Did you manage to get a look at the approaching ship, sir?" he asked.

"Yes, Captain." She fired on our heli-jet. We need to scan that ship and see what she is carrying. Do we have anything on the base capable of that?"

"No, sir, but I know a ship that does," said Captain Morgen.

Major Sian Campton, commander of DO3, was contemplating her next move. The water levels above them had dropped to only ten metres. Should they stay on the station or radio the general and get moved to Antarctica? The problem would be if DO3 was exposed to direct sunlight. The polymer construction was superb for underwater use but would be completely useless if exposed to sunlight. The chemicals in the polymer mix would harden and crack once exposed, so the base would start to crumble down around them. She had to think about the safety of the 180 personnel on the base.

They had been harvesting frozen methane gas and several types of edible seaweed and marine life. The methane tanks could be a problem if they became warm due to the sun. The food from the sea was frozen and should be OK to transport. The base still had enough food supplies and water for at least another few months; however, with the rate the water level was falling, they probably only had a few more weeks. She decided to contact the general to see what the situation was on Antarctica and whether they could house her teams.

"Hello, is that McMurdo base? Major Campton calling. Is General Payton there, please?"

"Payton here. What can we do for you, Major?" he said.

"General, just wanted to check on your situation on Antarctica. I believe we only have a few more weeks before the water level above us dissipates and the station becomes unliveable. Can you collect us … and do you have the room?" she replied.

"Presently, Major, I can't help you. We have a situation developing here. We're about to be attacked or invaded by a ship full of armed assailants."

"OK, sir, I understand. We'll continue collecting food and water to bring with us when the time comes."

Gerald and his extended family were enjoying an evening meal of tinned salmon, fresh bread, frozen salad, and sparkling water when there was a loud bang on the cabin door.

"Who can that be?" said Gerald.

"You'd better see who it is; might be important," said Val.

Gerald got up and opened the cabin door. In the doorway stood the camp commander, Captain Morgen. "Good evening, Gerald. Hope I'm not disturbing you."

"No, we're just having an evening meal, Captain. How can we help?"

"Can we go somewhere and talk? I have an important message for you from the general."

"Sure. Let's go into my study. Follow me. Hey, guys, I'll be with you in a minute. Just going to my study with the captain."

"OK, Gerald. I don't know how to put this, but I'll come straight out with it. We need your help. There's a big cruise liner headed our way full of armed people," said the captain.

"What has that to do with me. You're the soldiers and isn't your ship, the *Niagara*, armed to the teeth?"

"We need to borrow you and your ship, as the general wants to scan the ship before we take any action. It may have women and children aboard; it would be a bad day for the world's population if we have to sink her."

"My God, I thought we had left all this behind with the demise of the world's populations," said Gerald.

"I understand you used this equipment when you were in the Lake District and you destroyed a boat full of people. It must have been devastating to you," said the captain.

"It was awful; we were very saddened by it," said Gerald.

"We are faced with the same situation but potentially on a bigger scale. We don't want to take lives if it can be avoided."

Remembering how he felt that day in the Lake District, Gerald reluctantly agreed to help. "OK, Captain, what do you want me to do?" he said.

Maria, Natasha, and the other family members were having a meeting to discuss their options. Food supplies were plentiful, but oxygen was going to be a problem much earlier than they had thought it would be. Originally, they thought that the oxygen would last at least twelve to eighteen months for the six of them. At its present rate of usage, they would only have another three-months supply left. They had already cannibalised the oxygen supplies from the two pods and were contemplating taking the oxygen from one of the remaining two escape shuttles. That would give them another couple of weeks' supply on top of the station's oxygen. The carbon dioxide scrubbers were another problem. Even if they had enough oxygen, the carbon dioxide scrubbers needed renewing in six weeks, and they didn't have any more spares on the station.

"I suggest we gather all food and water supplies and take both shuttles to Antarctica to join the general and his group," said Maria.

"I don't think we should be too hasty. It's still not safe down there," said Adam.

"If we can't find a solution to the oxygen supplies and carbon dioxide scrubbers, we'll have no choice but to leave the station," said the professor.

"Why don't we take the oxygen supplies from one of the shuttles and the carbon dioxide scrubbers from the pods and one of the shuttles?" Adam said.

"Look, team, the scrubbers aren't compatible with the space lab, so they won't work," said Natasha in a defiant voice. "We'll need both shuttles, one to take supplies with us and one to take us, so we need to decide how long we wait before leaving the station. There are no other options."

"I agree with Natasha, so that's settled. We leave in another four weeks That will give us some leeway should our calculations be wrong," said Maria.

The *Lily Rose* had been commandeered by Captain Morgen. They placed a three-inch gun on the bow, a ship-to-ship missile battery on the stern, and twenty armed soldiers as part of the complement. Gerald was one of the crew, as he was the only one who knew how to operate the scanner and pulse cannon.

"Right, we're fully loaded. Let's get under way. We must get to the cruise liner before she gets too close to our base or her five-inch gun could cause havoc should they start firing," said Captain Morgen. The *Lily Rose* left the haven of McMurdo dock and set off towards the cruise liner.

"Gerald, how long does it take to fire up the scanner?" asked the captain.

"It will need a couple of minutes to warm up once we start it," he said.

"OK, the minute we spot the cruise liner, fire it up. What about the pulse cannon?"

"I don't think that the pulse cannon will stop an almighty cruise liner – that's not what it was designed for," said Gerald.

"If we can just slow it down, that would give us time to prepare back at base," said the captain.

"Captain, how fast do you want us to go? Because of the additional weight, if we move too quickly and try a sharp turn, we'll capsize," said Gerald, thinking they may have to veer away from the cruise liner to avoid being rammed.

"We need to ensure we get close to that liner before she makes port. She was about an hour out. If we go at thirty knots, we should intercept her ten miles from the base."

Maria and Natasha had also been measuring the temperature changes since the three asteroids landed on the planet. They had moved up at least one or two degrees. Although the temperature shift did not sound like much, it was enough to affect the climates in the earth's regions; the planet was becoming wetter.

The other issue they found was that the frozen methane that was trapped on the deep ocean floor was beginning to thaw out as the ocean floor continued to rise. Once this was released into the atmosphere, there would be dramatic climate changes. The earth would experience global warming on an unprecedented scale, the cloud cover will get much denser, and there would be more extreme weather during the different seasons. The oxygen production on the planet had been badly affected, with most rainforests now underwater. However, on the plus side, Antarctica was higher in the water and trees were starting to appear.

"Maria," said Natasha, the rate of rise on the ocean floors seems to have slowed down. Around Antarctica, it's stopped rising and the water levels have stabilised. What was the Indian Ocean is now above sea level; most of the Pacific is also above sea level. All the original continents are now fully submerged except parts of Australia and Corvo Island and Antarctica. There are new pieces of land being formed by the rising seabed, and there are already new types of plants growing."

Lily Rose was now in visual range of the incoming cruise liner. Captain Morgen was using the long-range binoculars, trying to make out its name and size. "Looks like she's called the *Lunar Star*. She is about sixty thousand tons and is moving at about twenty knots. I can make out the five-inch gun mounted on the bow," he said.

"We need to get closer for me to scan her interior" said Gerald, "how close" asked the captain, "within half a mile" said Gerald, "that will be close they will be able to hit us with the five-inch gun before we close to that range" said the captain.

"I'll plot a zig-zag course at close to forty knots. That should make it difficult to hit us accurately," said Gerald.

"OK, let's go," barked the captain.

Gerald opened the throttles on the turbo engines, and *Lily Rose* quickly got up to speed. She was within three-quarters of a mile when the first shell hit the water about forty metres in front of them. She continued her zig-zag course, with shells getting closer each time.

"Gerald, alter the zig to a longer frequency; they're picking up our range!" shouted the captain.

Just as Gerald altered the course, a shell exploded close by. Some of the fragments injured marines that were on deck.

"Gerald, can you use the scanner yet? We're getting mighty close to being hit!" screamed the captain above the roar of the turbines.

"Just a few metres more!" He turned *Lily Rose* away from the cruise liner just in time. Where he had been, a shell landed in the water and exploded.

"Did we get it!" shouted the captain.

"Yes, we got the scan; now let's get out of here!"

Lily Rose motored away on a different zig-zag pattern and got out of range of the five-inch gun. "Let's look at the scan," said the captain.

The scan of the interior showed that there were four hundred passengers on board and about one hundred armed personnel. "Just as the general thought, the ship has women and children on board," said the captain.

"You can't fire on that ship. It would be murder," said Gerald.

"We don't intend to," said the captain. He called his marines together to outline a plan for the cruise liner. "Right, men, get the ship-to-ship missiles ready. We're going to take out that five-inch gun."

"Hold on a minute, Captain. You said you were not going to fire on her!" shouted Gerald.

"Look, we're only going to disable the bow-mounted cannon, not fire on the rest of the ship," said the captain.

The *Niagara* had just unloaded the last of her passengers when the shortwave radio crackled into life. "Come in. This is the *Lily Rose* calling. Captain Morgen here."

"Come in, Captain. What's the situation?" said the general

"We've engaged the cruise liner and taken a scan. You were right. There are about five hundred people on board, four hundred passengers and about one hundred armed personnel," said the captain.

"What's the plan, then, Captain," asked the general.

"We'll disable the five-inch gun and the funnels with our ship-to-ship missiles, and then we'll try to disable the engines with the pulse cannon," said the captain.

"OK, but make sure you don't harm the passengers. It's important that these people survive," ordered the general. "Over and out."

Major Campton had been picking up the radio traffic on their long-range audio sets. "Major, I wish we could be there to help. We have plenty of medical supplies should they be required," said Sergeant Major Jan Fraser. She was now second in command of DO3 since the lieutenant was killed.

"I know, but we have to obey the general's orders. When this situation is finalised, he will send someone to pick us up," said the major.

Work on DO3 was continuing. Food and water were still being harvested from what was left of the ocean, as they were only in twenty metres of water. They had stopped mining the methane, as they would have no way of shipping it. DO3 had a couple of mini submarines that could each carry four people and several escape pods on board that would cover the rest of the personnel should they need to evacuate DO3. She had a limited armoury with weapons for twenty marines.

"We should prepare ourselves to be ready when the general sends someone to collect us. I want us to be ready to evacuate within two minutes of the siren," said the major to Sergeant Major Fraser.

"Yes, ma'am. We'll start drills today to make sure we're prepared," she said.

"Marines, ready the ship-to-ship missiles and target the five-inch gun first," barked the captain to his soldiers.

"Captain, you will only target the five-inch gun?" asked Gerald apprehensively.

"We'll fire the missiles at the bow gun and once disabled move in closer to use your pulse cannon," said the captain.

"Ready, sir," said the marine commander.

"Launch missiles!" ordered the captain.

"Missiles away!" said the marine commander.

They all watched from the main cabin as two white smoke trails streaked towards the cruise liner. Thirty seconds later, they saw the bow of the liner light up and then heard the explosion.

"Right, let's get in closer. Open her up, Gerald!" shouted the captain.

They reached the liner five minutes later to see black smoke billowing up from the bow area of the ship.

However, she still had not slowed down and was travelling at the same speed towards Antarctica.

"Gerald, fire up your pulse cannon and try to disable her engines!" screamed the captain.

Gerald obeyed immediately and thirty seconds later fired the pulse cannon at where he thought the engine room would be. Within seconds, there was an explosion from the stern of the ship. As the *Lily Rose* rounded the stern, they could see a gaping hole just above the waterline, big enough to drive a car through.

"Oh, my God, she will sink if they hit rough seas. What have we done?" said Gerald.

The big cruise liner began slowing down, and on deck a big white sheet was being waved. "I guess they have had enough," said the captain.

"Enough! We have probably killed several people on that ship. Of course, they have fucking had enough. Wouldn't you after that attack?"

"Now, Gerald, calm down. We had no choice. They could have killed hundreds had they reached the McMurdo base with that five-inch gun. At least we have prevented further bloodshed with a loss of a few lives."

The *Niagara* was racing to catch up with the captain on the *Lily Rose*. They were about twenty minutes behind her. "*Niagara* here. Come in, Captain Morgen," said the general over the ship-to-ship communications system.

"Captain Morgen here, sir," he said.

"Captain, give me an update. What's happening?" he asked.

"We have disabled her bow gun and slowed her down with the pulse cannon, sir," said the captain.

"How many casualties did we inflict?" asked the general.

"We aren't sure yet. They have raised a white flag so we can talk with them shortly."

"We'll be with you in fifteen minutes. Don't go aboard until I have reached you," ordered the general,

"Yes, sir," said the captain.

"Hello, attacking vessel. Come in, please. It's the captain of the *Lunar Star* here. Pease stop firing at us. We've several people injured and several dead!"

"*Lily Rose* assault ship here. Tell all the armed personnel to throw down their weapons and we'll cease hostilities," said the captain.

"*Lily Rose* assault ship? What the hell do you think you're playing at! This is a pleasure cruiser not a battleship!" shouted Gerald.

The *Niagara* came into view fifteen minutes later and moored up alongside the *Lily Rose*. The general came aboard. "Gerald, many thanks for letting us use your home and for supporting the defence of the base," he said.

"General, I'm not happy we caused some loss of life" said Gerald.

"A few losses to save a few hundred is all right in my book, as unfortunate as it is," said the general.

The general contacted the captain of the *Lunar Star* and explained why he attacked them; they should not have shot at his heli-jet. The captain explained why they did. Earlier in their voyage, they were attacked by pirates using a helicopter and small boats and thought that they were the same pirates trying to attack them again. After all the confusion was cleared up, the general explained that they had set up a community at the McMurdo base on Antarctica and would like to invite them to join it. The captain gave the general the approximate breakdown of people on board: one hundred children, two hundred women, and two hundred crew and men. Ten had died on the bow gun during the missile attack. Five crew members and five other men had died in the engine room explosion. All women and children were safe.

The *Lunar Star* still had two engine rooms and engines working and could make the journey to Antarctica. They had about two weeks of supplies left on board, and the general told the captain that they had enough accommodation built to house everyone and plenty of supplies on the base. The general apologised for the loss of life but was concerned that their ship could wreak havoc if they started firing their cannon at the base with the one thousand people already living there.

Maria, Natasha, and the family members were now a few days away from exiting the space lab; their four-week window that they set themselves was almost upon them. All of them had been spending the last few days loading supplies and plant seeds on to one of the escape shuttles, named ESC Earth 2. Natasha would pilot this shuttle, and Maria would take all the families on to the other shuttle, named ESC Earth 1. They still had enough food supplies for all of them to stay in space for another nine months. Unfortunately, the oxygen supplies would only last another four weeks. They were all looking forward to getting back down onto the earth. Even though they exercised daily and had a great healthy routine, this was no substitute for the real thing. They would have to plan their route meticulously, as there would be no room for any errors when flying back to Earth. They would need to enter the earth's atmosphere at exactly the right point or they would bounce back off into space.

"Now listen up, all of you. When we get into the escape shuttles, you must obey every word of the command pilot without question. Do we all understand that?" asked Natasha.

"Yes, sir," said the professor, Adam, and the children. Maria was collecting all the data they had and putting it on to several digital recorders, plus duplicating the information onto hard disks. Maria would carry the digital recorders, and Natasha would carry the backups. This was just in case one of them didn't make it.

"Come in, DO3. This is the *Niagara* calling. Captain Morgen here."

"This is Major Sian Campton. Nice to hear from someone again," she said.

"Hello, Major. We're about one hour away from your location. Are you ready to evacuate the station?" asked the captain.

"We'll be ready. I have one hundred and eighty personnel, including myself, and plenty of equipment, plus several large containers of food and water to load aboard," said the major.

"It's going to be a tight squeeze. This ship is only supposed to carry a crew complement of one hundred and eighty personnel with associated supplies to be at sea for about one month. I have one hundred and twenty crew and marines aboard, so we are going to be one hundred and twenty over the limit," said the captain.

Unbeknown to both the captain and major, someone else was listening in to their radio communication. The leader of the pirates based somewhere in the seas around what was left of Australia were on their way to DO3. These pirates were made up of several factions: Chinese, Koreans, Somali, Japanese, and several Australian outbackers. They had an armed helicopter based on the leader's ship and ten heavily armed vessels of different tonnages. They were like a small army of about one hundred and eighty men. The leader's ship was an old container ship of about twenty thousand tons, and she was heavily armed with three-inch guns. They were about an hour behind the *Niagara* in reaching DO3. They had been monitoring communications for several weeks and were in desperate need of fuel and water, so it was music to their ears when they heard about the supplies on DO3. They planned to attack the *Niagara* once she was loaded up, take prisoners to increase their little army, and kill anyone who tried to stop them.

The crew and passengers from the *Lunar Star* had been on Antarctica for four weeks now and were settling into life amongst the other settlers. There were now around twenty-three people at the base, including the army and navy personnel. They even had a small cemetery where the people who had died on the cruise liner were interred.

They were now growing food in the rich soils that have become available due to the permafrost thawing out. The Scottish fishing fleet have been fishing every day, catching a variety of different species. There were several rivers flowing on the continent now, so fresh water was in abundant supply. The only thing that they didn't have were farm animals, so obtaining milk was a problem. The base food stocks currently had a large supply of powdered milk for use on the ships, but that was no substitute for the real stuff.

The cruise liner had been repaired; the gaping hole had been patched up so she was seaworthy. They were manned with marines and had front and rear missile batteries placed on her, plus several two-inch anti-aircraft guns. She was presently out at sea with the general and several marines, plus all her civilian crew on a training exercise, but no one knew where. If they did, no one was saying anything. The general armed the cruise liner to protect the ship should she be attacked; their mission was still to rescue any people still alive in the Southern Hemisphere. Maybe she was heading towards a group of survivors.

The *Niagara* docked with DO3, which was sitting in thirty feet of water, just enough draught for the ship. The station was protruding out the water by about twenty feet. Captain Morgen climbed onto the station-docking platform to be met by Major Campton.

"Hello, Major. Are you ready to disembark?" he asked.

"Yes, Captain. My crew have been training for this eventuality, and we have all the supplies ready to go aboard," she said. It took around fifty minutes to load supplies and personnel onto the *Niagara*.

"Right, close all sea doors and seal all the hatches; we're ready to depart," said Captain Morgen to the ship's navigator and ship's captain. "Set course for Antarctica and let's get out of this place."

They had just departed DO3 when a fleet of ships came into view. The fleet had a helicopter flying in front of it, and the helicopter was heading their way. "I thought you only had a few ships based at Antarctica, Captain. Is it the general coming to give us an escort back to base?" asked the major.

"No, Major, we only have the cruise liner, *Lily Rose*, a small launch, and the Niagara based in Antarctica, so don't know who they are," he said.

They found out soon enough that this fleet was not friendly when a shell landed close by them. By this time, the helicopter had reached them and was bellowing out a message on its speakers.

"This is General Hiro speaking. Surrender your ship and allow us to take your supplies and no harm will come to you. If you don't surrender, we'll attack you. You have one minute to acknowledge."

Unbeknown to the pirates, *Niagara* had a ship-to-ship missile battery on her, with a complement of ten missiles. "Marines, get the missile batteries fired up and target the control room on the lead ship in their fleet," ordered the captain.

"You realise, Captain, that the minute we open fire on them, all hell will rain down on us. Their helicopter is armed to the teeth and could inflict some serious damage," said Major Campton.

"With all due respect, Major, I'm commander of this mission, and we will strike quickly and try to deter them. If not, they will capture this ship and cause more misery for any survivors," replied the captain.

"This is space lab calling McMurdo control – come in, McMurdo control!" shouted Maria down the communications link.

"McMurdo control here. Sergeant Kawloski here," said the sergeant.

"Can I speak with the general, please?"

"I'm afraid not, Commander. He is out on manoeuvres with the *Lunar Star* and *Lily Rose*," said the sergeant.

"When is he due back? We're going to leave the space lab in two days, and I need coordinates for the base and an airstrip to land on," said Maria.

"Commander, we don't have a return date for the general, but I can make sure an airstrip is prepared. I'll let you know the coordinates in twenty-four hours."

General Payton had been concerned when he heard about the attack by pirates on the *Lunar Star*, and he had been monitoring all radio communications since. He managed to pick up the band frequency the pirates used and had been following their discussion about attacking the *Niagara*.

The *Niagara* fired off a salvo of ship-to-ship missiles before their minute was up. Thirty seconds later, there were explosions on the container lead ship. As luck would have it, they knocked out the battery of three-inch guns as well as the control room. Seeing this, the pirate general started a rocket-strafing run on the *Niagara*. The first salvo landed short of the ship. The second salvo hit the stern and blew out a few deck plates. Several personnel from DO3 were injured in the attack. The captain ordered all his marines on deck to fire at the attacking helicopter. In the meantime, the other nine ships in the pirate fleet started firing their small calibre and three-inch cannon weapons at the *Niagara*.

"I told you they would throw everything at us. I'm not worried for myself but for all the non-combatant personnel that were on DO3!" shrieked the major.

"Major, do you really think they would have allowed us to live if we had given them the ship. There wouldn't be enough food for them and us. They would have killed most of us," said the captain.

The captain had just finished replying to the major when a shell exploded on top of the missile battery, killing the four marines manning them and injuring several others. "Shit, the container ship still has an active three-inch gun firing, and they have just taken out our ship-to-ship missile battery."

The other smaller ships were still racing towards them, firing their smaller calibre cannons. The pirates were trying to disable the ship rather than destroy her. The situation was now looking desperate for the *Niagara* and her passengers – no main weapon left and only small handheld rocket packs plus a few marines to defend the ship, "Major, we may have to surrender the ship to at least keep some of you alive," said the captain. The captain was looking through his binoculars to work out which ship to target first with their short-range weapons when one of the attacking ships suddenly burst into flames, then another, then another, and another explosion on the container ship. "My God, they must have some old clapped-out ships in their fleet and the sudden burst of speed to get to us has overworked their engines to the point they exploded," said the captain.

"Let me look," said the major. "Another ship has just had an explosion on her deck; that's four of them disabled and still another five coming our way!"

In the meantime, the attacking helicopter veered off and headed back towards its fleet of ships, it had just reached the container ship when it too exploded in mid-air before it could land. Then they spotted something coming towards the pirate fleet from the left side. "Oh, my God, it's a huge ship and a smaller cruiser coming to join the attack against us. We have had it this time!" shrieked the major.

The captain took the binoculars from the major and scanned the area to the left of the pirate fleet. "I think the pirate fleet have had it, Major. It's the *Lunar Star* and the *Lily Rose*, and they're attacking the pirate fleet," said the captain.

Sure enough, the general on the *Lunar Star* and Gerald on the *Lily Rose* were attacking the pirate fleet. Gerald had used the pulse cannon on four of the ships, which had caused them to catch fire and explode, and the general used his ship-to-air missiles and ship-to-ship missiles to destroy the attacking helicopter and finish off the container ship. Seeing the size of the *Lunar Star* coming towards them made the remaining five pirate ships turn tail and run for home. The other ships were ablaze and sinking. There were no survivors from these ships. The pirate general had been killed in the helicopter; *Niagara* had four dead and twenty injured.

The *Lunar Star* and *Lily Rose* pulled up alongside the *Niagara,* and the general came aboard to meet with Major Campton and the captain. "Thank God, sir. Where the hell did you come from? We were told that you were on manoeuvres somewhere to the south of Antarctica," said the captain.

"The pirates thought that also. We had intercepted their radio band frequency, and when talking to McMurdo base, we let them think we were to the south on exercise," said the general.

"How did you get here so quickly?" asked the major.

"As soon as you left, we were running about one hour behind you to the west of your position," said the general.

"So, you knew the pirates were going to attack us, then?" asked the captain.

The major got extremely angry and said, "So you could have prevented this attack and the loss of life we had on the *Niagara*!" she shouted at the general.

"No, Major, we couldn't. If we hadn't drawn out, the pirates they had a strong enough fleet to devastate the McMurdo base and kill many of the people living there," said the general.

"But, sir, could we have not found their base and attacked them there?" asked the captain.

"I'm sorry we lost a few of our marines, but it was important to take out this threat. They will not try to attack the base now because we have destroyed their big container ship and some of their heavily armed ones. Now let's take your wounded and other personnel onto the *Lunar Star* and get back to base," said the general.

It took the *Lunar Star* and the rest of the ships twenty-four hours to get back to McMurdo base. The food and supplies were distributed amongst the residents of their new village, the injured were taken to the base hospital, and the dead had a ceremony and then were buried in the new cemetery. The general was in the control centre on the base when a call came in from the space lab. "Hello, space lab calling. Commander Kuzuhara here. Come in."

"General Payton speaking."

"Hello, Dad, do you have a landing strip prepared for us and the landing coordinates? We're going to leave the space lab in five hours," said Natasha.

"It's general to you, Commander, and yes, we have the landing strip prepared and the coordinates have been sent to your lab computer," he said.

"We are going to take both escape shuttles. I'll pilot ESC Earth1 with all our supplies and a copy of our data files, and Commander Francis will pilot ESC Earth 2 with our families and all our original data files. We intend to depart ten minutes apart. I'll leave first in five hours, and ESC 2 will depart the station ten minutes later," said Natasha.

"How long will it take before you land at McMurdo base once you depart the space lab," asked the general.

"ESC Earth 1 should be with you twelve hours after we depart and ESC Earth 2 ten minutes after that." said Maria.

"So we expect you tomorrow around midday. We all look forward to that. Have a safe journey. Over and out," said the general.

"Sir, do we need to make sure we have emergency crews standing by when the shuttles land in case we get any problems when they land on our makeshift landing strip?" asked Captain Morgen.

"Yes, and I want constant radar monitoring of the skies and seas just in case we encounter any more unexpected craft," ordered the general.

"OK, sir, we'll take every precaution possible, as we know your daughter is on one of the shuttles," said the captain.

Work had continued on the base to increase the amount of homes and to build a perimeter wall around the base not facing the sea. They had found a plentiful supply of steel brace girders used to shore up sea walls. They were about four hundred millimetres wide in an S shape, with flanged edges for strength and to interlock with each other, and they were six metres long. They had a pile hammer on the base to bang them into the ground. With the warming of Antarctica, these steel braces sunk into the ground to about two metres and when locked together, they formed a formidable steel wall that would take a battleship to break through it. The wall was built about half a kilometre from the sea, and once finished, it would completely circle the three quarters of the base and new village. The base was to the west and the village to the east. The ground between them was used to grow vegetables and fruit. The wall would finish at the sea behind the base and by the sea, just past the village. There would be no openings in the wall, so the only way in would be by seaport. Additionally, to the west was a mountain range and to the east a river. These natural defences would add to the steel wall. Gerald and his extended family were now living back on *Lily Rose*. They didn't want to live in one of the new houses that had been built; they were eagerly awaiting his brother's arrival and plan to offer them a berth on the *Lily Rose*.

Maria was closing all systems that were not necessary to run the space lab. She left all the tracking devices and the station defences on. The McMurdo base wanted to keep the lab running until she ran out of fuel for geostationary orbit adjustments. Natasha adjusted the LRT to maintain a widespread scan of the outer universe to make sure they got early warning of any additional incoming asteroids or objects.

"I think we're about done here. Let's get our passengers loaded onto the shuttles," said Natasha.

"All right, Natasha. Team, please move one at a time towards the shuttle escape doors," said Maria.

Maria loaded the children first and strapped them into the last two seats at the back of the shuttle, then Adam her husband in the row of seats in front of the children. "Professor, I want you to sit in the co-pilot's seat next to me. Should anything go wrong, you will need to pilot the shuttle," she said.

"What, me? I don't know the first thing about flying a shuttle," he said.

"It's relatively simple, Professor. Once we're moving, there are two controls – one for engine burn and a joystick for attitude control. The coordinates for our landing are programmed into the shuttle computer so the shuttle will correctly calculate angle of entry."

"Then why do you need me to take over the controls when everything is computer controlled?" he asked.

"There is only one manual operation required once we break through into the earth's atmosphere. This switch here needs to be moved from space to Earth," said Maria.

"What situation will stop you from activating that switch?" asked the professor.

"Once we break through into the atmosphere, the extreme pressure can cause a temporary blackout that can last about fifteen seconds. One of us needs to resist the urge and activate the earth switch to take manual control until the computers take over."

Maria then said to Natasha, "We're loaded and ready to go. It's up to you now to lead the way and hope the computers have it right."

"Main engine burn, release docking clamps. I'm off and running. See you back on Earth," said Natasha.

"OK, Commander. Good luck," Maria said.

After their run-in with the pirates, the *Lunar Star* and the *Niagara* were fitted with everything they had in the base stores: anti-aircraft missile batteries, three-inch cannons, and ship-to-ship missiles, plus a helicopter deck for the *Lunar Star*. Gerald gave the general permission to take out the scanner system and pulse cannon from the *Lily Rose* and had these fitted to the *Lunar Star*. The *Lunar Star* was kept fully fuelled up and stocked with enough long-life stores to be at sea for six months with three thousand people on board. That would be fifteen hundred over its recommended capacity. The wall would have defence weapons stationed every-one hundred metres to ensure it would be difficult to get too close to the steel wall. Even though it would take a huge force to break through, it could still be scaled with ropes. Volunteers were selected from the village inhabitants to form part of the defence force, including the marines and navy personnel. They could put together a force of about six hundred defenders. There were still scientific research stations all around the Antarctic continent, where around one thousand scientists and researchers were still working, even though most of their home countries no longer existed.

Gerald and the *Lily Rose* were used to visit these sites on a weekly basis, taking any food and water requirements with them to restock their supplies. It was on their visit to Halley base, formerly owned by the UK, that Gerald learned something of interest that he must tell the general when they return to the McMurdo base. The scientists from the base had been studying the Mona 3 asteroid that was sitting on top of the Vinson Massif mountain range. Apparently, a crack had started to appear around its centre, uniform and straight, not what you would expect from rocks cracking. Gerald asked if these cracks were due to the asteroid cooling down too quickly. Unsure, they were still researching it. Gerald left them with a long-range radio for contact if there were any more developments.

Maria broke through the earth's atmosphere with ESC Earth 2. It was a bit of a bumpy ride, and she did pass out for several seconds – ten, to be precise – but the professor took control and managed to activate the earth switch and control the craft for those ten seconds. "Thanks for that, Professor. I'll take over now," said Maria.

"You're welcome. You had me worried for a minute," he said.

"I think it was about ten seconds, actually, Professor," Maria said jokingly.

The on-board computer then took control of the shuttle and aimed it towards the Antarctic base at McMurdo.

"Hello, come in, McMurdo base. ESC Earth shuttle 2 here. Commander Francis calling."

"Hello, shuttle 2. General Payton, McMurdo base. Over."

"General, we'll be with you in thirty minutes. ESC 1 should be with you ten minutes earlier," said Maria.

"We have not heard from the ESC 1. I thought it left before you," said the general.

"It did, sir, exactly ten minutes before. She should be landing soon. Perhaps her communications device has broken down after coming through the atmosphere," said Maria in a concerned voice.

"We'll continue monitoring communications and trying to contact shuttle 1; you just make sure that your craft gets down safely commander. Over and out," said the general.

Maria checked all her instruments to make sure that the shuttle was still on course and the coordinates that were input to the ship's computer by the space lab were correct. All the data looked correct, and the flight and compass headings would put them down at McMurdo base, so hopefully they'd at least make the base. "Everyone OK back there? We will shortly be coming into land. Please check that your safety harnesses are secure. Adam, check the children's; Professor, check yours," ordered Maria.

Natasha broke through into the earth's atmosphere not exactly where she thought the shuttle would. She blacked out for a few seconds, and when she awoke, she was in the lower atmosphere. She quickly flicked her Earth switch, and the space lab computer took control before it started to roll. If she had been five seconds later, the roll would have been irreversible and the shuttle would have plummeted to Earth. She regained her composure and radioed McMurdo base.

"Hello, McMurdo base. Commander Kuzuhara here. Come in," she said into the headset. All she could hear was a crackling in the headset. There was no reply. Natasha thought it was because of the communications blackout zone that she got no reply, so she wasn't unduly worried. She checked her instrumentation, and to her surprise, the shuttle was heading to the other side of Antarctica and not the McMurdo base; now she was worried. As she travelled lower in the Earth's atmosphere, she tried her communications set again.

"Hello, McMurdo base. Come in, please. It's Commander Kuzuhara here," she said. Still a crackling in the headset and no reply. Natasha could see through the clouds. Lots of green down there – no snow or ice cover as you would expect on Antarctica. She was coming in fast.

"Shit, I cannot see any landing strip down there. I must be way off course. All I can see are fields of green," Natasha was saying to herself. Unfortunately for her, the space lab computer had decided that both craft couldn't land at McMurdo base, just in case the landing strip wasn't cleared in time for shuttle 2 to land, and to avoid any chance of a collision, the space lab computer planned a landing spot further north, as she only had cargo aboard. Natasha had no control over the shuttle now, for the computer from the space lab was dictating the landing. She came lower and lower, and suddenly she touched down with a thud. The ship slid across the grassy surface and clipped a few rocks on its slide before coming to an abrupt halt. Natasha came to about twenty minutes after the shuttle came to a halt. She was a bit groggy because the impact of landing caused her to pass out.

"Hello, shuttle 1. Come in. McMurdo base here. Over."

"Hello, McMurdo base. Commander Kuzuhara here. Over."

Now the fucking radio decides to work, she thought.

Maria could see the base now as they broke through the dense cloud cover. There were mountains almost completely circling the McMurdo plains. The shuttle started to bank right and start a circular decent. Suddenly, she could see the crude landing strip. "Christ, it does not look long enough to land the shuttle on," she said to herself.

"What was that, Commander?" asked the professor.

"Oh, nothing. Just talking to myself," she said. She didn't want to frighten her passengers but was worried that the landing would be a close call.

"Come in, shuttle 2. McMurdo control here. Over.

"Shuttle 2 here. Commander Francis receiving. Over."

"You're on the final approach. You will need to touch down at the top end of the landing strip or you will overshoot," said McMurdo control.

Maria took a huge risk and turned off the auto-guided landing controls; she took manual control of the landing. She was fighting with the controls to touch the shuttle down earlier and quicker than the auto system would have. She was getting lower and lower, landing wheels out. "Right, crew, it's now or never." There was an almighty bang as the shuttle hit the landing strip, then another bang as the landing wheels folded under the shuttle's weight. The nose dug into the strip, and the shuttle slid for four hundred metres before coming to a halt.

"God, that was close. Everyone all right back there?" said Maria, she got no response to her question

"Hello, McMurdo control. We are down and safe. Any word from Commander Kuzuhara in shuttle 1?" she asked.

"No, not yet, Commander. Glad, you made it back safely – only hope Natasha makes it too," said the general, who wasn't known for his sentiment. Several vehicles came out to meet them. On the lead truck was Major Campton. She wanted to be one of the first people to greet them. Maria unbuckled and went back into the rear of the shuttle to unharness the children. Adam got out of his seat to help Maria.

"Come on, kids, let's go. That was fun, wasn't it?" said Adam in a relieved voice.

"Yes, Daddy, can we do that again? It was fun!" both Alana and Sean screeched.

Major Campton reached the shuttle first as Maria was emerging from the main exit door. She stepped out and fell over in a heap, giggling to herself.

"Maria, are you OK, and what's so funny?" she asked.

"I'm laughing more in relief that we made it down to Earth safely and forgot to move slower. All that time in zero gravity has made my muscles a little weak," said Maria, still giggling to herself. "I had better warn the others."

"Get over here, medical team. We need to help the passengers off the shuttle!" bellowed the major.

"Hello, shuttle 1. Where the hell are you?" the general said.

"I'm somewhere to the north of you. Let me check the compass reading. Hang on ... I'm at latitude sixty degrees and longitude zero degrees," said Natasha.

"Sergeant, where is that?" asked the general.

"One minute, sir. Let me bring up the map on the system. Mm, that would put the shuttle in ... Aha, I have it now. Queen Maud Land, somewhere near the Sanae base."

"Captain Morgen, how long will it take you to get to the shuttle?" asked the general.

"If I took the heli-jet, probably seven hours. By sea, it's around four days," said the captain.

"Sergeant, radio the Sanae base to let them know the situation. Captain, you take the helicopter to pick up Commander Kuzuhara and I'll ask Major Campton to take the *Niagara* and pick up the supplies," ordered the general.

"Come in, McMurdo base. What's happening? Is anyone going to speak to me?" asked Natasha.

"OK, commander, keep your hair on and stay put. We're sending Captain Morgen with the heli-jet to pick you up; he will be there in about seven hours," replied the general.

"Seven hours is a lifetime. Did Commander Francis make it to the base?" enquired Natasha.

"Yes, she landed safe and sound about twenty minutes ago. It was a close one. It was a good that you didn't land here, as we wouldn't have had enough time to clear the runway," said the general.

Maria, Adam, the children, and the professor were released from the base medical facility after a few hours of tests. They were all still a little unsteady on their feet, but other than that, they were all given a clean bill of health.

Adam's brother, Gerald, was waiting outside the medical facility with Valerie, their children, Maria's mother, Mary, and Maria's uncle, Tom. On seeing them emerge, they all rushed at once to have hugs and kisses. Many tears flowed until finally Maria said, "OK, team, it's so nice to be back on Earth with our families. What's been happening? What have we missed since being in space?"

Everyone was trying to say something all at the same time: "Well, we were attacked by pirates."

"We were attacked in Scotland."

"We met a load of fishermen."

"I managed to rescue your mother and uncle."

"Oh, and we rescued lots of flour to make bread."

"We're living on the *Lily Rose*, not in one of the new homes."

"Everyone please stop. Does anyone know what happened to my daughter-in-law, Natasha!" screamed the professor at the top of his voice.

"Steady on, Professor. We have just learned that she landed in Queen Maud Land to the north of here and that they are sending a heli-jet to pick her up," said Gerald.

"Oh, thank you, thank you. That is fantastic news," said the professor.

"Hey, brov, I have several rooms left on my *Lily Rose* which you and the family can have if you don't want to live in one of the new homes," said Gerald.

"Can you fit in Commander Kuzuhara and the professor?" asked Adam.

"Well, let me see. Me and Val are in two-berth cabin one; you and Maria can have two-berth cabin two; Lauren, Jade, and Alana can share the three-berth cabin three. Jamie and Sean will be in two-berth cabin four, Mary in one-berth cabin five, Professor Kuzuhara in one-berth cabin six, Natasha in two-berth cabin seven, and that leaves three-berth cabin eight for Tom.

Natasha was trying to pass the time while waiting for her pickup by going through her cargo manifest. There were six hundred packets of dried soup and the same number of packets of dried egg yolks, powdered coffee, dried tea, chicken curry, and beef curry. "All food can be rehydrated with water. But why is everything in packs of six hundred?" she said to herself.

She was contemplating what life would be like now that she was back on the earth. It was so structured up in space. When she heard the roar of a turbo engine coming closer, she thought it must be the heli-jet. She got out of the shuttle main door in time to see the McMurdo base heli-jet landing about fifty metres away. Out stepped a handsome captain. *Wow,* she thought, *there is life after space.*

"Good afternoon, Commander. Lovely day for a landing," said Captain Morgen, who appeared to be trying to make conversation with the dark-haired beauty without out sounding stupid.

"Captain, nice of you to finally get here," said Natasha, trying not to seem interested and quite nonchalant in her reply.

"Do you need anything from the shuttle? If not, lock her down, as the *Niagara* will be here in a few days to offload your supplies," said the captain.

"Now just one minute, Captain. I outrank you, and I'll make the decision when to lock my shuttle down," she said.

"Yes, ma'am. When you're ready, we'll head back to base." He said this in a much more formal tone.

On the way back to the base, she thought to herself, *He knew our families would be joining us, the wily old fox.* "Six hundred divided by one hundred days equals six people," she said aloud softly.

CHAPTER SIX

CRETACEOUS

The earth movements had now settled down. What was the Indian Ocean is completely dry and over-grown with vegetation. The Atlantic Ocean was also completely dry, with some strange huge trees and with some forests growing on the plains and slopes. There was an exception. An area 140 miles east of Corvo Island was linked to the deep oceans where Portugal used to be by a 2-mile-wide shallow sea. The top half of the Pacific has also dried up, with very limited vegetation growing.

It had been a year and a half now since the collapse of humanity and the asteroid impacts. Where you had oceans, you now had dry land; where you had dry land, you now had very deep oceans. If you could see the earth from space, there would be more land than oceans. These oceans were much deeper than the previous ones, some going as deep as twenty miles. The only remaining land prior to the time of the asteroids was Antarctica, parts of the Azores which form mountain ranges now, and parts of Australia. There were still shallow seas around Antarctica which joined up to the deep sea, where South America, North America, and Africa had been; and it is still joined by the old south part of the Pacific Ocean to what was left of Australia.

The general and his team had managed to bring most survivors from around the Southern Hemisphere to McMurdo Village, as it is now called. The village inhabitants now number around three thousand people, including around four hundred of the one thousand scientific community. They had not seen the remainder of the pirate fleet since their last encounter, but they were constantly monitoring radio communications and keeping all the ships fully armed when they got out of McMurdo Harbour. It was becoming a major problem to keep all inhabitants happy and well fed. You could only eat so much fish, seaweed, fruits, and vegetables. They didn't don't have any livestock, as farm animals did not survived the destruction. They were mounting an expedition soon to the Azores, and perhaps they could dedicate part of this trip to searching for new food alternatives.

Commanders Francis, Kuzuhara, and friends, plus their families, were now all living aboard the *Lily Rose* with Gerald's family and Maria's mum and uncle Tom. Maria's day job was based on the *Niagara*, and she formed part of the scientific group whose job it was to analyse any finds they made and to monitor the new oceans and new vegetation growing on the dry sea-beds. The weather on the planet had completely changed. The air was much denser and the climate more humid. The scientists believed this was due to the release of all the methane that was trapped on the old ocean floors. There was ice forming at the north of the planet, but the south currently seemed completely clear of any frozen particles.

The science community from Halley base were still monitoring Mona 3, as the crack around the centre was getting wider. It was about five centimetres now, and there were some strange sounds emanating from inside the asteroid. The general was readying an expedition as requested by the scientific community to visit the other asteroid, William 6, which landed on the Island of Corvo at what was the Azores group of islands. The scientists wanted to see if this asteroid was cracking at its middle like Mona 3 and try to identify the sounds, if any, coming from the inside. The general had asked Major Campton to lead this expedition supported by Captain Morgen and Commanders Francis and Kuzuhara. It would require loading the heli-jet and several vehicles onto the *Niagara* and sailing her up to where Portugal had been, making a journey inland to William 6.

Alun Morgen and Natasha Kuzuhara were now an item. Natasha was immediately attracted to Captain Morgen, who was of mixed parentage, with a welsh mother and Greek father. He had dark hair, eyes of brown, and stood six feet three inches in his socks. She first noticed his good looks when watching him climbing down from the heli-jet during her rescue from Queen Maud Land. Once they reached the McMurdo base Natasha asked her father, General Payton, about him. She wanted to know every detail. However, the general could only talk about his service record, which was exemplary, but he didn't know much about him socially.

"Look, Natasha, if you want to find out more about Captain Morgen, go and have a chat with him," said the general.

"Oh, Father, you don't know much about relationships, do you?" she said with a big grin on her face.

Over the next few months, they were working closely together, going on several rescue missions, and their relationship blossomed. At first, it was a bit awkward, but as they got to know each other better, things moved quickly, Natasha thought she would never find love again after her husband and daughter had died. Natasha also sought approval from her father-in-law, Professor Kuzuhara, as she didn't want to offend him by starting a relationship after being married to his son. The professor was delighted about her finding someone else.

"Natasha, Takao would have wanted you to move on and not keep yourself locked away," he said.

"Oh, thank you," she said, feeling very humbled towards him.

After some time, Natasha asked Gerald if she could bring him aboard the *Lily Rose* to live with them.

"Of course, you can, Natasha. Life must go on. We're the last of the world's population. Where are, you going to find, another man like him?"

The *Niagara* was now fully loaded and ready to head off to the Azores Island Corvo. They had kept the crew complement to a minimum, enough to operate the ship; they wanted to make sure there was enough space to accommodate a larger marine complement and scientists. It would take around eight days to get to the Azores or, to be more precise, to reach 140 miles to the East of Corvo in the shallow sea, plus another three-fourths of a day by vehicle to reach what was once Corvo Island, for the terrain would have some mountain regions to negotiate.

In eight days, *Niagara* reached the coordinates where 140 miles east of Corvo had been. The trip was uneventful. They didn't encounter the pirates and didn't see another ship en route. The ship moored up on what had been the Atlantic Ocean floor, 140 miles away from Corvo. The scientists were quite surprised to see dense forest just inland of where they moored.

"That just can't be possible. How can the area be so full of trees and plants so quickly after emerging from the deep seas!" exclaimed Professor George Munro, the leader of the scientific community.

Major Campton sent the heli-jet to William 6 ahead of the main expedition to scan ahead and provide feedback as to which vehicles would be required for the trip.

Captain Morgen and Commander Kuzuhara, along with six marines, formed the crew complement of the heli-jet, along with some communications equipment and some food and water supplies. As the heli-jet flew further inland, the forest got denser and they could see birds flying around below them, as well as some animals of unidentified species, although they were travelling quite fast so identification of what was down there would be quite difficult.

"Come in *Niagara*. This is Captain Morgen here. Over," he said.

"Major Campton here. What have you to report? Over," she said.

"Major, you may have to break out the deforest vehicle, as from up here, the forest is extremely dense. It will be difficult to get to Corvo by a direct route," explained the captain.

The *Niagara* unloaded three heavy-duty habitation trucks that can traverse any terrain. They were eight-wheeled vehicles with independent drives for each wheel. They can carry ten persons and had living accommodation for each of the ten. Additionally, they had enough capacity to carry food and water to last the ten people for fifteen days. They also unloaded the deforest vehicle, which had a caterpillar track system: four independent tracks, two sets at the front and two sets at the rear of the vehicle. The unique thing about this vehicle was its tree, vegetation, and rock removal system. It could remove trees as tall as forty metres, pulverise rocks with its sonic system, and clear vegetation, creating a four-metre-wide path. They also unloaded the multi-action protection vehicle, or MAP, as it was known to all military personnel. This was a fully armoured lightweight tank, armed with rockets, anti-aircraft missiles, and a laser cannon. It carried five people and was light enough to travel over any terrain but heavily armoured enough to withstand a lot of punishment. It even had a three-layer skin system to repair breaches, called timinium repair. The expedition would consist of twenty marines and ten scientists, made up of archaeologists, botanists, food specialists, and Commanders Kuzuhara and Francis as terrain specialists, the MAP and the captain with the heli-jet to command the marines.

The general was picking up some strange radio communications between two factions within the pirate group that attacked them. One group was determined to try to attack the McMurdo base, and another group wanted to join the community there. There were only five ships left in the pirate fleet, four smaller motor fishing trawlers of around fifty tons, and a larger fast-moving pilot tug vessel of about two thousand tons, called The Storm. The pilot tug vessel was armed with three-inch guns and carried a crew complement of twenty men. The fishing fleet carried smaller-calibre weapons and had fifty men spread amongst the other four vessels. "We better warn the expedition that they could have some trouble on the way back," said the general to Sergeant Kawloski.

"Yes, sir. I'll contact them on the secure channel scrambler," he said. The general readied the *Lunar Star* just in case they were needed. He also asked Gerald if they would support any rescue mission should it be required with the *Lily Rose*. Valerie and Mary were not happy putting their home at risk again. They didn't like having to move constantly into temporary accommodation at the base; it was always a big upheaval for the children.

"Gerald, do we really have to move out again?" enquired Valerie.

"I know it is inconvenient but just think of all the lives we saved the last couple of times. It is worth the upheaval for me," he said.

They don't normally get an opinion from Maria's uncle Tom, but on this occasion, he was quite agitated. "Now listen here, lassie. If we all took that attitude, then lots of people we know would not be here now," he said before storming off to his room.

Major Campton had remained on the *Niagara* to direct operations for the expedition. She had the minimum crew complement of thirty people and thirty marines to protect them should they get attacked. Her radio operator was receiving a message from McMurdo base. "All right, sir. I'll relay the message to the major. Over and out," said the operator.

"Major just received a message from the general. He had been monitoring the pirate frequencies. We need to ensure we are careful on the return trip, as they may attack us," said Corporal Francesca Litel.

"Thanks for the message. I'll ensure we double our night-time lookouts in case they try to attack us here," she said.

The major moved the *Niagara* and anchored her a few hundred metres off-shore. This would give them more room to manoeuvre should they be attacked. It was now night-time when they'd anchored. Many strange noises were emanating from the forest on the foreshore, some that they had never heard before, deep roaring, which made the blood run cold and sent shivers up their spines.

The expedition had cut their way twenty miles inland just as nightfall descended upon them. Some of the trees they had been cutting down had not been on the planet since the age of the dinosaurs during that period. The scientists were having a field day. All these new discoveries created an air of optimism and confidence amongst the team that they would also find some alternative food sources.

The captain landed the heli-jet close to the vehicles. He was a little concerned about the strange animal noises coming from all around them in the forest. They were not sure, but the strange roaring sounded like some enormous animals. In the interest of safety, the captain insisted that all personnel sleep in their vehicles. For the marines and scientists, this wasn't an issue, as their vehicles were designed for such a purpose. However, for the people manning the MAP conditions, were a little cramped, as most of the room was designed to take armaments and supplies. They could only move their seats back a little way. Natasha and the captain bunked in one of the heavy-duty trucks; the other marines stayed with the Heli-jet and bunked on board. Captain Morgen, Natasha, Maria, and the head scientist for the expedition had a meeting on board the heavy-duty truck they were in to plan for the next day's events. They planned to try to travel forty miles in a day, as that would get them to their objective in three days. That would mean the scientists wouldn't get as much time to study the plants and fauna as they had during their first day.

The McMurdo base radar was picking up a large vessel moving towards them. It was registering about twenty miles out from the base. "General, we're picking up a fast-moving vessel heading our way. Its present position is twenty miles out," said Sergeant Kawloski.

"Sergeant, I want to know it's every movement whilst I prepare the *Lunar Star*," said the general. The large two-thousand-ton tug was heading towards the McMurdo base. They had transferred some of the men from the rest of their fleet to bring the complement up to fifty crew and soldiers. Additionally, they moved some of the smaller-calibre anti-aircraft guns onto the deck. She was more like a small destroyer now. She had two sets of three-inch guns and five forty-millimetre-calibre anti-aircraft guns.

The leader of the pirates thought that by attacking under the cover of darkness, they would have the element of surprise. Unbeknown to him, the base had a sophisticated radar system and could pick up a rowing boat at twenty miles. The general launched the *Lunar*

Star within thirty minutes of picking up the incoming vessel; she should intercept the large vessel ten miles from the base. The *Lunar Star* was now heavily armed and a match for anything the pirates could throw at them. The *Lunar Star* reached the location, and they expected to encounter the incoming ship but found nothing. There was an unusually heavy sea fog in the area, and visibility was down to about fifty feet. One could pass a huge object and never see it if it was more than fifty feet away. Even sound was dampened in the fog.

The general radioed back to McMurdo base to see if the vessel was still on their radar screens. "Hello, McMurdo base. General Payton here. Over."

"McMurdo base here, Sergeant Kawloski. Over."

"Sergeant, do you still have that vessel on your screens? We can't find it out here in this heavy fog," said the general.

"Yes, sir, she has now passed you and is still heading our way," said the sergeant.

"How far past us is she?" asked the general.

"The vessel is about five hundred metres off your stern and speeding up."

The captain was first to wake up and take a stroll outside the habitation truck. "Oh my God," he said to himself. "Professor Munro, wake up. You need to come and see this!" he shouted.

Professor Munro was a little groggy from being roused so quickly from his slumber. Still, he jumped down from the vehicle and went over to join the captain. What he saw next made him reel back in disbelief. There were animal tracks all around their camp, but these were no ordinary tracks. They were made by a creature from a time as far back as the Cretaceous period. Natasha and Maria had roused from their sleep and joined them.

"What are we studying, gentlemen, some sort of new plant, eh?" said Natasha in a sarcastic voice.

"No, my dear. These are fresh tracks left by a nasty predator from the Cretaceous period," said the professor.

"How can that be? They all died out a few million years ago," said Maria.

"No, they're definitely fresh tracks, and they have been made by velociraptors," said the professor.

"You're kidding me, Professor," said Captain Morgen.

"No, absolutely not. Look at the claw configuration – a velociraptor. We better keep all the scientists in the vehicles when travelling through this forest," he said.

"OK, Professor. I'll pass the message on, but we still need to investigate any new food sources. Perhaps we can eat these velociraptors," replied the captain.

Lunar Star came about and started after this mystery ship. She had about a half-kilometre head start, plus it took the *Lunar Star* a little while to come about, as she was a big ship. "Engine room full speed ahead. I need maximum engine power to catch this vessel," barked the general down the ship com line. The *Lunar Star* started to accelerate after the vessel. The fog was too thick to see any distance. All they could do was chase them at maximum speed. The base was only thirty minutes from their position.

The pirate vessel, *Storm,* was just entering Ross Bay. She started firing all her three-inch guns, immediately McMurdo base came into view. The first shots landed short of the dock. The next salvo hit the harbour goods warehouse, punching holes in the roof and destroying some of the mechanical stores and some spare fishing nets. Being late at night, fortunately no one was in the building at the time. *Storm* was about to fire off another salvo when the first ship-to-ship missile hit her forward three-inch gun. The second missile took out her control room, and the third destroyed the stern three-inch gun. Just coming into view behind her was the *Lunar Star...* As she got close, she fired the pulse cannon at *Storm*'s engines, there was an almighty explosion. The ship split into three pieces, and she quickly sank to the bottom. There were seven survivors pulled from the water. The rest of the fifty-man crew either drowned or were killed by the missile impacts.

The new pirate leader and all his command officers died in the attack.

The next morning, Alun and Natasha took up the heli-jet to scout further ahead. They left the six marines behind to help defend the expedition should any animals attack them. They decided to fly straight, as the crow flies to William 6, a flight that would take them about two hours at quarter speed. The rest of the expedition was cutting their way forward also in a straight line towards William 6. Maria was in the lead vehicle behind the deforester when it came to an abrupt halt about twenty miles in. She radioed them, asking why they had stopped.

"Commander we've hit something solid. We must go back to get around it. Must be quite big," replied the driver.

Maria and her crew and Professor Munro climbed out of the lead habitation truck to see what the obstruction was. What they saw came as a bit of a shock to the group. They had hit a concrete construction sticking about ten feet out of the ground and running into the forest east to west for as far as they could see. It had windows every ten feet – or to be precise, they were square holes where windows would have been. Maria and the professor climbed to the top of the construction to get a better view. They seemed to be standing on what would have been the roof. They moved about twenty feet towards the back of the roof.

As they were walking towards the back, Maria noticed what looked like a part of a huge white letter. She called the professor over. "Professor Munro, look at this. Obviously, this ancient civilisation could write," she said.

After clearing some of the mud and debris from the white letter, it became apparent what it was. They both stared at each other for a few seconds, each waiting for the other to say something. Maria was first to get her words out. "But that's ridiculous," she said.

"I'm still trying to make sense of this," said the professor. What they were actually looking at was a capital *H*, something you would have seen on top of many modern skyscrapers today had they survived. It was a helicopter landing spot, marked with a big letter *H* in a white circle.

"You know what this means," said Maria.

"No, what are you trying to get at?"

"When we were scanning the earth from the space lab in this area, we saw a road with white lines down it and buildings two miles below the surface, near the Azores," she said, so we were not imagining it.

Natasha and Alun Morgen reached the coordinates where William 6 had landed but could not find the asteroid. All they could see was dense jungle at the height they were hovering. "I think we need to get higher," said Alun.

"We should see the asteroid, as it measured two miles in height," said Natasha.

Alun took the Heli-jet to about three hundred metres high, then he could see something: twelve asteroid-sized circles, six miles in diameter, three miles across, and 267 metres tall, with runways coming out of twenty-four locations across all twelve circles.

"We had better get back to the expedition and report our findings. It's going to blow them away," said Natasha.

The seven survivors of the pirate fleet were being questioned by the general to understand why they were desperate to attack the McMurdo base, knowing they would be destroyed. The pirates explained that they were very low on fuel, which would typically not be a problem in normal circumstances, but they needed their ships to collect water, as the area they lived in had no natural source. They knew that McMurdo base had a fuel dump and were prepared to try anything to get some of it, even if it meant they died in the attempt. They were that desperate.

"What about your other ships? Why did they not support your attack?" asked the general.

"These ships carried mainly women and children as well as crew for them. They voted not to attack the base," said the highest-ranking pirate.

"So... what's going to happen to them?" asked the general.

"They will probably head back to our base in Australia. We aren't able to contact them, as our pirate leader took all their communication devices to stop them contacting you," said the pirate.

Natasha and Alun Morgen re-joined the expedition to find them still examining the concrete structure. They had posted armed guards to support them, as they weren't sure whether they would get attacked by the velociraptors that had been in their camp earlier. The captain called together Professor Munro, Maria, Natasha, and along with himself, they sent a radio link to Major Campton for a discussion on what they had found at the site where William 6 had landed.

"Right, Captain and Commander Kuzuhara – what have you to report?" asked Major Campton.

"We could not find William 6, but what we did find were twelve asteroid-sized circles, three miles by six miles and about two hundred and sixty-seven metres high, with two runways out of each circle covered by thick jungle," said Natasha.

"I think the asteroid is still there, but it has split into twelve pieces," said Professor Munro.

"Why do you think that, Professor," asked Maria.

"Were on this expedition because Mona 3 is doing the same thing; it is starting to split," said the professor.

"What about this wall, then? Or is it a building?" asked the captain.

"I'll let Maria answer that one," he said.

"We think that this building was originally a tall structure, but due to being under the sea for so long, silt and mud had almost covered it," she said.

"OK, enough about the structure. Why do think this is significant?" asked Major Campton.

"Major, this is not just some ancient structure. The building has a helicopter landing pad painted on it," said Maria.

"Don't be so ridiculous. How can this ancient civilisation have had helicopters, and how were they able to build modern skyscrapers?" asked Major Campton in a sarcastic voice.

"I would not scoff at this, Major. We saw buildings and a road with white lines running down it from the space lab in this area," said Natasha defiantly.

"Let's not argue about this, team. Continue on your journey to the site where William 6 landed," ordered the major.

The general was picking up a radio broadcast from the scientists investigating Mona 3. There were shouts of panic, screaming, and an awful grating sound as if the ground were breaking up.

"Hello, come in, Halley science team," screamed the general into the microphone. "General, it's happening. Oh, my God, it's starting to open—" The messages ended then and the radio just crackled. They also heard a blood-curling roar just as the signal cut off.

"We'd better send someone over to the Halley base and on to the site of Mona 3 to find out what happened," ordered the general.

"Only the *Lily Rose* can make that journey, as the *Lunar Star* needs to stay here in case of any more pirate attacks," said Sergeant Kawloski.

The general decided to talk with Gerald directly rather than send a messenger to ask him if they could borrow their home again. "Hi, Gerald, can I come in?" he asked after knocking on the main control room door of the *Lily Rose*.

"Sure, General, come in. I'm assuming you want to use our ship again," he said.

The expedition took another three days to reach the site of William 6, and they cut an almost maze-like path to get there. They found more buildings en route. Seen from the air, the pattern represented streets of a big city. More and more everyday objects were also found: tins of food, bottles, plastic pens, and modern-day cars.

"So, the general almost got it right. These objects were not planted by aliens but are the remains of civilisation from over two hundred and fifty thousand years ago. This find will put our scientists back a few years," said Professor Munro.

"What you're saying, Professor, if I understand you correctly, is that humans have existed on this planet a lot longer than we thought," said Maria.

"No, not exactly. Humanity had progressed to a level of technology and science, then was wiped out by an unknown catastrophe. What we're finding are the remains of a modern-day civilisation," said the professor.

"That would mean that the general was almost correct," Natasha said. "He still thinks someone targeted us from outside our solar system. We should know our space lab was attacked several times. What I mean is that objects were sent in our direction to knock us out of orbit or destroy us like the Russian/Chinese lab was."

The *Lily Rose* was loaded up with ten heavily armed marines and the general. Gerald was asked to support the mission by captaining the vessel; it would take them four days to reach the Halley base.

"General, why are we heading off in such a rush?" asked Gerald.

"We think that the scientists were being attacked and the quicker we get there, the more of a chance of helping the team," said the general.

The *Lily Rose* reached the Halley base without any incident, no pirates or other distractions, and they were met at the quay by one of the British scientists, Edmund Sachs, who was the base leader.

"General, thank God you got here. We've not seen or heard from our science team since they set out for Mona 3 five days ago," said Edmund.

"We did get a garbled message on the radio we left them. It didn't sound good. I think they were attacked," said the general.

"What do you mean *attacked*?" asked Edmund. "By whom?"

"We aren't sure, that's why we're here. Grab some supplies and join us. We'll sail over to the base of Vinson Massif mountain and try to find them," replied the general.

Two scientists from Halley base joined the team on the *Lily Rose*. It would take them about twelve hours to reach the base of Vinson Massif mountain. The general loaded several motor-cycles on to *Lily Rose* before they sailed, for it would be a quicker way to reach the mountain – or what was left of it. It had flattened out somewhat after Mona 3 landed on it.

The expedition set up camp at the coordinates where William 6 had landed in a heavily forested location. They set up a perimeter defence system using infrared beams to mirror panels and lasers to target anything that would beak the beams. These would be set up around the whole camp to detect an intrusion at about ten feet out from the vehicles and at three height levels. They were camped near one of the runways that came from a circular section of William 6, and they intend to explore the section in the morning, as they have arrived close to dusk. During the night, something had broken the perimeter infrared beams. The laser defence system had hit something.

"Captain, over here. I found our intruder!" shouted Professor Munro.

Maria and Natasha followed the captain to see what the professor had found. They all recoiled in horror. Lying in front of them was a velociraptor, green and yellow in colour, with big red eyes and huge four-inch razor sharp teeth. It was about nine feet tip to tail and when standing was about seven feet high. The laser defence system blasted a hole one inch in diameter right through its body, around where its heart would be. It would have died instantly.

The *Lily Rose* reached the Vinson Massif mountain range in ten hours, quicker than expected. They couldn't see Mona 3, yet this asteroid was three miles long and two miles high. It would have been visible even from the sea. The general had the motorcycles unloaded and sent a team of four marines led by Sergeant Grenfold and two scientists led by Edmund Sachs to look for the science expedition from the Halley base. The terrain was much lower and flatter due to Mona 3's weight pushing the mountain down. The team reached the coordinates where Mona 3 would be, and all they saw were high-sided cliffs with dense forested areas on their summits and a runway coming down from the cliff.

The scientific team travelled around the base of the high cliffs to see how far they stretched. After a few hundred metres, the lead motorcyclist came to an abrupt halt, causing the others in the team to skid on the grassy surface. "Why the hell have you stopped?" shouted the marines at the back of the group

"I think I've just found one of our scientists," replied Edmund Sachs, the lead rider. Sticking out from the base of the cliff were a pair of legs, and Sachs recognised the boots on the legs.

"How could a scientist get under the cliff?" asked Sergeant Grenfold.

"He either dug his way in and the tunnel collapsed or the cliff fell on him," said one of the other scientists.

"I don't think the cliff fell on him. Let's assume he dug his way in and the rest of the team are trapped in that tunnel and presumed dead," said the sergeant.

Natasha and Captain Morgen left the heli-jet behind with ten marines to protect the camp and climbed into one of the habitation trucks, as they wanted to be with the team when they reached a section from the meteor William 6 at the summit. The expedition made its way up the ramp leading to the top of the meteor section. It was quite a steep climb, as they had to negotiate a rise from 0 metres to 267 metres in quite a short distance. The ramp was about ten metres wide. It took them about forty minutes to reach the top, and what they saw next left them all stunned. The circular section of William 6 was like a miniature world in itself – forested, small lakes, and herds of extinct dinosaurs, including Corythosaurus, triceratops, diplodocus. You name it, they were all there. The expedition followed the ramp down into the interior of the asteroid section to an area by the back wall that had no trees or grass or animals near it, and they found a series of caves with huge glass doors on them.

The team from the *Lily Rose* reached the summit of a ramp leading up into the Mona 3 asteroid section; from this height, they could survey the land. Mona 3 had split into twelve sections just like William 6, and each section was covered in forest.

"My God, look at this," said the lead scientist to the marine commander.

"What is it you see? Oh, wow." There were herds of dinosaurs of several periods roaming around each of the forested sections of Mona 3. There were also several flying species of pterosaur.

The *Lily Rose* team contacted the general, who was still on the ship. "Come in, General Payton. Mona 3 team here, sergeant Grenfold. Over."

"General Payton here. What have you to report sergeant?" he said. "Well, sir, you aren't going to believe this," he said.

"Spit it out, man. What is it?" barked the general.

"We've reached the summit of a section of Mona 3, and we can see the asteroid has split into twelve sections. Additionally, there are dinosaurs everywhere you look," said the sergeant.

"Have you lost your senses, man? How can there be dinosaurs? They went extinct millions of years ago," said the general.

"Hello, General. It's Professor Edmund Sachs here. I can assure you that the sergeant is not going mad. There are herds of dinosaurs of several species roaming around the inside of all the asteroid sections."

"Did you find your missing scientists?" asked the general, trying to bring some normality back to the conversation.

"Yes, I believe we have," said Edmund.

"What does that mean? Have you or have you not found your missing scientists?" asked the general quite sternly.

"General, we've found one of our scientist's legs sticking out from under a cliff face and will have to assume that the asteroid section fell on the whole team, killing them," said Edmund.

"OK, then I'd get yourself back to the ship, because where there are herds of dinosaurs, there are going to be several predators."

"Will do," said Edmund. "OK, team, we're heading back to the *Lily Rose* as fast as we can,"

Whilst the general was waiting for his team to return, he tried contacting Major Campton on the *Niagara* to get an update on what they had found. "Come in, *Niagara*. General Payton here. Over." He didn't get a reply.

He thought that the high areas surrounding him were blocking the signal, as they were using normal radio sets. Incoming objects had destroyed all the satellites in orbit for communications prior to the William 6 and Mona 3 asteroids landing. All communications were now by old-fashioned radio waves.

Natasha, Maria, Professor Munro, and Captain Morgen were in the first vehicle to reach the giant glass doors. They were wide open, and the team drove through the doors, passing a console in the centre of the cavern. These doors were big enough to glaze a whole street of houses and protected an opening twelve metres wide by twelve metres high. They were on sliding carriages for ease of opening. Once inside, they found themselves in an enormous cavern, which must have been four hundred metres in diameter and about thirty metres to the ceiling. The floor of the cavern was smooth like polished marble. Around the wall of the cavern, as far as the eye could see, were steel doors, most of which were open.

"Good God, this is almost like an old Roman colosseum and we're standing on the arena floor," remarked Professor Munro.

"I think we should look in one of the open steel doors to see what was in there or what's still in there," said Maria.

"Excellent idea," said Natasha.

The professor went into the nearest open door and let out a loud shriek of excitement. "Maria, Natasha, Captain, come and look at this. It's absolutely fantastic!" he bellowed.

Maria was first into the room, followed by Natasha. "Wow, that's neat," said Natasha.

"Why would you do that?" asked the captain. What they saw when they got into the room were several glassed compartments with straw bedding in them. They would be big enough to house five large animals. There was a control panel on each glass door and several nozzles sticking out from the back wall of each compartment.

"It looks like some kind of sleeping dormitory," said Professor Munro.

"You know what this means?" said Maria

"No, what are you getting at?" said the captain.

"What are you saying?" asked Natasha.

The Halley scientists and marines arrived back at the beach area where *Lily Rose* was moored. "Sergeant, glad you're back. Did you encounter any problems?" asked the general.

"We had a couple of nasty surprises but managed to avoid getting trampled," he said.

"Trampled!"

"Yes, sir. We ran into a herd of slow-moving dinosaurs about fifty strong."

"What were they called?

"Diplodocus. Very large creatures. As far as our historical data says, they were herbivores so they only eat vegetation. They were just so big that you had to avoid them or they could step on you before you knew it," said the professor.

"We better get back to McMurdo base and let our teams know about these beasts. They will no doubt spread out from Vinson Massif over time, and we need to make sure they don't overrun our settlements."

"What I'm trying to say is that someone or something loaded up these creatures to this asteroid with the purpose of colonising a new planet. I don't think that they were expecting any life to survive after the asteroid impact, ensuing tsunami, and blast from the North Pole after Maria 2 exploded," he said.

"I must examine these chambers further to determine how they transported these animals through space and how they survived the journey. They must have been travelling for a few thousand years," said Professor Munro.

"What brought you to that conclusion, Professor?" asked Maria.

"Our nearest star is the Alpha Centauri, about four point three light years away to travel here from there. Even at fifty thousand miles per hour, it would take eighty thousand years – and what speed were the asteroids travelling at, Natasha?"

"We tracked William 6 at two hundred and fifty thousand miles per hour," said Natasha.

"So, it would have taken William 6 about sixteen thousand years at that speed to travel here from Alpha Centauri," said the professor.

"No animal could survive that length of a journey, so they would either need to breed en route or be put into a suspended sleep of some kind," replied Maria.

"What do you think these nozzles at the back of the chamber are for?" asked Captain Morgen,

"They're varied colours, so I assume that one colour delivers a sleep potion and the other colour probably delivers a wake-up potion," said Professor Munro.

"Professor, if this is one chamber of many in this section of asteroid, then with eleven other sections, there must be thousands of creatures that have been transported here," said Natasha.

"I would think you're probably correct, which would mean that if Mona 3 has the same capability, then we'll have thousands of creatures shortly at the Vinson Massif site. We had better warn the general," said Professor Munro.

"What about the doors that aren't open? Should we not investigate those as well whilst we're here?" asked Maria.

"That was going to be my next port of call. Why have only some of the doors opened?"

After their encounter on Vinson Massif mountain, the *Lily Rose* picked up what was left of the Halley research team from the Halley base and set sail for the McMurdo base. It took them another twenty-four hours to reach the base. During that time, the general had time to do some thinking. If this smaller asteroid contained these creatures, then William 6 must contain a darn sight more. *I'd better warn the Niagara expedition,* he thought. *We also need to warn the other research stations on Antarctica that these creatures will eventually populate the whole continent and give the teams the option to come and live in McMurdo village.*

Professor Munro moved out of the open chamber towards one of the locked doors, and he noticed some sort of hieroglyph painted in red at eye level on the grey door. He had'nt noticed anything on the cell with the open door.

"Where are you going, Professor," asked Natasha as the professor swept past her to go and look at the door on the open chamber.

"I'm just checking on something," he said. The professor looked at the hieroglyph on this door and noticed it was coloured green and shaped like an herbivore dinosaur head. He rushed back to the unopened door and looked at the red hieroglyph head, which had big teeth in its jaw. "Hmm, just as I thought," the professor mumbled to himself,

A somewhat puzzled Maria, Natasha, and Captain Morgen asked him in unison what he meant.

"I'm afraid we will need to get out of here pretty sharpish," he said.

"Why do we need to do that? We've only just got here," said Maria.

"The open-door cells contained mainly herbivore dinosaurs and maybe a few small predators like the velociraptor that was killed at our camp yesterday evening. The doors that aren't yet open contain much bigger predators. This cell has one or several tyrannosauruses, and they are much larger than a velociraptor," said the professor, without taking a breath as he spilled out a long mouthful of words.

"How much bigger?" asked Captain Morgen.

"Ten times larger and ten times heavier than the velociraptor," said the professor.

"When do you think, the doors will open on these things, Professor?" asked Natasha.

"Well, it is my belief, and it is only an opinion, that the people who sent these dinosaurs wanted the herbivores to establish themselves first with a few small predators and then they would release the big boys; and by the sound coming from behind this closed door, I suppose they didn't want the predators to eat everything before they could get a foothold on their new planet."

"Come in, *Niagara*. This is General Payton calling. Over."

"*Niagara* here. Over."

"Major, you need to get the expedition team back to the ship as soon as possible."

"What's the hurry, General?"

"The team have reached William 6 and are exploring," said the major.

"Major, we've just returned from Vinson Massif, and there are dinosaurs everywhere. We believe they came from Mona 3, which has split into twelve sections," said the general.

"Maybe that's not the same for William 6. The team has not reported in since they entered the asteroid section. If they had found dinosaurs, surely, they would have contacted me," said the major.

"Major, that wasn't a request. I want all the team back on the *Niagara* immediately, and get back here ASAP," ordered the general. "Do you understand?"

"Sorry, sir. I'll contact them immediately. Over and out," said the major.

"Let's take some pictures and make our way back to the habitation vehicle. We need to get back to camp," ordered Captain Morgen.

The professor wanted to look at more, especially the control console in the middle of the cavern before they left. "Just a minute, Captain," he said. "I want to look at the control console, for it may give us more information as to what's going to happen next."

"OK, but no more than ten minutes. Right, men and ladies, let's get back to our vehicle," said the captain.

"I'm going to join the professor because my materials expertise can help him," said Maria.

"No longer than ten minutes."

"Professor, wait a minute. I'm coming with you!" shouted Maria.

When they reached the console in the middle of the cavern, it was about three metres in diameter and stood about 1.5 metres tall. The professor climbed up onto it to get a better look at the controls. "Maria, come and look at this," he called.

Maria climbed up and joined Professor Munro on top of the console. She was taken aback at what the professor was studying. There was a plaque about three hundred millimetres' square depicting our planet and another planet in a distance galaxy, with lines of travel drawn and arrows indicating direction. It showed that William 6 and Mona 3 had travelled to our planet sometime in the distant past and then travelled back to its origin – and now new arrows showed it is travelling back here in our time.

"My God, are you thinking what I'm thinking?" screeched Maria.

"Yes, it is implausible, but the evidence is in front of us. Most of the dinosaurs didn't die out because of the Chicxulub asteroid on the Yucatan peninsula sixty-five million years ago. They were transported away from the earth by some unknown civilisation and sent back to our world," said the professor.

"Does that mean that the dinosaurs didn't originate on our planet?" asked Maria.

"No, I don't think so, but if it were true, then that would throw some theoretical spanners into the archaeological world, what's left of it."

"Professor, Maria, time to go. There's an awful noise coming from the predator chambers. I think the doors are about to open so let's get moving!" shouted Captain Morgen.

"Captain, we're coming!" shouted both Maria and the professor as they scrambled down from the console and ran to the habitation truck and climbed in. They both got into the truck just in time, and then an almighty roar reverberated around the cavern. As they drove off, they could see a huge shape walking into the cavern.

"Come in, William 6 expedition. Major Campton here. Over," she said.

"Captain Morgen here. Over."

Captain, please return to the *Niagara* as soon as possible, orders of General Payton," said the major. "We are on our way back to our base camp; we need to stay ahead of the predator dinosaurs that have been released from the chambers in one section of William 6."

The major said, "Slow down, Captain, and take a breath, will you?"

"Sorry, Major. So much going on here that I'm trying to get it out in one go. We've been inside William 6 and found sleeping chambers for herbivores and predator dinosaurs, and as we were leaving some of the big Tyrannosaurs came out of their chambers," he said without taking a breath.

"OK, Captain, just get the team back safely. Can you do the journey without any stops?" asked the major.

"No, we'll have to stop, as we don't want to travel at night, but I can fly ahead and be with you in a couple of hours, but the team will take time travelling in this dense forest."

"OK, see you in two hours or so. Over and out," said the major.

"Come in, McMurdo base. Major Campton calling. Over," she said.

"General Payton here. Over," he said.

"I've spoken with the expedition, and they are going to be back on board the *Niagara* in two days," she said. "Did they encounter any dinosaurs?" asked the general.

"Yes, their camp defences killed a small predator called a velociraptor, and they saw other creatures. Additionally, they found dinosaur sleeping chambers in one section of William 6," said the major.

"Just as we thought. Mona 3 contained hundreds of dinosaurs, so we concluded William 6 would have a lot more, as it is twice the size of Mona 3," said the general.

"I'll put the ship's defences on maximum alert, just in case any of the predator dinosaurs reach us here before the expedition returns," said the major.

"OK, Major, keep us informed if the team runs into any trouble. Over and out," said General Payton.

"Major Campton calling. All shore-based personnel please return to the *Niagara*. I want all weapons manned day and night. We need to be ready to support the return of the expedition, and I want the ship at the ready to depart once all are loaded. Over and out."

When Captain Morgen and the habitation trucks reached their base camp, it was a complete mess. The Heli-jet had been completely smashed, and a lot of their equipment was damaged beyond repair. "What the hell could have done this?" asked Captain Morgen.

"I think maybe one of the bigger dinosaurs, something like a diplodocus, may have wandered into the camp when we were in William 6," said professor Munro.

"A diplo what?" asked Natasha.

"A diplodocus is a huge plant-eating animal. Some could weigh up to fifty tons or more, so they would not notice trampling on a Heli-jet or vehicle," said the professor.

"We had better be careful on the way back, as I wouldn't want to run into a herd of these creatures," said Captain Munro.

"Let's break camp and get going. We can radio the *Niagara* later to let them know we're all travelling by vehicle," said Maria.

The expedition travelled back along the path they cut on the journey to William 6; it was slow going, for the terrain had turned boggy due to the heavy rain that had been falling since their departure. The team had only covered 60 of the 140 miles in the first day and had decided to set up camp because night was about to fall. All the perimeter defences were put on to protect the camp whilst they slept, although they had posted a guard as an additional precaution.

Captain Morgen woke Natasha at six in the morning. He put his hand on her mouth to stop her making a sound. "Natasha, wake up. I think there's something prowling around our camp," he said quietly to her.

She woke up trying hard to catch her breath, flailing her arms at the captain to indicate she needed to breathe.

"Sorry, but I didn't want you to make a sound. I've just seen one of the tyrannosaurs outside our window. It looked absolutely massive," he said.

"I don't understand. If it's in our camp, surely the defence lasers would have killed it, wouldn't they?"

"I know there must be something wrong with our defence perimeter," said Captain Morgen.

By this time, Maria and Professor Munro were awake, as the noises coming from outside the habitation truck were quite loud.

"Shush, everybody. Don't make a sound; we have a huge visitor outside," said the captain

Prowling around the camp and bumping into the vehicles was an eight-ton juvenile tyrannosaurus, a deadly predator which could swallow a human being in one go even at that size. The captain got on the radio and warned the other members of the expedition to stay inside their vehicles and make as little noise as possible. Eventually, the dinosaur left the camp. It couldn't find any food so went to look elsewhere. The captain climbed out of the habitation truck to check around the camp. A few things had been knocked over, but other than that, all seemed OK. Then he suddenly remembered they had posted a guard. Where was he?

Back at McMurdo base, the general was briefing all the people about the dinosaur threat and had warned them that if anyone was going to venture outside the camp towards the hills to take armed protection with them. The village at the camp was surrounded by a four-metre-high steel wall, but some of the dinosaurs were much taller and they would need to fire warning shots from the defence anti-aircraft guns to frighten them off or, if need be, kill them, which they had hoped to avoid. Using the long-range binoculars, the lookouts had already spotted flying pterosaurs and herds of herbivores at around twenty miles away. At the rate they were moving, in a couple of days, they would be at the camp wall.

"Now I need some volunteers to be spotters outside on the hills overlooking our camp," said the general to the assembled meeting.

"I'm happy to take my turn, General," volunteered Gerald.

"That is very kind of you, but I need you here to captain the *Lily Rose* should we be attacked again. Thanks for the offer."

"Now then, anyone else, you will be supported by a couple of armed marines. Come on, we need to know when these beasts are getting close. Surely someone will volunteer," said the general, more forcefully this time.

Captain Morgen continued looking around the camp for the guard he had posted when he made a grisly discovery. Just behind one of the habitation trucks, he found blood-soaked ground and a pair of boots with partial legs in them, with an arm lying nearby. "Fucking hell, no wonder the guard didn't warn us. He must have been taken by surprise and was taken in one bite by that huge tyrannosaurus!" he shouted out.

Natasha was first to reach the spot the captain was looking at. She let out a blood-curdling scream. "Shit, shit!" she screamed, just as she did when she saw the Russian cosmonaut outside the space lab window.

By this time, Maria had caught up with Natasha, and she also recoiled in horror at what she saw. "Oh, my God, that poor man."

"I don't think he even had time to let out a scream – it was that quick," said Captain Morgen.

"We had better check why our perimeter warning system didn't destroy that creature," said Maria.

Professor Munro was already at the perimeter security generator, looking at what was left of it. "Over here!" he shouted.

"Looks like the dinosaur entered our camp after being hit by the laser and trampled the generator," said Captain Morgen.

"Does that indicate some level of intelligence?" asked Natasha.

"Could be, because if you were going to attack the camp, this is the exact spot where to enter," said Captain Morgen.

"Let's get everyone ready to break camp in twenty minutes. We must do the last eighty miles back to the *Niagara* in one trip. We can't afford to stop overnight, as we have no perimeter protection," said Maria.

"I'll radio ahead to let the *Niagara* know that we'll be travelling back in one trip by vehicle, as we have no heli-jet now, and to make sure they are ready to sail as soon as we get there," said Captain Morgen.

"Come in, *Niagara*. Captain Morgen here. Over," he said.

"Major Campton here. Where the hell are you? I was expecting you back yesterday. What's your situation? Over."

"We started our journey back yesterday. The heli-jet was destroyed in our base camp and we stopped overnight and lost one marine, eaten by a predator dinosaur. Please be ready to depart once we are back. It will be very late in the day, as we still have eighty miles to go. Over," said Captain Morgen, panting as he finished.

"We will be ready. Just make sure you get back safely, and, Captain, try to speak more slowly next time. You'll give yourself a heart attack at this rate. Over and out," said Major Campton.

A couple of volunteers stepped forward to support the lookout patrols; to the general's surprise, they were two of the pirates who had survived the attack on McMurdo base. The people at the meeting were unhappy to have two former pirates responsible for the security of the village, and many voiced their concerns that these men would just run away and desert their posts.

"People, people, let's keep this an orderly meeting," shouted the general.

"But, General, why can't more of your marines take on this responsibility?" shouted one protestor.

"We're very short-handed, we have most of our teams away from base at the moment, and I need my marines to support the evacuation of the many science stations around Antarctica," he said.

One of the volunteering pirates shouted above the noise of the crowd, "Please listen. Yes, we were pirates, but only to make sure we could protect our wives, sons, and daughters. The pirate general threatened all our families if we didn't support his fleet. We're free now and want to give something back to this community," he added solemnly.

This speech by one of the pirates seemed to calm the crowd, and someone from the back shouted, "Let's give them a chance, but if they try to run away, the marines should shoot to kill – that's what I say."

All the gathered assembly shouted in agreement. "OK, then, it's agreed," said the general. "You two will support the first patrol that we send out later today, but heed the warning, if you prove to be reliable, then we'll welcome all of you to our new village."

The William 6 expedition set off early to make up time for yesterday. The rain had stopped, and the sun was drying the ground as they went. They had travelled about thirty miles and had passed the hidden city when the expedition decided to stop for a twenty-minute break. The captain warned everyone to stay within the convoy perimeter. The MAP stood at the ready to defend the camp should it be necessary. Suddenly, the trees in the distance started bending and waving around and there was an almighty crashing sound as boughs were being broken and trees were falling and being trodden on. One hundred metres in front of the expedition over to their left, a huge beast was emerging from the thirty-metre-high trees. It appeared to be running as fast as it's huge bulk would allow.

"Now I wonder what that huge monster is running from," said the captain.

Just as he finished his sentence, a deafening roar pierced the air and an adult tyrannosaurus of about twelve tons crashed through the trees to the other dinosaur's left and knocked it over, right across the path they had cut. The action was over quickly, as the tyrannosaurus finished off the diplodocus. It was so busy eating it's fill that at first it didn't notice the expedition parked just off the path they had cut a couple of days earlier. When the tyrannosaurus had finished eating, it surveyed the area to ensure no other predator would eat its kill. Suddenly, it saw the expedition and started moving towards them.

"Good grief, that Tyrannosaurus has just spotted us. It thinks we're going to eat its kill," said Professor Munro. The captain ordered the MAP to the front of the convoy. The dinosaur was still moving towards them. The MAP fired over its head with the laser cannon. It kept coming. The MAP then fired directly at the dinosaur with the laser cannon. All this did was glance off its shiny hide.

"Fire one of the rockets to explode above it!" shouted the captain. The MAP commander fired the rocket as commanded, and it exploded directly above the tyrannosaurus's head, causing it to stop momentarily as it shook its head, trying to re-orient itself before toppling over. The beast had been knocked unconscious by the explosion.

"Right, let's get past as quickly as possible and continue onto the *Niagara*," commanded Captain Morgen.

At McMurdo Village, the first of the big dinosaurs started to appear on the plains outside the perimeter wall, mainly herds of herbivore animals. There was plenty for them to feed on: grasses, small bushes, and a limited number of trees. At present, they were not a threat to the village but were being watched constantly to ensure they were kept away from the perimeter wall, although it was strong enough to stop most of them. Anything over twenty tons could damage or bend the wall.

The first combined marine and pirate patrol set out from the village to the hills surrounding the village. It would give them a good vantage point to survey the whole perimeter wall and the plains between the village and the hills. The patrol consisted of two heavily armed marines and two former pirates who were lightly armed with rifles and pistols. They also carried an old two-way radio system to communicate any findings back to base.

Whilst in the hills, the patrol spotted what looked like a huge black cloud in the sky above them. On closer inspection through their long-range binoculars, they saw swarms of huge strangely coloured insects which looked like wasps. They were green and red, not the normal yellow and black. The only difference was these wasps were ten times bigger than anything currently on the planet.

"We had better warn the village to keep everyone inside their homes. I would not like to get stung by one of these buggers," said Corporal Littleton.

In the middle of the swarm, there was an ominous black shape. It was at least one metre in length and was being protected by a group of wasps about half its size.

This was the queen and her drones, looking for a new nesting site.

"Come in, General Payton. Corporal Littleton here. Over," he said into the two-way radio

When the general responded, he said, "General there's a huge swarm of giant wasps heading your way. There must be at least one hundred thousand insects."

"OK, Corporal, but that should not worry us here. I'm more interested in the predator dinosaurs" said the general.

"But, sir, these wasps are huge. The smaller workers are about one hundred millimetres in size, but there's a queen and drones. The queen must be at least one metre in size and her drones about half that."

"They sound like they could be dangerous. I'll warn the base and village to keep under cover until they pass us. Unless you're threatened by them, stay where you are and keep monitoring the dinosaurs. Over and out," said the general.

The expedition had just started to cut a path past the fallen tyrannosaurus when Professor Munro jumped out of the habitation truck to cut a twelve-inch- by-three-inch-thick slice of meat off the dead diplodocus.

"What the hell are you doing professor?" cried Captain Morgen.

"We didn't just come here to investigate William 6. We're also supposed to be looking for alternative food sources," replied the professor.

"Professor, we'll need to be careful about eating that. Some reptiles' flesh contains deadly bacteria which no amount of cooking will sterilise," said Maria.

"I know that, but if this meat proves edible, then we have a new food source rather than that damned fish all the time," he said.

"Come on, get back in the habitation truck. That tyrannosaurus could wake up anytime soon," ordered Captain Morgen.

The expedition made their way past the unconscious tyrannosaurus, making sure not to touch it with any of the vehicles. They had travelled another thirty miles in three hours when they decided to have another comfort break. They were still twenty miles from the *Niagara*. This was a big mistake; the tyrannosaurus woke up about an hour after the expedition passed it. Slightly disorientated, it started smelling the air. Like a shark in the water that can detect blood from miles away, the dinosaur could smell the blood from its kill still wafting in the air and set off following the scent.

There was an awful smell in the habitation truck that was carrying the diplodocus slice of meat. It smelt like gone-off sewage, so the team welcomed the break to open the doors and air it out. It had been ten minutes since they stopped for their break when they could feel the ground vibrating under their feet. It was a rhythmic *thud, thud, thud*.

"What's that sound," said Natasha to Captain Morgen.

"I don't know. What do you think that is, Professor?" asked Captain Morgen.

"The ground is shaking as if somebody is thumping it with a sledgehammer," he said.

"I think that's the sound of something very heavy running," said Maria,

"I don't like it. Everyone back to the vehicles. Let's get moving," ordered Captain Morgen. Just as they started moving, the captain could see something a few miles down the track behind them moving at speed. "Shit, it's that tyrannosaurus we knocked out earlier following us!" he screamed. He radioed all vehicles to speed up.

The black cloud of insects was now directly above the village. Everyone stayed inside their cabins, except for five of the marines who were armed with flamethrowers and small-calibre machine guns. The swarm descended onto one of the empty cabins. The queen smashed through the roof followed by her drones. The rest of the swarm completely covered the outside of the building up to two metres deep. It looked like one giant ten-metre diameter beach ball.

"We need to move that swarm on. It cannot be allowed to settle here!" shouted the general to flamethrower-armed marines through his two-way radio.

"All right, sir. We'll try to disperse these insects," they said.

The marines fired the flamethrowers at the outside edge of the swarm of insects. As each one died, it was replaced from the inside of the ball by more insects. They kept firing, and more and more insects died until the hundreds of large drones appeared at the outside edge of the swarm. They flew straight at the marines, with the flamethrowers stinging them repeatedly until the marines stopped firing the flamethrowers. They then retreated into the centre of the swarm. The five marines that had been stung died instantly. They had turned completely green in colour, and they smelled of honey. The swarm continued to cling to the empty cabin, totally ignoring anything happening around them.

"We must move this swarm on. If they decide to attack the village, there will be many fatalities," claimed the general down the two-way radio to his troops.

The expedition was racing against time to reach the *Niagara*. Following closely behind them was a huge adult tyrannosaurus causing ground vibrations as it was running.

"I thought these huge beasts could only run for a limited time due to their bulk, a bit like lion's short bursts of speed and then they need to rest," said Maria.

"I think we got that one wrong too," said the professor.

The expedition was now just two miles from the *Niagara* when disaster struck; the deforestation vehicle lost a track and was blocking the path.

"For God's sake, get that vehicle out of the way or that fucking monster behind will catch us!" screamed Captain Morgen. The MAP moved from behind the convoy and pushed the vehicle into the forest.

"Perhaps we can come back for that later," said the commander in the MAP.

"Yeah, let's get the crew from the deforester into one of the habitation trucks!" shouted Captain Morgen.

The whole operation took nearly forty minutes to complete, by which time the tyrannosaurus was just half a mile behind them. The MAP stayed at the back of the convoy to stop the dinosaur should they need to. *Thud, thud, thud!* The tyrannosaurus was getting closer by the minute. Just as they got onto the beach, it broke out of the forest four hundred metres to the right of them and was blocking their route to the *Niagara*.

"Gerald, come in. It's General Payton here. Over."

"Gerald here. Over."

"What range does your flare cannon have? Could you reach us here in the village with a shot?"

"Yes, General, we have a two-mile range with this cannon. Why the hell do you want me to fire at the village?"

"We have a huge swarm of giant wasps settled on one of our empty cabins. We tried flamethrowers, but that just aggravated them and they killed five of our marines."

"I thought the intense heat from your flare cannon would get rid of them," said the general.

"You realise, sir, that it will radiate heat at two hundred degrees centigrade for about twenty feet from the impact point. I hope no other cabins are nearby," said Gerald.

"I will give you exact coordinates to the centre of the empty cabin. The nearest populated cabins are forty feet away."

"All right. Let me have the numbers," said Gerald.

"It's fifty-four degrees east, thirteen degrees west," said the general.

"Here goes nothing. I'm firing in five, four, three, two, one. The shot is on its way!" shouted Gerald over the radio.

Just as Gerald finished speaking, the huge distress flare crashed through the centre of the swarm and ignited in a blinding flash. The queen and her drones were incinerated in an instant. The rest of the swarm flew away as fast as their wings would carry them. The general could feel the heat from where he was standing about thirty metres away. God knows how hot it must have been for the wasps at the point of impact.

The tyrannosaurus seemed to break through the forest at the right point to stop the expedition reaching the *Niagara*, as if it had some level of high intelligence. "How the hell did it manage that!" shouted the captain down the radio to rest of the convoy. The tyrannosaurus moved menacingly towards them when the first rocket from the MAP streaked past them; however, it seemed ready for that and moved swiftly down to its right to avoid the explosion. In one movement, it raced forward, smashing its huge clawed feet into the driver's cabin of Captain Morgen's vehicle, killing the driver instantly. Using its huge teeth, it started ripping at the metal and glass to get into the interior of the habitation truck.

Everyone inside the habitation truck jumped out the rear doors and ran towards the vehicle behind them. The *Niagara* started firing her cannons at the beast, but to no avail. The tyrannosaurus continued ripping the habitation truck apart until it found what it was looking for. Its head emerged from the shattered vehicle with a slab of meat in its jaws. It found the slice professor Munro had cut from the dead diplodocus. The tyrannosaurus took one look at the assembled group from the shattered habitation truck, then turned and ran off into the forest.

"My God, that creature definitely has an intelligence level we would have never imagined. It followed us to retrieve its food, it planned its attack, and it even stopped us reaching the ship. We need to be careful in the future should they decide to attack the base," said the professor with an air of someone who had just found the answer to the meaning of life.

CHAPTER SEVEN

LIFE

McMurdo base is counting the cost of the wasp swarm attack: five dead, one cabin destroyed, several others damaged, and a clean-up job that would take a few days. General Payton was concerned about the *Niagara*. After all, his daughter and several of his senior officers were on this mission. He couldn't afford to lose any of them, but he knew the risks being a soldier himself. He was still miles away when Sergeant Kawloski nudged him.

"General, General, are you OK, sir?" he asked.

"Yes, just thinking about our expedition," he said.

"Sir, I'm picking up telemetry from the space lab. We're tracking another object coming in from deep space," he said.

"How big? What is it? How far away and how long before it reaches us?" blurted out the general. It wasn't like him to get ruffled like that.

"I'm not sure how long it will take to reach us. From the readings we're receiving, the object is in the same size category as William 6, probably of that ilk. It's still a few hundred thousand miles away. At its present velocity, I would say about ten days to reach the moon," said the sergeant.

"Ten days? That does not give us long to prepare. Contact the expedition again. I want them back in the next few days," ordered the general.

"Yes, sir, will do," said the sergeant.

The expedition crews were boarding the *Niagara*. They had lost personnel, one marine and one driver, and some pieces of equipment: the deforester, one habitation truck, the shield generator, and other small items without much to show for all the time and effort put into this mission. They could hear many sounds coming from the dense forest – mighty roars, screams, and noises that couldn't be explained.

"By the sounds coming from the forest, I'd say all the creatures that landed in William 6 are out of their chambers," said Professor Munro to his gathered audience. Captain Morgen, Natasha, Maria, Major Campton, and the professor were on a conference call to the general at McMurdo base.

"General, you were right. These asteroids have been sent here by someone outside of our solar system. They were not sent here to destroy the planet but to repopulate it with other species," said Professor Munro.

"Repopulate? We were already populated. Those bastards destroyed most of the life as we knew it. It doesn't make any sense," said the general.

"Professor, tell the general about the plaque we found in the sleeping chamber hall," said Maria excitedly.

"What plaque? You never told me about that, Professor," fumed Major Campton.

"Yes, we found a brass plaque about three hundred millimetres square depicting pictures of William 6 and Mona 3 and a distant planet with arrows showing direction of travel," said the professor.

"What is so interesting about that? We know that William 6 travelled here," said the general.

"Two things about this are of interest to us. Firstly, William 6 was on our planet sixty-five million years ago, collecting animals to take back to a planet in the Alpha Centauri star system. Secondly, the Chicxulub asteroid didn't destroy all the dinosaurs. They had left the planet by then, which means there's other intelligent life outside our solar system."

"I thought you all ought to know there's another object heading our way. The space lab picked up its telemetry, and early indications show it is as big as William 6, but I need Natasha and Maria back to understand the data."

"How long before you get back, Major?" asked the general.

"If we leave now, about seven days at maximum speed," said the major.

"OK, see you in seven days. Safe journey."

"Right, team, are we loaded up yet?" shouted the major over the ship-wide communications system.

The ship's captain responded with, "Locked and loaded."

"Right, let's get moving," replied the major.

The general is addressing the new village council to let them know about what was found at the site of William 6 and about the incoming space object. He wanted to make sure everyone was aware of the potential danger of another asteroid striking the planet. "So, General, what do you expect us to do if another object is going to strike the planet. It's a matter of where and when, isn't it?" said the council leader.

"You're absolutely right, Professor Kuzuhara," replied the general.

"However, we'll know more when Commanders Francis and Kuzuhara get back from their mission and study the data, which will be in four days' time," said the general.

"What about the beasts on the plains … and will we get another insect attack!" shouted someone from the assembled council.

"I've posted lookouts on the hills. We can get an early warning about any impending threat to give us time to respond, but that's about all we can do for now," said the general.

"Are our perimeter walls strong enough to stop any incursion into the village," asked another councillor.

"Sergeant, you can answer that one; you built it," said the general.

"All I can say is that wall is built of steel interlocking panels at least half an inch thick. It can stop a tank due to its interlocking sections, and because it is buried two metres deep into the ground and four metres above ground with soil piled up behind the panels, it will stop most things," said the sergeant "I heard that some of these big dinosaurs are at least fifty tons in weight. Hope it stops them?" asked another worried councillor.

"I'm sure it will keep everything out of the village. If something does break through, we have armed towers to stop it," said the sergeant.

"What you mean, like that tyrannosaurus that the *Niagara* and MAP couldn't stop?" said someone sarcastically.

Niagara was underway. It would take at least seven days to return to McMurdo base even at full speed, which they weren't going to be able to keep up, as the engines would need a breather at some point. The journey back would give the professor time to write up his notes and time for him to reflect on all the amazing discoveries that they have made.

Captain Morgen and Natasha made some time to catch up with their ongoing relationship. It had blossomed from pure lust to a real love affair; they found it extremely difficult to be apart from each other. Although they loved each other unconditionally, they both had duties to perform concerning their positions in the hierarchy of the base.

It was the first time in many years that Natasha had opened her feelings to someone other than Takao and her daughter, Natasha, whose name she took after their deaths. She felt vulnerable now during this time.

Maria was looking forward to seeing her husband and children again. This adventure was almost like her time spent on the space lab, always looking forward to getting back to her family each time she went up there.

Professor Munro just couldn't get enough hours in the day, as he was frantically writing up notes about the trip. Although he would have no scientific forum to present them to, he loved the adulation of his fellow scientists and continued to work feverishly on them.

The major was thinking about finding someone to be attached to. She wasn't getting any younger and would have liked a family, a warm and tender husband and a couple of children. She wasn't as tough as her military persona portrayed.

All the personnel on the *Niagara* were contemplating their futures. With all this new life on the planet, how would they survive? What happens when they run out of fuel and armaments for the ship? Would they have enough food to survive? Would they eventually be overrun by the predator dinosaurs?

Suddenly, the ships speakers sprung into life, shattering everyone's peace and quiet. "Ships on the horizon. All naval personnel to battle stations," came the call from the duty officer. They were still twenty miles away from McMurdo base.

"What now?" said Major Campton.

McMurdo base was still receiving data from the space lab. The object seemed to be slowing down, although the sergeant was not an expert on these things.

"General, I think the object is slowing down," said Sergeant Kawloski.

"Are you absolutely sure about that, Sergeant?" he asked.

"No, not really. It's just that the signal from the object is taking longer to reach the space lab than earlier," said the sergeant.

"Therefore, I need Commanders Francis and Kuzuhara back; they would know how to understand the information the space lab is sending us," muttered the general under his breath.

"Sorry, sir, I didn't catch what you said," said the sergeant.

"Not to worry – it wasn't important," said the general.

Gerald and the *Lily Rose* and one of the Scottish fishing boats were being used to collect scientists from the international stations scattered around Antarctica. The Antarctic Peninsula to the west was now overrun with herds of herbivores and several large predators that came from Mona 3. This peninsula was quite low lying and covered in trees and grasslands, great news for the herbivores and even better news for the predators. Grave news for the humans. The former American Palmer and British Rothera stations were next to be evacuated on the peninsula, as they were most at risk of attack. The stations based to the far east of Antarctica were less of a problem, as the dinosaurs would need to work their way around the coast to get there, which would take them months. The interior had high mountainous regions, which made it almost impassable to heavy, large animals. After the stations on the peninsula were evacuated, there were plans to collect scientists from former British Halley, Argentinian Belgrano II, and Germany Neumayer stations to the north of the peninsula, but they needed the *Niagara* for that, as they had larger populations. The *Lunar Star* was considered but couldn't get close enough to shore, meaning several smaller ships would be required to ferry them from the stations, which would rather defeat the object of conserving fuel and making the trip in one go.

On the sixth day of their return journey, the captain was on the bridge of the *Niagara* with Major Campton, and they could see five ships coming towards them in a tight attack formation. "Right, Captain, get your marines ready. I want them fully armed and ready to repel boarders," she said.

"OK, Major, we'll be ready for those damned pirates," he said.

"Missile batteries get ready to fire when I give the order," she barked down the ship's communications system.

"We've targeted the lead ship in the flotilla," said the gunnery officer.

Maria was looking at the incoming fleet through the long-range binoculars when she spotted something strung across the control room of the lead ship. It was a huge white banner, but she couldn't read what was on it, as they were still too far away.

"It's strange they have not started firing at us," said Captain Morgen.

"Nothing strange about it. They're just trying to get closer because we're probably out of range of their cannons," said Major Campton.

"Get ready, missile battery. Just a few metres more."

Just as she was about to give the order to fire, Maria rushed onto the bridge of the *Niagara* shouting, "For God's sake, don't fire yet, Major! I think they're surrendering and not attacking us.

"Missile battery, hold your fire go to standby and await further orders!" shouted Major Campton.

"Captain, use the long-range binoculars and see if you can read what's on their banner!" ordered the major.

"OK, now let me see. It says, 'Please don't shoot. We have women and children on board and wish to surrender'," he read.

"Thank God you stopped us, Maria," said the major.

"Let's try the radio and see if they answer. "Hello, pirate ships. *Niagara* here. Over," said the radio operator. They tried again but got no reply.

Unbeknown to the *Niagara*, the ships had no radio communication. That's why they were sailing in such a tight formation, so as not to lose anyone during the night.

"Major, we're getting no reply," said the radio operator.

"I hope this is not a ploy to bring our guard down so they can get closer to open fire on us," said Captain Morgen.

"I don't think that's the case. Look through your binoculars. They have children up on deck waving towards us," said Maria.

The *Niagara* docked with the lead pirate ship, and their officers came aboard. They explained why they were surrendering and that they wanted to join the McMurdo village. They could offer the village the twenty goats they had on board and the fifty hens and five roosters to supplement the base's food supply. This would give them fresh eggs, milk, and meat, of course. There were five ships in the flotilla, with fifty crew and men, plus forty women and children split evenly among the five vessels. They were out of water and almost out of fuel, so many of the children were quite dehydrated.

"Let's get those ships fuelled up and supplied with water and get back to McMurdo base," ordered the major.

"Sir, we're receiving a message from the *Niagara*. Do we want to take this?" asked Sergeant Kawloski.

"Yes, put it through to my office," said the general.

"Hello, General. Major Campton here. Over."

"General Payton here. Over."

"Sir, we've encountered the remaining pirate fleet," said the major.

"How many losses did we suffer, Major? Just give me the bad news, no long monologues," said the general.

"We didn't engage them in a firefight, they surrendered to us; they have forty women and children amongst them and about fifty men," said the major.

"That is good news. No losses, just gain. They will add to the community, I'm sure," said the general.

"Even better news: they have goats and chickens that we can use for eggs, milk, and meat," said the major.

"General, Commander Kuzuhara here. Are you still receiving telemetry from that incoming object?" she asked

"Yes, we are, but no one can accurately quantify the data. We need you and Commander Francis back here," he said.

"We're still about a half a day's sailing away from base," said the major.

"OK, Major, we'll see you in twelve-hours. Over and out," said the general.

All the ships travelling back to McMurdo base had been refuelled, and the ship's doctor had administered salt tablets and water to those women and children who were most in need on the pirate ships. The major, Captain Morgen, Maria, Natasha, Professor Munro, and the pirate ships' captains were meeting on the *Niagara* to discuss the journey home.

"Where is your home base?" Captain Morgen asked the pirate captains.

"We were based at the far western tip of what was formerly the continent of Australia, on a small five-by-ten-mile strip of land that survived the rises in sea level," they said.

"What did you do for food?" asked Maria.

"We were lucky that quite a few goats, chickens, and sheep survived with us, but we needed to sail out each week to find water," they said.

"What happened to your sheep, as we only found goats and chickens on your ships?" asked Natasha.

"We ate them," they said.

"Where did you go to find water?" asked Professor Munro.

"We found another island not too far away, about two days' sailing, that had running water, but making the weekly journey was consuming our fuel to the point we would eventually run out and all die of thirst," one explained.

The discussion continued for a couple of hours. It transpired that the original pirate leader found them collecting water from the island and forced them to join his crews. If they didn't, all their families would have been killed.

Niagara and the remaining pirate ships reached McMurdo base without further incidents in eleven-hours. All the pirates and their families were quarantined for twenty-four hours to check their health and to debrief them. Once released, they were reunited with the seven survivors of the attack on the base. Some of them had family amongst the forty women and children; they were all housed and settled into the village. The goats and chickens were separated into small lots with the intention of breeding more to ensure fresh eggs, milk, and meat to supplement the fish, seaweed, and vegetables that most of the village had been living on. This influx of animals and people gave new hope to the village that they would survive and manage to live on the newly changed planet. The pirate trawlers were converted back to fishing boats to provide more fish and increase the fleet size to eight ships.

Later that day, Natasha, Maria, the general, and other scientists met to analyse the data received from the space lab. "Oh, my God, this new object is another asteroid and it is much bigger than William 6, probably twice the size," said Natasha to the assembled group.

"How long before it impacts with Earth?" asked the general.

"We aren't sure yet, General, as it appears to be slowing down. At its present speed, about two days from now," replied Maria.

"Where on the planet is it due to make landfall?" asked professor Kuzuhara.

"Looks like somewhere in the Northern Hemisphere" said Natasha.

"If it hits the water, there will be another tsunami of huge proportions. If it hits land, then all life on the planet will be destroyed," said Maria.

"We need to keep monitoring that object – or let's call it an asteroid and give it a name. Sergeant, what's your first name?" asked the general.

"My first name? Oh, it's Fred," said the sergeant.

"OK, Fred 12 it is, then," said the general. The assembled group burst out into spontaneous laughter. That was the first space object to get a quirky name.

Gerald and his extended family were discussing living space; did they want to move into one of the new village cabins now that all the threats to the base were gone or would they stay on the *Lily Rose*.

"I vote we stay. I've got used to the luxury and the fact I've my own room," said Mary.

"I agree. We should stay on board because otherwise we'll have to share a cabin and facilities," said Valerie.

"I vote we stay on board because there is still a risk of a dinosaur breaking through the perimeter wall, and I'd much rather be here if that happens," said Maria.

"OK, that settles it. Unless you've anything to add, Tom, we stay on the *Lily Rose*," said Gerald.

They had just finished their discussion when there was a loud bang on the main control room door. "I'd better go and see who that is," said Gerald. He opened the door to an excited Captain Morgen.

"Oh, one minute – let me get my breath back. Is Maria in? She needs to join Natasha at the control centre. There have been further developments with Fred 12." He was giggling as he said it.

Maria could hear the conversation and moved quickly to the door. "What developments, Captain?" she asked.

"I'm not sure, but Natasha and the general need you to get to the control centre ASAP," he said.

Maria made her way over to the base control room, and as she entered, she was greeted by Natasha, who grabbed her arm and said, "Come and look at the pictures that have been sent back by the space lab," with her arms flailing around.

Maria moved over to the screen, making sure to avoid Natasha's flailing arms. "Here we go again. Now when did we do this last?" she said aloud, which brought a giggle out of Natasha.

"What's that all about?" asked the general.

"Nothing, sir. Just a joke we both share about the space lab."

"This is no joking matter, Commanders. Tell me what's happening with Fred 12," he said, twittering to himself.

"I think that the asteroid has impacted with the space lab. When did you receive these pictures?" said Maria.

"About five hours ago," said Natasha.

"Try contacting the space lab again."

Sergeant Kawloski sent a signal to the space lab, there was no reply, although it would take about thirty seconds before the lab responded, "no response, absolutely nothing, it's dead" said the sergeant. They all stood in stunned silence for a moment until a loud banging on the control room door woke them out of their stupor,

"See who that is," said the general.

Captain Morgen went to the door and opened it. The duty corporal was standing there gesturing him to come outside.

"Quick, everybody outside!" shouted the captain.

The whole group rushed out of the control room and looked up at the sky, where the corporal was pointing. They could see a bright light streaking across the night sky heading towards the new ocean where South America once was.

"What the hell is that? Surely not Fred 12 already making planetfall!" screamed the general.

"No, sir, I believe that's the space lab, as the size and vapour trail would be much larger if it were the asteroid," said Maria.

"Where the hell is the asteroid? It can't be far behind the space lab," said Natasha.

"Strange how the only areas of the planet not affected by the earthquakes and rising water were the most sparsely populated on the earth. Was it predetermined by the senders of the asteroids? What else is going to happen to us," said the general.

He had just finished speaking when one of the villagers came running over to him. "General, the ground is shaking near the perimeter fence, and we've spotted a couple of large tyrannosaurus making their way towards us!" screamed the villager.

The guard towers in the perimeter wall managed to scare off the rampaging dinosaurs, and the village once more settled down to life on Antarctica. The general was still concerned about Fred 12. It had been a few days since the space lab crashed to Earth. When would the asteroid impact the planet, and what did the future hold for planet Earth?

About the Author

A. A. Caddy was a former global manager in the automotive industry. He is a husband and father of two, based in the East of England. From an early age, Alan loved science fiction stories and films, and this was the inspiration for his novel. He started his novel seventeen years ago; however, having a young family and working in a fast-moving industry, he put his writing on the back burner. Since taking early retirement to pursue other interests, he made it a priority to complete his novel, 2047, the first in a trilogy.

Lightning Source UK Ltd.
Milton Keynes UK
UKOW04f0658220817
307660UK00002B/226/P

9 781543 485516